GYPSY FOR GOD

Endorsements

Gypsy for God is a heart-warming story of how a woman facing major changes in her life determines where her future lies. Her strong faith in the Lord, a loving, supportive husband, and a community of believers enable doors to be opened, true interests, and a sense of purpose to be revealed.

As the story unfolded, it touched our hearts as the couple discovered a love for worldwide travel and a passion for the mission field of homelessness, poverty, and human rights. Yvonne Morgan combines a fascinating travelogue with her tale of discovery and fulfillment. There are distinct parallels to life in this story, including the changing of careers after many successful years, learning to travel to different countries, and experiencing the disparity of wealth and need in faraway lands. *Gypsy for God* kept us spellbound as it swept us along, experiencing frustration, hope, and elation. It reminded us not to give up on our dreams, the value of family, and to remember that God is always with us.

We thoroughly enjoyed this book and recommend it as a must-read.

—**Karen Ruhl**, Publisher and Editor-in-Chief, *Faith On Every Corner Magazine*

—**Craig Ruhl**, Managing Editor, *Faith On Every Corner Magazine*

Gypsy for God is an outstanding story of courage, faith, and what it means to surrender to God's will, even when it feels incredibly beyond our comfort zone. Also, Yvonne Morgan's writing is warm and relatable. I couldn't put it down. I can't wait to see what she'll bring us next!

—**Jessica Brodie**, author, editor, blogger, and writing coach

Gypsy for God is a delightful travelogue that includes a beautiful and important story that results in transformation for Kathleen, the heroine, her family and church, needy children in numerous locations, and ultimately the readers. Don't miss the vital information at the back of the book, so you and your church or organization can also be involved in changing the world.

—Delores Liesner, author of *Be the Miracle, Guideposts* journalist and freelance writer.

Gypsy for God relates a story of universal appeal about the search for self, for purpose, and for faith. Yvonne Morgan skillfully takes her readers on this empathetic and heartwarming journey.

—William Bernhardt, national bestselling author of *The Last Chance Lawyer*

GYPSY FOR GOD

Yvonne M. Morgan

PUBLISHING THE POSITIVE
Plymouth, Massachusetts

A Christian Company
ElkLakePublishingInc.com

Copyright Notice

Cover and Interior Design:
Editor(s): Sue A. Fairchild, Deb Haggerty

PUBLISHED BY: Elk Lake Publishing, Inc., 35 Dogwood Drive, Plymouth, MA 02360, 2023

Library Cataloging Data
Names: Morgan, Yvonne M. (Yvonne M. Morgan)
Gypsy for God / Yvonne M. Morgan

332 p. 23cm × 15cm (9in × 6 in.)
ISBN-13: 978-1-64949-928-8 (paperback) | 978-1-64949-929-5 (trade hardcover) | 978-1-64949-930-1 (trade paperback) | 978-1-64949-931-8 (e-book)
Key Words: Purpose; God's not done with us yet; Mission; Changing the world; hope; strength; world travel
Library of Congress Control Number: 2023940203 Fiction

DEDICATION

To my wonderful sister-in-law, Leticia. Thank you for your help and suggestions. I really appreciate your support.

To all the middle-aged women searching for a purpose in their lives as families grow up and leave home. God is not done with us yet.

Psalm 92:12–14 (NIV); "The righteous will flourish like a palm tree, they will grow like a cedar of Lebanon; planted in the house of the LORD, they will flourish in the courts of our God. They will still bear fruit in old age, they will stay fresh and green."

ACKNOWLEDGMENTS

I want to thank the following people who were instrumental in preparing this book for publication:

Larry J Leech II—who did my initial edits. He is a saint.

Deb Haggerty—Editor-in-Chief with Elk Lake Publishing, Inc. Thanks for taking a chance on me.

Cristel Phelps—Elk Lake Publishing, Inc. Acquisitions Editor

Sue A. Fairchild—Elk Lake Publishing, Inc. For sticking with me and teaching me to be a better writer.

Leslie Stobbe—for recommending me to Elk Lake Publishing, Inc.

CHAPTER ONE

This was the worst Friday of my career. A beep from the computer reminded me of the meeting that marked the end of life as I knew it. My heart thumped wildly in my chest. A sense of dread enveloped me.

The door to the conference room stood open. A cacophony arose from those inside. I sighed, then sucked in a long breath and strode inside with my head down.

Colorful streamers and banners decorated the walls while balloon bouquets adorned eight tables. I wanted to hide from my friends and coworkers and walked like someone going to the gallows as I made my way to the center of the room. Smiles and laughter erupted around me. Friends smiled at me, but numbness kept me from responding.

On a side table sat a giant cake covered with colorful icing flowers and the words "Happy Retirement, Kathleen" in bright red icing. My heart ached even more.

The one bright spot came as I realized that these fifty people came to wish me well in the next chapter of my life. But then a rising fear overtook me, and panic made me think about escaping to the nearest exit. *Will I ever feel useful again? Because right now, I feel like a failure.* I disguised my feelings by pretending to smile back at friends and coworkers. *What does God have planned for my future?*

Yup, Kathleen Johnson, put out to pasture after almost thirty years of faithful service at Smith Accounting, Inc. Discarded like an old rag. My face flushed and my throat tightened at the injustice of the situation.

I had planned to work until at least sixty-five, not fifty. But everything changed a few months ago. After years of climbing my way up the corporate ladder, I discovered the company placed more importance on saving money than remaining loyal to their long-term employees.

The options came down to retiring or moving up north to Canada, far away from my family and friends here in Arlington, Texas. I had wrestled with this decision for days and lost lots of sleep over it, eventually choosing the unwelcome retirement, or maybe it chose me. But now, the decision haunted me as thoughts ran wild in my mind. My work had brought meaning to my life. So now, where would I find my worth or purpose?

The slow traffic on the way home on 1-20 south of the metroplex had given me too much time to think about my sad situation. Now, I couldn't wait to fall into my husband Sam's arms. *Thank God for a husband who knows how to comfort me.* My cat Rex greeted me at the door and the emptiness of the house echoed the emptiness of my soul. I rubbed Rex's head as he brushed against my leg and purred loudly. "Where's Sam?" I asked but got no reply. "I guess he's still at work."

More dark thoughts popped into my mind. *Sam and I are the same age, but his company values the wisdom that comes with age and years of faithful service. God hasn't forgotten him as he did me. He still can contribute to society.*

GYPSY FOR GOD

The ugly thoughts shifted. *Am I too rigid in my routines and inflexible about trying anything new, as Sam so often tells me? So what if I expect everything planned out in my life and everything in its place? What's wrong with starting every day the same way, driving the same route, or stopping at the same local coffee shop?* I appreciated how Courtney, the coffee shop morning employee, prepared my coffee—black with one sugar—and handed it to me when I walked through the door each morning. *Will she wonder where I am come Monday?*

I walked down the hallway toward the kitchen, glancing into both bedrooms, the den, and the formal living room to check for Sam. My heart ached to feel his reassuring arms around me.

I plopped into a kitchen chair and let my head rest on the table. Helping my clients audit their annual financial statements and following a regular morning routine gave me a sense of purpose. Now, my world crashed around me and left me reeling. *I don't think I can live without my routine.* A profound gloom washed over me afresh as I contemplated the challenges of finding a new daily routine. *To say I'm a creature of habit is a considerable understatement. But after today, all that changes.*

Sam arrived home a short time later with a bouquet of flowers he hoped would cheer me up. The bright yellow roses arranged with fresh baby's breath and dark green foliage brought a momentary smile. After thirty-one years of marriage, Sam understood how much I struggled with change.

I slipped into the kitchen with the excuse of looking for a vase and to avoid answering the inevitable questions he would ask. But more than that, the painful answers I would have to give. When I reentered the living room, I found Sam perched on the dark brown leather couch with a huge smile.

3

"How was the retirement party?" he asked.

"I enjoyed it. All the usual friends and coworkers looking for a free piece of cake attended," I said. "They served an Italian cream cake that tasted yummy. I brought a piece home for you."

"Cake, yum. Hold on," he said, heading toward the fridge. "I think I'll try a bite now instead of waiting till after dinner."

I giggled. After all our years together, he still made me laugh and smile. Even with his hair graying around the temples, my heart fluttered at the mere sight of him. I counted it as a blessing when I met him all those years ago at Dallas Community College north of the city. Sam had studied management and I accounting. After graduation, we moved into the same apartment complex to maximize our time together, my favorite thing. Marriage followed a year later, and then, we purchased this lovely ranch style home where we had lived ever since.

However, my failings began to haunt me soon after marriage. After enduring several miscarriages, we stopped trying when we discovered my body was incapable of bearing children. Years of depression left me a shell of a human and tore at the fabric of our marriage. The bitter disappointment consumed me and forced me to search for a purpose besides motherhood when Sam refused to discuss adoption as a solution.

I threw myself into my career instead and found a purpose there. I also used cats to fill the void of my empty uterus. The pitter-patter of their little paws allowed me to pretend that a herd of kids ran through the house. Eight cats over the last thirty years helped me to fill my maternal needs. I loved them all, but they were poor substitutes.

Sam reemerged from the kitchen and sat beside me. After wolfing down the entire piece of cake and dropping crumbs into his lap, he said, "Yum."

Sam's arms folded around me then, and my smile faded as a tear unwillingly ran down my cheek. "What am I going to do with myself now?" I asked while he lovingly caressed my cheek.

"You'll figure something out, babe. For the next few days, take things easy. I think you need some time for yourself. Maybe you can reconnect with the person God intended you to be." He ran a thumb over my wet cheek. "Once you do that, I know you'll find some kind of new career that'll be life-changing and rewarding."

I turned away. "It'll all work out, just like that verse you have posted on the fridge."

Sam got up and returned a moment later with the sticky note on his fingertips. "Here it is, Romans 8:28; 'And we know that in all things God works for the good of those who love him, who have been called according to his purpose.'" Then he added, "God has a plan. Just wait and see."

Does God have a plan for me? How can a retired, routine-obsessed, middle-aged lady have a purpose?

Later, as I lay wide awake, I heard the grandfather clock in the hallway. *Tick, tick, tick* echoed through my mind. Each tick reminding me I had no purpose.

Tick—unworthy.

Tick—loser.

Tick—irrelevant.

CHAPTER TWO

I jumped up out of bed, my heart thumping in my chest. Dazed and confused, I looked at the clock on the nightstand. 8:00 a.m.

I had not slept this late in years. My routine did not allow it. *Why is it so late? Have I overslept?* I groped around for my robe and slippers as I tried to poke my brain into action.

Then, the events of the previous few days flooded back. My heart sank again when my brain registered that the events of yesterday had really happened.

My brain still in a fog, I shuffled into the kitchen, shaking my head to clear the cobwebs from my mind. Sam sat in his favorite chair, reading the Saturday edition of the *Dallas Morning News*. A pot of freshly brewed coffee awaited me. The nutty aroma with a hint of cinnamon filled my nostrils and made my mouth water. I poured myself a large cup and sat down in the chair next to Sam.

He flashed an encouraging smile in my direction. "Now that you're an officially unemployed bum, how does it feel?"

I appreciated that he tried to lighten my mood, but his antics weren't working.

"Useless? I feel totally useless."

My mood darkened even more as I rehashed the events of the previous day. "How am I going to fill my days?" I asked, not expecting a reply. "The weekends will be fine, because of the normal weekend routine. But what do I do on Monday morning when you head back to work? I'll be alone in this empty house with nothing to do."

I loved our house but sitting alone in it day after day made it sound more like a prison sentence than something I should cherish and enjoy. A deep sigh escaped my quivering lips, and I took a long draw on my coffee, hoping to hide my feelings. *How long will it take before this magic brown liquid sweeps away the fuzziness in my mind?*

"Why can't I find a purpose, one that helps people somehow? I want to make their lives better."

"Don't worry, honey, you'll be fine," Sam said. "I know you. You'll find something new that you'll love too." He paused to sip his own coffee, then said, "Hey, how 'bout we escape somewhere for the weekend? You know, get away and give you a chance to clear your mind. Leaving town may change your perspective enough to allow you to think of new things to try."

I liked the idea. "Where shall we go?"

"How 'bout we head over to the Great Piney Woods area? I bet we could find a little motel on a lake far away from everything, maybe do some hiking or fishing."

Biting down on a smile, I said, "Great." I gulped a mouthful of my coffee and savored the warmth of it.

We sat in a comfortable silence for a while, sipping coffee and imagining the details of a weekend getaway. A slight giddiness welled up within me at the idea of a weekend away, and I jumped up to get my cell phone. Searching the internet saved me from thinking about my problems.

With a renewed energy, I looked for a cute cabin near Tyler, Texas. An attractive little inn near the Lake of the Pines caught my attention after only a few minutes of searching. Their website showed availability for this weekend, so I snatched up a room for two nights.

"I found us a great place. How about we leave in about thirty minutes? Can you get packed that quickly?"

Sam looked up from his newspaper. "Wow, was that all it took—planning a weekend getaway—to bring a smile back to your beautiful face?"

My cheeks flushed. Smiling, I ran to the bedroom to throw some stuff into an overnight bag, then yelled from the bedroom, "You know me. Planning things fulfills a need within me and gives me purpose. I guess that's the good part of my control freak personality."

Jeans or shorts and simple tops worked best for me, so I made quick work of packing. With the fall weather cooling the temperatures, I also threw in a couple of sweatshirts for the crisp nights. Within a few brief hours, the beauty of nature would surround us with pine trees reaching to the sky, birds chirping happily, and crisp, clean air to breathe. A few days away might do the trick.

When we'd packed the car with the bags, snacks, and hiking gear, we pulled out of the driveway and headed east just as the sun reached its noon apex.

"Thank you, Jesus," I whispered as I tried to relax.

Even on a Saturday morning, Dallas traffic slowed to a crawl in its usual spots, adding about an hour to the drive. When we cleared the city limits, my shoulders released the week's stress, and my body tension eased. Christian music played on the radio, and I lowered my window to feel the coolness of the breeze on my face. About halfway through the two-hour drive, the scent of pine blew in through the windows and cast long shadows across the lane as they obscured the sun.

I inhaled deeply. "I think this might be the perfect thing for my mental health."

"See, sometimes I have good ideas." Sam smiled at me, then returned his attention to the road. "You look a little brighter already."

The earthy aromas flooded my senses, stirring up memories of laughing and relaxing times on vacations with Sam as we hiked and relaxed. By the time we pulled up to the inn's door, all my gloomy thoughts had disappeared.

I planned what to do first while we walked into the warm glow of a roaring fire in the inn's lobby. Sam checked us in, and I walked over to the enormous windows and looked out over the tranquil pond.

"This place feels like a slice of heaven," I said.

Sam wrapped his arm around my waist as we headed down the long hall to our room. The pastel shades of the inn calmed my soul, and we talked about what we should do. Since the early fall sun sat low in the sky already, we put off hiking until the following day. Sam unlocked the room door to reveal a space full of peace and serenity.

A small gasp escaped my lips. Crisp, clean sheets covered a king-size bed bathed in vibrant amber sunlight. The large French doors faced the lake and led to a cozy veranda. Two worn wicker chairs beckoned guests to sit a spell and take in the incredible views.

Green-headed mallards swam lazily across the still waters, trailing a shimmering wake behind them. We stepped out onto the veranda as a gaggle of geese honked nonstop overhead. Crickets chirped their melodic songs and made the woods sound alive with activity. A light breeze rustled through the trees, causing a cascade of withered leaves to float down to the mossy earth.

My soul sang a new song filled with bliss.

"I love this place, and I love you for coming up with the idea. This trip was just what I needed. Thanks for your loving support." I wrapped my arms around Sam's waist and leaned against his chest.

"We're a team, honey, and when you hurt, I hurt. But we'll get through this together just like we always have with our gigantic problems." Sam reached down to wipe away the tear that appeared on my cheek.

I slept deeply that night and awoke refreshed the following day. I threw back the curtains and allowed the sunlight to wash over me.

"Hurry up, lazy," I called to the still form of my husband. "I want to get this day started."

"I'm glad to see your enthusiasm for life has returned," he said, then swung his legs out of the bed.

A few minutes later, we'd donned our hiking boots and loaded a backpack with snacks and water for our day of adventure. After a wonderful breakfast of eggs, bacon, and homemade blueberry muffins in the hotel's restaurant, we headed out to explore. We found a small country chapel near the lake and joined the service. The simpleness of the small chapel, with its wood pews, creaking wood floor, white slat walls, and warm glow from the candles burning on the small altar added to the sense of sacredness, and the congregation's warm welcome after the service made us feel at home.

"Now, my soul feels as refreshed as my body and mind," I said as we headed out into the woods to commune more with nature. "You know, I think we need to get back into church on a more regular basis. It might help me figure out the plans for the future."

"I think that might help both of us. Sometimes it feels like God is so far away. I think it's me who lost the connection. I'm up to going back more often," Sam agreed.

As we walked a well-marked trail, the sounds of the leaves crunching under our feet echoed through the trees surrounding us. The sun streamed through the pines, causing shadows to dance on the ground. A deer crept by in the shadows and disappeared in an instant. The cacophony of bird noises made it hard to hear each other, and by the time we reached the end of the five-mile hike, a small stream of sweat ran down my back.

"You're glistening," Sam said, handing me a handkerchief hidden in his pocket.

"Hush, silly, you know it's sweat," I said as I wiped my brow. "But thanks for trying to make me feel better. It got warmer than I expected."

We made our way back to the inn to clean up before dinner.

"Wow, I feel like a new person. Maybe this retirement life won't be too bad," I said as I headed into the bathroom. "I think a soak in the tub will help me relax even more."

I filled the spa-like tub with steaming water, then poured in a generous splash of the lavender bath salts provided by the inn. Before long, the entire room filled with the scents of an old English flower garden.

I inhaled deeply as I stepped into the tub, then surrendered to the luxuriously scented water and let my mind drift away from the worries. Releasing a note of contentment, I ducked below the water.

I soaked so long that my fingers and toes looked like they belonged to ninety-year-old women. I wrapped myself in a warm terry cloth towel hanging on the back of the door and relished its softness as I stood in front of the mirror.

Wiping away the steam from the glass, I stared at myself for the first time in a very long time. *I guess I could look a lot worse at my age.* I jiggled the flab that hung below my arms and poked my plump, round belly. But I cringed at the dark bags under my eyes and the way they stood out against my ashen skin.

Sam often called me his vampire because of the paleness of my skin. *Maybe I should put on a little under-eye cream to hide the bags.* Even though wet, my gray hairs still showed, and I told myself it could be much worse after all the stress I had endured these last few weeks of employment. Part of my retirement plan needed to include more exercise to improve my overall health and maybe tone up a few areas. *Well, at least Sam loves me no matter how I look.*

I headed out of the bathroom to dress for dinner. "Sam, do you think I'm fat?"

"There's no way I'm answering that loaded question, babe. But I'll say I think you're beautiful, and I love you just the way you are." Sam sidled up and took me in his arms, offering a peck on the cheek.

"Perfect answer. Thanks." I snuggled into his arms for a moment before saying, "How about we check out that small diner we saw at the end of the lane in front of the inn for dinner? I'm starved."

Sam agreed and soon we were walking down the lane toward a sign that blinked "Home-cooked Meals." Those words drew us in, our stomachs rumbling in unison.

I ordered a cheeseburger after spying the server carrying one to another table. Sam ordered a chicken-fried steak. When our order arrived, my mouth watered as the delicious smell of grilled meat filled my nostrils. Sam's chicken fried steak hung over the edges of his plate, doused in white gravy. I wolfed down the burger as ketchup and mayo oozed out the side and over my fingers. Expecting both of us to get indigestion from the fatty indulgence, I dug out my packet of Tums. Another fun side-effect of getting older.

After dinner, a shared slice of lemon meringue pie completed the evening meal. Now overstuffed, I sat back and tugged on my tightening pants as I smiled at Sam. A small burp erupted from my lips, and we both laughed.

As I thought of the indulgent meal we'd just partaken, fresh fear arose and drove my peace away. *What if we can't afford to do these kinds of getaways without my salary? What other things will I be forced to give up because of the change in my circumstances?*

"Are you okay?" Sam asked, reaching across the table for my hand. "You look pale. Is everything okay?"

"I'm fine. I think it's from all this rich food." I hoped Sam would not hear the lie.

The next morning we pulled away from the canopy of trees shading the front of the inn, returning to our "normal" life. As the view of the lake disappeared, my mind once again raced with unsettled feelings about my future, and a small tear ran down my cheek. I brushed away the ugly thoughts and focused on the peacefulness of the drive with my favorite person.

Two hours later, the familiar surroundings of our home greeted us, and I sank down into my big, overstuffed chair and let its softness wrap around me as Rex wrapped himself around my ankles.

Sam settled on the couch across from me. "You look better after the weekend away."

"I feel slightly better, but I'm still unsure what my future will hold," I said. "Maybe something will just drop into my lap. I want to work. But I just don't know what kind of work I should pursue. I feel like I'm starting all over again."

"Well, what would be your dream job? Is there something you always dreamed of doing but never pursued?"

"I'm not sure. I stopped dreaming many years ago because they always seem to end badly."

Yet I pondered Sam's questions, searching my soul, trying to find an answer to what things brought me joy. *What did I enjoy most in life?*

"Maybe I should pray about this situation a little more than I have so far," I told him.

I just hoped God would give me an answer that I liked.

CHAPTER THREE

One morning several weeks later, I stared at the plethora of lists I had made, trying to figure out what jobs would give me the most security, satisfaction, and a chance to find a new routine. One by one, I wadded up each list into little balls and tossed them toward the trash can.

That evening, Sam retrieved some of the balls of paper from the floor. "No luck?" he said, bending down to kiss me.

I glared up at him from the chair at the dining room table and shook my head, then returned to the scribble pad while he unfolded some of the day's failures.

He read through them silently, then, touching my shoulder, he plopped down in a chair next to me. A warm smile spread across his face, and his eyes locked onto mine.

"I love you," he mouthed, and his eyes echoed the same.

The warmth of his love reached deep into my soul and soothed me like nothing else.

"I spotted a theme from several of the items on these lists," he continued. "Several things seem to relate to traveling activities. Is there something travel-related you'd like to do?"

I shrugged. "Sure, I love to travel, and I love planning our trips. It'd be a dream come true to become a travel agent. But who am I kidding? I'm a fifty-six-year-old retiree. Who'd hire me with no background in the industry?" I sighed. "I can picture the rejections now. I walk into a travel office and tell them I want to be a travel agent. 'Do you have any experience?' they ask. They'd laugh me out the door once I told them no." I turned back to my notepad. "No, thank you. I don't want to go through any more humiliation."

"You don't know until you try, do you?" Sam pressed. "What do you have to lose? And with your attention to detail, thoroughness, and a fastidious nature, you'd be great at it. Besides, think of some of the places we could explore so you could recommend them to your clients." Sam sat at the edge of his chair, his excitement obviously growing as he talked about the idea.

My shoulders slumped, and I dropped my head. I did not dare to dream. And I wanted to remain realistic about my opportunities since I did not expect many to materialize.

Sam saw my look and continued to encourage me until I finally agreed to do some research to get him to drop the subject. But I expected this dream to fizzle out quickly.

The following day, I sat down to research the training required to become a travel agent. I expected to click page after page, my soul drowning a little more with each new search.

After two hours of searching, however, I had found some interesting information. Much to my surprise, there seemed to be very little effort involved in becoming a travel agent.

I should keep this part quiet so Sam doesn't gloat about being right.

A small pulse of excitement ran up my spine. *Please don't get your hopes up,* I warned myself. My heart could not stand any more disappointments. "Our Lord, please don't tease me if this kind of work is not possible," I whispered toward the ceiling. "Please show me the path to take for my next career. Amen," I added sheepishly, trying to make the cries of my heart sound more like a prayer than a desperate plea.

I hoped God would give me a verbal answer. I looked up, half expecting to hear a voice. I couldn't remember the last time I had prayed on my own. Most of my prayer life happened only in church or if something terrified me. "Maybe I should pray more often," I confessed to the heavens in hopes God would hear me and help. "Maybe praying would keep me out of these kinds of situations in the first place."

As I continued my research, it did seem easy to become a travel agent, especially if you wanted to do it from home. But I needed to make a few decisions before I began the initial process. The advice recommended picking between corporate travel or leisure travel.

Easy enough, I want to help people have fun.

I would focus on leisure travel.

Additional recommendations suggested specializing in a theme of travel, like adventure or romantic getaways or by destination, like beach or European trips. People like to think they are working with an "expert" on the type of traveling they want to do. Focusing on one primary area would allow me to market myself as an expert in that kind of travel.

My thoughts ran wild with the possibilities. My heart leaped at the thought of helping people plan trips. I wanted to explore the entire world but was afraid to leave my comfort zone full of electricity, clean water, excellent hospitals, and well-supplied air conditioning. I also loved nature and discovering out-of-the-way spots to unwind and relax while on vacation. An excited flutter rose at the idea of planning trips for others to national parks in the United States or other wilderness areas. That didn't sound too dangerous.

But what about Europe? I'd always wanted to explore another continent—as long as my needs were met, that is. I could seek out luxurious spots in foreign countries. Surely most of them had the amenities I sought.

STOP. These decisions can wait until I actually work in the travel industry.

Another interesting piece of advice suggested working with a "host agency" as an independent contractor to learn the ropes before venturing out on my own.

Who do I know in the travel industry who could help me?

A face popped into my memory, someone whom I'd worked with years ago. She'd quit the accounting firm to start a travel agency in town. I pushed my fear of change aside and picked up my phone.

"Thank you, Jesus, for showing me this opportunity. I'm sorry I doubted you. Please help me achieve my goals," I whispered while dialing my old friend Jane and waiting to see where the future would lead me.

During dinner that night, I shared the details of my searches with Sam instead of hiding them. And his encouraging smile made me appreciate him more.

"You sound a little more positive than you did last night," Sam said. "I thought you might just blow off the whole idea of working as a travel agent and go with some accounting temp agency since you don't like change. I'm proud of you, babe."

"Confession time. I almost blew it off but thought maybe taking a minor risk to research the possibilities wouldn't hurt too much. I also applied to several accounting temporary employment agencies online, though, just in case. You know me. I need some kind of backup plan." I shrugged.

Sam laughed, grabbed my hand, and held on tightly. "That's one thing I love about you, your predictability and your dependability." He smirked while he rubbed my hand with his thumb. "You'll be fine, Mrs. Johnson. With a little time and effort, you'll land on your feet. In fact, I predict someday you'll look back on all of this and thank God for forcing you to change jobs. You'll find a new career field that'll bring you much more happiness."

From your mouth to God's ears.

CHAPTER FOUR

ONE YEAR LATER

One afternoon, while sitting at the dining room table, I set about to research options for a trip to Spain.

Jane had quickly taken me on and helped me get all the training I'd needed. Since getting my license, most of my travel business involved setting up trips for individuals or small families. I had gained lots of experience helping families plan trips to Disney World and helping couples plan honeymoons to tropical islands in the South Pacific. But now, Sam and I would be embarking on an exploratory trip to Spain. I had helped clients plan similar journeys, so this should be easy for me to replicate.

"Any thoughts on things you want to see or do?" I asked Sam.

"Nothing I can think of right now. Both cities offer lots of options for things to see and do from what friends told me. But I trust you to pick out the best things. I'm just hoping this trip will convince you to travel more."

My primary purpose for this first trip outside of the US would provide me with many opportunities to experience other cultures. While there, I planned to check out several new hotels in Madrid and Barcelona in order to refer them to clients.

The secondary purpose of the trip included helping me overcome my fear of the unknown and of change. We'd never traveled abroad in the earlier days of our marriage because of my stupid fears. With so many other positive changes in my life, this might be something to change too. I determined I wanted to travel the world. What did I need to make myself comfortable in faraway places? My list included modern medical systems, porcelain toilets, clean drinking water, and air conditioning for warm weather areas.

Okay, maybe I still hold onto some of my fears.

"We'll see. Jane is forcing this trip on me, so I can research these new hotels. I don't feel like I can tell her no, since she has helped me so much."

"I'm praying this trip is the beginning of many fresh adventures for us," Sam said.

Both of us hoped this trip would help me conquer my fears.

I looked back at the website I was browsing and did not respond to his comment. "I've found lots of museums we could explore, as well as a palace. How do you feel about visiting a palace?"

Sam laughed. "Sounds good. You can pretend you're a princess."

"There are several helpful websites that provide sample agendas for two days in Madrid. Each recommends a stroll through the streets of the *El Madrid de los Austrias* first followed by the Bohemian *Las Letras* neighborhood for shopping and food." I scribbled down the information. The itinerary included a few days in Madrid before heading to Barcelona by train for several more days.

"They also suggest taking in the museums and palace on the second day. I think I'll adopt this plan for our time in Madrid. Now, I need to look at things to do in Barcelona," I said.

Sam nodded in agreement from his spot in his chair, nose in a newspaper.

I continued, "The same website suggests a sample two-day itinerary for a visit to Barcelona. For day one, the site recommends visiting the old Gothic area of town, which includes the harbor, open-air market, and a ride on the cable car. For day two, the sights of the modern parts of the city with highlights on the famous works of Antoni Gaudí are recommended. What do you think?"

Sam looked up from his newspaper and nodded. "I think they sound like good plans to start. We can adjust them if we see something else we want to explore."

I wasn't sure I wanted to explore. If I *had* to go, sticking to a well-planned itinerary seemed fine by me.

"Thanks for all the hard work," Sam said.

I laughed, trying to hide my discomfort about the whole thing. "I just pulled these from a website. Not much work for me. That's the benefit of traveling to popular European destinations—relying on the work of others. I don't think these types of recommendations would be available in some of the faraway lands you want to explore though. So I would need to begin from ground zero, and I'm not sure I could."

My attempt to put off my adventurous husband didn't work though.

"I'll take whatever I can get." Sam smiled. "And I think you could do it easily. You don't give yourself enough credit."

I smiled and began to make a list of things we'd need to accomplish before going. A plan always helped me relax. I would need to call Sophie, our twelve-year-old cat-sitter, to make sure she could look after Rex while we traveled. She and her mom lived next door and she loved animals—a perfect fit when we wanted to get away.

I secretly hoped she would not be available, though, so I didn't have to make the trip.

No time like the present.

I picked up my phone and dialed our neighbor's number. When Sophie's mother, Sue Talbert, answered, I said, "Hey! Long time no chat. We really need to get together for some coffee soon."

I heard Sue exhale through the phone. Since her divorce when Sophie was only a baby, Sue had struggled to meet all her financial obligations on a single income. She had also tried to keep up a social life but had never managed to find a balance that worked for her. Before long, she'd given up and put all her efforts into raising Sophie.

"I would love that, but I've been so busy working two jobs and going to Sophie's extracurricular stuff. Maybe next month sometime?"

"Well, actually, we're going away for a week next month," I said. "I'm wondering if Sophie can watch Rex for us?"

"Oh, okay. Let me give her the phone. We'll talk soon."

I felt bad at brushing Sue off and vowed to try and get her over for coffee soon. I knew she was busy since her husband had left her to be the sole provider for Sophie. *Maybe I should invite her to our new church.*

Soon Sophie came on the line and when I told her what we needed, she said, "Let me check my calendar, Ms. Kathleen."

Rex and I both liked Sophie, and she watched him for a reasonable price.

"Yup, I sure can. Same plan, as usual? Feed him twice a day and love on him?"

"Yes. Do you still have a key?"

"Sure do. You're all set, Ms. Kathleen. And as always, I will have Mom text you if there are any problems."

I told her to tell her mom I'd call soon for a coffee date, then hung up the phone and held my head in my hands, a sigh escaping my quivering lips. *I guess I'm flying to Spain in a few weeks. Lord, please don't let me die on this trip. And if there is any way, please stop this from happening. I'm afraid.*

CHAPTER FIVE

A few weeks later, a flash of excitement and even a slight joy arose from my toes and spread throughout my body as the plane touched down in Spain.

"Maybe international travel won't be as bad as I expected." I smiled at Sam.

"See, I told you so," Sam said.

Even the tiredness of an all-night flight did not dampen my spirits as I soaked up the sunshine and the smell of orange and jasmine wafting through the air while we waited outside the airport for our ride.

As we rode the taxi to the hotel, I spotted some old-world architecture set between modern skyscrapers. For our three nights in Madrid, we would stay in a hotel with that same old-world feel.

Stepping into the hotel's circular lobby felt a bit like stepping into a piece of history—with its marble columns and multiple stairways leading to the mezzanine level adorned with beautiful stained glass. The lack of an elevator added to the feeling of days gone by as we lugged everything up two flights of stairs to our room. We opted for a quick nap to ease the jet lag before exploring this new world.

After our nap, we checked out the area closest to the hotel, still stumbling around in a fog of jet lag. I hadn't expected to feel this groggy from traveling.

"Do you feel as out of sorts as I do?" I asked Sam.

"I do. And I can't seem to shake it. I'm glad we're keeping the evening light. I don't think I'd be able to do much until I get a good night's sleep."

"If we travel more in the future, I think we need a routine that includes a quick nap for starters then to keep our activities light on the first day to allow for our heads to clear from the jet lag."

"Deal."

A good night of rest refreshed both of us and cleared my head of the travel cobwebs. After breakfast at the hotel, we ventured out again into the city of Madrid, known for its unique air because of the combination of its high altitude and mountain breezes. The flamboyant nature of the city displayed itself in the arts, architecture, and music, along with its famed flamenco music and dances, bullfights, fantastic beaches, and abundant sunshine.

We selected the San Miguel market for our first place to visit. Traditionally, the Spaniards considered lunch as the main meal of the day. We also discovered many restaurants provided a *menu del dai*—menu of the day. This option included a starter, a main course, and dessert, all for one low price. Some places even offered a glass of wine as part of the price.

We grabbed lunch at one of the many stalls in the market to sample the local cuisine from the *menu del dai*. At that first lunch, I discovered my new favorite dish— *paella*, a delicious meat dish with rice and a lot of savory spices of saffron, paprika, and rosemary.

"I think I like the seafood paella the best," I told Sam as I wiped my mouth with the linen napkin.

"I think I like mine with the spicy sausage. But both are great. I don't think I'll be able to eat much for dinner tonight," he said, patting his stomach.

"Remember what the receptionist told us about dinner here in Spain? Most Spanish people don't eat dinner till after nine because of the afternoon siestas and big lunches. And most restaurants won't even open until that late," I said, pulling out my notebook to jot a few notes. "You might be hungry again by bedtime. After we explore a little more, we'll head back for a siesta, too, since all the stores close up for those two hours."

"I like your way of thinking, my dear."

After waking from our siesta nap, we opted to snack on tapas for dinner. These smaller, sharable plates allowed us to sample many other various local dishes. I loved the *patatas bravas*—potatoes with a spicy sauce—and the bacon-wrapped dates with goat cheese.

"These are delightful. This might be my new favorite dish."

"You might have a whole list of new favorites by the time we're done." Sam laughed, then took my hand. "Okay, now what? I feel fully awake now, so I don't want to go back to the hotel yet."

I consulted the small file I'd been carrying with me with the information I'd gleaned from the internet. "Well, there's a spot where we can watch the flamenco dancers perform. Do you think you're up to it?"

Sam stood from his chair and held out his hand for mine. "Lead the way, my darling."

We walked down one of the busiest streets in the city, called Gran Via to a local flamenco bar called *Las Tablas*. The women in brightly colored, polka-dotted dresses with shawls draped over their shoulders, stomped, swirled, and swayed to the traditional music.

When we finally made it back to the hotel well after midnight, we both fell into bed, exhausted from the day's activities. Despite being dog-tired, I hoped tomorrow offered even more fun adventures.

My stress level rose with the start of the second day when I attended a short, work-related meeting with the Board of Tourism for Spain. The country wanted our agency to push Spain as a prime European destination to increase tourism dollars. To show me more of their city, they had agreed to give me tours of some of the other hotels.

"I love the things I've seen so far," I told the board while standing outside the second hotel, "so I'll have no problem encouraging clients to travel here."

"Thank you," Fernando said. "We wish you could stay longer in each city and see other parts of our beautiful country."

"Well, this is my first exploratory trip and my first overseas, so I kept the trip a little shorter, because I didn't know what to expect. Next time, we'll stay longer. I'm looking forward to the palace this afternoon and our time in Barcelona," I said.

"Make sure you visit the beach in Barcelona," Mateo said.

I agreed and was soon heading back to my own hotel to meet up with my husband, the stress in my shoulders evaporating.

"I'm glad that's done," I told Sam as we headed out for our own day. "Now, I can be a real tourist. Spain does offer lots of options, though, so I'll recommend it often to my clients."

"And in the future, maybe we can spend more time here and experience more of the local flavor," Sam said.

I agreed, much to my own surprise. "This might be the beginning of a new me."

Since the meeting had run longer than I'd expected, we opted to skip the museums and focus on something I wanted to see—the Royal Palace. As a child, I loved reading all the fairytales, but Cinderella always remained my favorite.

"I'm not sure if I'm unique in this, but I really wanted to be a princess as a little girl," I had told Sam years ago. He'd laughed at me, but, over the years, had called me his princess and tried to make me feel like one every chance he could.

Now, as we looked up at the palatial building, I said, "I can't believe I'm walking into my first genuine palace."

"This is one of the few official heads of state residences open to the public," Sam said while reading the brochure. "Could you imagine living here?"

The opulence of the palace left me almost speechless, and I walked around with my mouth agape. After walking through the gilded gates and past the marble façade, two enormous staircases stood on each side of the room. Bronze statues, crystal chandeliers, and ornate paintings filled the room so much my eyes did not know where to look first. The elegance continued from room to room and overwhelmed my senses. I twirled in circles as we walked, trying to see everything.

Inside the throne room, I pointed and said, "Look at the lions at the foot of the throne. I love the colors in the room too. Gold and crimson remind me of royalty, so maybe we can decorate one of our rooms like this."

"As you wish, my princess," Sam said, bowing to me.

We both laughed, drawing stares from some of the other visitors.

The hours slipped away as we explored many of the 3,418 rooms. My feet hurt by the time we finished the tour.

"Wow, can you believe some people live like that?" I asked Sam. "Now, I'm worried that our place back in Texas will feel like a dump compared to the palace's grandeur."

"Don't let the green-eyed monster of jealousy make you think what we've got is not good enough," he warned. "We've a good life, and remember, massive problems come with that kind of wealth."

"Okay, I know. Well, at least I'm your princess, right?"

Sam pulled me into his arms and kissed me. "You are and always will be."

We tried a different tapas restaurant for dinner that night, ordering six new items. I got the *patatas bravas* as one dish, and we grew a little more daring and tried cuttlefish, but I wasn't a fan. Sam finished the fish, while I enjoyed the mussels. We then scarfed down bacon-wrapped dates, fried calamari, and finished the meal with *Jamon Serrano*, a traditional ham dish.

"I'm not sure I'll be able to walk back to the hotel after all this food," Sam said.

"Me either. Maybe we can catch a cab instead."

The waiter explained where to catch a ride back to our hotel, and we walked hand in hand to the corner.

"What an adventure. I'm so glad we made this trip together. I can't imagine being here alone." I leaned into Sam's shoulder as we walked.

"Does that mean you'll be up for more adventures in the future?" Sam asked.

"Let's just enjoy the moment. I'm not ready to make any promises."

Oh, Lord, please. Don't make Sam want to go on any more international trips. This has been great, but I'm not sure I can do this again. Fear rose into the back of my throat. *Please help me.* I let my shoulders drop as we walked and let out a small sigh. *Lord, I tried a new adventure but now I want to go back to the comfort and familiarity of my old way of life.*

CHAPTER SIX

We embarked on the next leg of the journey with a three-hour, high-speed train ride to Barcelona. The train whisked us from luscious, green rolling countryside through the mountains at speeds of almost two hundred miles per hour. This sleek, new train ran smoothly across the rails and even offered a choice of eating in the dining car or at the walk-up cafeteria.

"I'm enjoying this train ride so much I think I'll recommend it to my clients," I said as I pulled out my trusty notebook. "It's a great way to experience the Spanish countryside without driving. They could travel between the cities for about the same price as a plane ticket and without the security hassles. And you see so much more than just looking down at the landscape from a tiny plane window," I said to Sam. "I'm also learning to enjoy the journey just as much as the destination."

"I'd definitely travel by train again," Sam said, staring out the window at the passing scenery. "Catching the train was so much easier than catching a plane with all the airline security."

I consulted my notes again. "For our stay in Barcelona, I picked a more modern hotel. I choose this one because of the easy access to the world famous beaches."

From the photos I'd seen of the hotel on the website, the place lacked the old-world charm of our previous hotel, but I wasn't prepared for how severe the difference would be.

When we entered the doors of the steel façade and stark lobby a few hours later, my heart sank. The place reminded me of many of the chain hotels in the United States—dull, boring ... same.

But then we entered our enormous room. Light poured in from the windows, and I noticed a glass door with a balcony overlooking the stunning azure waters of the Mediterranean Sea below. As I stood at the balcony door, a warm breeze blew in and the waves crashing echoed through the room. The sun danced on the water, while I stood transfixed by the scenery below.

"What a perfect location," I said.

"Perfect, just like you," Sam said, coming up behind me and wrapping his arms around my waist.

"You're making me blush, so stop it. This has been such an incredible trip so far. I don't know why we haven't done this sooner."

"Because you're a big, old scaredy-cat."

"Okay, maybe. But maybe that's all changed. I'm looking forward to checking out the city tomorrow." I turned to look at him. "Maybe we can spend some time on the beach too. I brought a ton of sunscreen, so I don't do a lobster impression. What do you want to do first tomorrow? I read we should check out the many works of Gaudí around town."

Our focus for the first day would include seeing many of the works of the architect Antoni Gaudí who had left his signature buildings all over this city. We started the tour of his work with the breathtaking church called *Sagrada Familia.*

"Here is what the brochure says about this place," Sam said, reading from the literature we'd picked up. "'This church is a special place that is an international symbol of architecture, as well as Gaudí's most famous work.' And here's another interesting fact—did you know that Gaudí died when he got hit by a tram, and they buried him here?" Sam explained, "This also says it's worth climbing to the top of the original towers to check out the magnificent view of Barcelona. We can ride up in an elevator and walk down the 504 steps to the street level if that's more your speed."

"I hope the view is worth it," I said, looking up at the massive structure. "That sounds exhausting just thinking about it."

"That's why I said to walk down and not up," Sam said, laughing.

A few moments later, I stood mesmerized by the view from the top of the tower. The sea sparkled in the distance, and the sun glistened off tall, modern glass buildings all around the cathedral. We could see the entire city spread out before us.

"Okay, this is certainly worth how much my legs will hurt on the way down."

We enjoyed the many other buildings and parks home to his works throughout the city that morning. I found Gaudí's style whimsical and beautiful, almost Dr. Seuss-like in its character. His use of color in his architecture also brought life to normally drab buildings. A trip to Barcelona would not be complete without exploring his influence in the town, and I made sure to make note of everything we saw, so I could recommend it to others.

After a large lunch from the menu del dai, like in Madrid, we opted for a siesta back at the hotel. Later that afternoon, we enjoyed a ride in the Port Cable Car across the Barcelona harbor.

The thrilling ride started high on a hilltop and swept down to the harbor area far below at ten feet per second, providing us with amazing views of the city and harbor areas as the sun set.

As darkness settled over the area, we set off to see the impressive magic fountain of Montjuïc. The water of the fountains danced and swayed to the music, rising higher and plunging down again, the colorful lights reflecting off the sprays in a rainbow of hues. The spectators applauded as the show finished.

"That fountain made a thrilling display," I said. "Who knew water could dance like that?"

"No kidding. That's a great way to wind up our day here. Are you hungry?"

"Yes, all this walking has worked up my appetite. Do you want our new normal dinner?"

"Of course," he said, and we ducked into a small place for tapas before wrapping up the night.

To start our second day, we made our way to the most famous street in the city—La Rambla, which stretches three-quarters of a mile with many terraces, street artists, florists, and kiosks spread out along the road.

We stumbled upon a local market near the port called the *La Boquería*. Inside, we found tons of stalls offering all kinds of produce, meats, and seafood. We wandered around the place and watched the locals do their weekly shopping. I observed that no one haggled over the prices, so I paid the asking price for my apple. We kept to our new style of eating a big lunch, and soon found a little local place near the beach for more paella.

"I think this is the best seafood paella yet," I said. "I would come back to Barcelona just for this."

"Me too." Sam stood, walked over, and put his arms around me. "So, what's next on our tour today?"

"I think we just keep exploring around this area," I said as I consulted my notes. "You know what? I don't want this trip to end. How 'bout you?"

"I don't want to go home, because this has been so much fun."

"Oh, I need to pick up a little something for Sophie since she's watching Rex," I said, looking around at the many shops.

"Aren't we paying her for watching him?" Sam frowned.

"Yes. But Sophie is just a kid, so I think she would also enjoy a little gift." I pulled him over to a shop with lots of little trinkets. "Let's just duck into this shop to get something. Look, what do you think about a little flamenco dancer figure?"

Sam shrugged. "Works for me if you think you must."

I paid for the figurine, then we made our way to the beach to find the Columbus Monument, constructed for the *Exposición Universal de Barcelona* in honor of Columbus's first voyage to the Americas. After gazing for a bit up at the 197 feet tall monument, we wrapped up the day with a lovely stroll along the beach from the harbor toward the hotel.

"Before we got here, I dreaded many parts of this work trip because I only focused on my obligations," I told Sam. "I reasoned that work and fun vacations needed to be separate things." I shrugged. "But now, I know that's wrong. So maybe in the future, we can add on some non-work-related travel to my work trips."

Sam put his arm around my shoulder and squeezed. "I like your way of thinking."

Our trip was quickly coming to an end, and I was surprised to feel disappointed. I had relished this new pace of vacation life. But all good things must end, eventually. Still, more shocking, international travel thrilled me, and I wanted to do more of it in the future. We would not wait too long to take another trip like this one.

A smile spread across my face while I pondered all the possibilities: Paris, Rome, London, and so many other places with good medical systems, air conditioning, and real toilets.

Thank you, Lord, for this new adventure you provided to me. Help me trust you with future trips. But please don't make me go to lands without modern conveniences. Amen.

CHAPTER SEVEN

That first Saturday home, at my women's Bible study, I decided to share about our trip. We had recently joined a new church and had been attending regularly. New friendships had developed through the church and this Bible study, giving us a sense of belonging to an extended family.

The women expressed their interest in our trip, and I hoped it would lead to some of them using my travel services.

Then we began our study of Zechariah and Elizabeth and how they had trusted God when their longing went unfulfilled. Their story reminded me of my history, so I used the opportunity to share with the women of the group about how I had become a travel agent. I told them my new career had fulfilled a dream for me and that God had led me to this new chance to start over. This was the first time I had acknowledged God's role in all the changes in my life in public, and I offered a quiet prayer of thanks while the other ladies continued talking.

A warm feeling spread over me, and a broad smile spread across my face. "I'm just so content with how life is turning out," I said then, looking up. All the other women stared at me, and I felt myself blush.

But then they all smiled.

God is good.

When we finished our study, I said goodbye to the ladies and walked to my car.

As I reached for my keys, I heard someone call my name. I turned to see Helen Carter walking toward me.

"Do you have a second?" she said. "I wanted to ask you about something."

Helen was the "idea" person in our group and full of a lot of spunk. But she liked to push her plans for the topics to discuss or alternative places to eat. She worked in the church, somewhere in the office. I didn't know what she did other than talking and coming up with ideas.

"What can I do for you?" I asked, hesitant to be pulled into one of her plans.

She planted herself right in front of me. I liked Helen a lot, but she could be pushy—such the opposite of me.

"I thought maybe I could pick your brain about some travel information. I work in the mission office for the church, and with those duties, I sometimes need help with the travel arrangements for the teams heading out of the country. Maybe you can help us with planning. What do you think? Have you ever been interested in helping plan a mission trip?"

The way Helen spoke almost made her question more of a challenge than an actual question. I gulped and tried to think of a way to answer without committing myself to anything.

"I have planned international trips but have only gone on one myself. Most of the ones I plan are to well-known places, like London or Paris." I took a sharp breath. "I don't have a lot of experience working with traveling to more remote locations. And I assume mission trips would be to remote areas."

I hoped that would be the end of the discussion. But it wasn't.

"How much different could it be? London, Paris, or some little town in the Andes Mountains of South America. Airfare, hotels, and transportation are needed no matter where you go. Easy, peasy," she said with a wave of her hand. "Plus, it would be so much fun to work together on such projects. Please say yes, please." She gripped my elbow and smiled brightly.

I gathered up enough courage to stammer, "Let ... let me think about it, and I'll get back to you in a few days."

"Great." Helen released my elbow and clapped. "We're planning out the church's trips for next year, so this will be perfect timing."

Why did it sound like she already knew I'd attend?

As she walked away, a deep sigh escaped my lips, and I plopped down into my car seat.

How would I get myself out of this situation? It would require a lot more work to plan trips to remote locations. *How do you go about finding hotels in parts of the world where they don't have internet?* And would I know if they were safe? Many of these places required visas and shots, and I didn't know how to find out about those items. So many questions whirled around in my head as I started my car. Would I be out of my league trying to plan something like this? I let out another sigh.

As I pulled out of the church parking lot, I yelled, "Dang it, Helen. I'm finally comfortable with my skills. I don't want to try anything new!"

I looked around to make sure my words had stayed within the confines of the car. With all the windows up, my outburst remained safely hidden from any big ears. I fumed the entire drive home.

Sam's car was not in the garage when I pulled in. "He must still be golfing," I said out loud.

Rex, our trusty Siamese cat, greeted me as I walked into the kitchen, purring while I stroked his head.

"How do I get myself into these messes?" I asked, but he offered no answers.

I moved to the kitchen and filled the kettle with water. A nice cup of tea might help me think better. It always did. I placed the pot of water on the stovetop and turned on the burner then got the cup and tea bag ready. I preferred traditional English Breakfast or Earl Grey tea to the other herbal varieties and chose the latter this time. While waiting for the water to boil, I heard my cell phone ping, so I walked over to check it. I clicked the message icon and recognized the number immediately.

"Thank you for offering your help to the mission team," Helen's voice message started. "I've already let the pastor know, and he's so thankful for your help. I'll call you in a few days to set up a meeting for you to attend so you can get more information about the trips. Talk soon!"

"Now what?" I said to Rex as I plopped down on the couch.

I soon became lost in my thoughts, trying to figure a way out of the situation. A high-pitched whistle from the boiling kettle brought me back to reality.

"I'm not sure a cup of tea will help me solve the problem this time, Rex," I said as he rubbed against my leg, and I prepared my tea.

As I walked back to the couch to contemplate this new snag in my life, Sam walked into the house. I quickly bombarded him with all the details of my latest troubles. He chuckled a little while I tried to explain how Helen had trapped me into helping. Finally, I stopped and glared at him.

"Why do you think this is funny?"

Sam swiped a hand over his grin. "You get yourself worked up over these so-called problems all because you don't like change or trying new things. But once you put your mind to work, you always figure out what to do. You're good at solving problems. You just need to stop worrying and realize it. What's that verse that the pastor shared last Sunday? Oh, yeah, 'I can do all this through him who gives me strength.'"

My mouth dropped open. "Since when do you have any Bible verses memorized?"

"I know." He shrugged. "I think that verse is the first one. It just spoke to me during the service, so I made a mental note of it. The verse keeps popping into my mind. And it fits this situation."

I stared at him, flabbergasted. The idea that Sam had memorized a Bible verse and quoted it to me made me lose my train of thought. I blankly stared at him. But in my heart, I believed he was probably right, so I would attend the meeting to get more information.

How difficult could it be, anyway? And if it's too hard, I can back out later on.

CHAPTER EIGHT

ONE YEAR LATER

I hated when Sam was right about something, mainly because he gloated. He had been right about me pursuing a new career and was right about me gaining a wealth of knowledge from helping the mission group. Over the last year, I had dug to find hotel gems in faraway places or figured out what shots and visas were needed for exotic locations. The whole experience had thrilled me and further cemented my new friendships at the church— including Helen, who wasn't so bad after all.

Now comfortable with sending clients to almost every corner of the world, I helped clients get off the beaten track. More and more clients wanted to see places left untouched by runaway tourism than places that put fast-food chain restaurants on every corner. The world became my oyster.

Well, at least through the internet. I still didn't want to venture into any of these remote places myself. I feared the unknown and uncertainty of such faraway lands. Other people might enjoy the adventure of new, unexplored worlds, but I didn't share those feelings. I longed to only stay at the best hotels in countries with sound medical systems, air conditioning, and modern amenities. I dreaded pit latrines and feared what might lurk inside them.

One evening, Sam came home from work a little early. My job blessed me with the option to work from home, and I loved the freedom that came with it. As Sam walked into the kitchen, I noticed the strange grin on his face.

"What's up?" I asked when he leaned down to kiss me.

"Promise me you won't panic," he said.

Just those words caused me to break out in a cold sweat, but I waited without saying a word.

"The company wants to expand internationally. They want me to do some traveling to scout out probable locations and then maybe even help set up some of the new offices," he said while observing my reaction.

I could squeak only out one word, "Where?"

"United Arab Emirates," he said as he sat next to me. "They want me to visit both Abu Dhabi and Dubai for future offices during a two-week trip." He added with a wide grin, "I'd like your help with the travel plans, and here's the best part—the company will pay for you to go with me. Won't that be great? You can finally explore some of those exotic places your clients visit."

"I can't," I said, trying to sound disappointed. "I'm too busy with work." I fanned my hand over my computer as if to illustrate the fact.

"I thought you might answer that way, so I did some research of my own. The country of UAE has a very modern Wi-Fi system. You can take your laptop and work from the hotel during the days, and we can explore the area at night." Sam grabbed my hand. "Please, honey. Say you'll go with me. I don't want to explore somewhere new while you sit at home. It'll be a great opportunity to get out of your comfort zone. Plus, the experience will enable you to help your clients who want to travel to or through the

Middle East. They have all the things you require for your comfort too."

His arguments impressed me. He must have planned his thoughts out well before this discussion. Any objection I raised, he gave me a reason to why it would work out fine. And many of my clients enjoyed traveling through the Middle East on their way to farther destinations.

He sealed the deal by saying, "They have new, state-of-the-art hotels and hospitals."

He understood me so well. He knew explaining the modern amenities could help me become more comfortable with the idea.

"Okay, maybe." I held up one finger as he started to rise, a huge smile on his face. "Let me do some research, and I'll let you know what I decide."

Sam grabbed me in a bear hug and lifted me from my chair, swirling me around in a dancing motion. His excitement overflowed, and he jumped up and down like a little kid on Christmas morning.

I didn't want to disappoint Sam but knew my fears would not allow me to enjoy this kind of trip. Sam always went along with my harebrained ideas. Now, I guess I needed to suck it up and return the favor. *But not without some research first.*

Unfortunately, my research over the next few days did not provide me with a viable way of backing out of the trip. We could fly to either city in the UAE from the Dallas-Fort Worth Airport. Some of the world's best airlines operated on these routes. All the major hotel chains listed properties in both cities. The tropical climate came as a bonus. And Sam's office provided the paperwork to get the visas needed for a two-week business trip.

What could a girl do but say yes and make her husband extremely satisfied? Besides, Sam would be by my side the entire time, and he could always calm my anxieties. The trip received my hesitant green light.

I walked into the kitchen to grab a glass of water. Rex followed me, hoping to receive a treat.

"I'm going to the Middle East, Rex. Can you believe it?" I said to the cat as I handed him some kibble.

Oh, wait. Maybe that can be my excuse. Maybe Sophie wouldn't be able to take care of Rex. I called her and prayed she would not be available.

"We'll be traveling again and need you to watch Rex," I told her when she answered the phone a few minutes later. "This time we'll be gone for two weeks. Will you check your calendar to see if you are available?" I crossed my fingers as I waited for her reply.

"Sure, Ms. Kathleen. I love watching Rex, and those dates are open," she said.

I mumbled, "Great."

"Something wrong, Ms. Kathleen? Did I do something wrong?"

"Oh, no, honey. I'm just not thrilled with the idea of the trip. But that's not your problem. Thanks for helping with Rex. He loves spending time with you. I appreciate it," I said and hung up the phone.

CHAPTER NINE

A few weeks later, I found myself at the airport waiting to board another international flight. The Emirates flight attendants greeted us and pointed down the aisle to our seats. The dark-eyed and dark-haired ladies looked stunning in their red caps with white scarves hanging below their chins.

After we settled in, another attendant delivered each passenger toiletry bags full of goodies in a brightly colored sack with an elephant motif. The crew also offered toys and goodies, boxes of crayons, coloring books, and puzzles to the children on the flight.

A crew member talked to the mom behind me, and I overheard the conversation. She explained the airline employed a nanny on board to help with the children during the long, twelve-hour flight. I made mental notes to share this news with my clients who traveled with children.

Next, the flight attendants distributed menus for the meals—an impressive selection including crepes, paella, and fresh fruits—certainly not like any other airplane food choices I'd ever eaten. The menu also offered us a selection of five different wines with the delicious dinner options. I went with the vegetable paella in memory of our trip to Spain. A few hours later, the flight attendants brought around hot cookies and ice cream for us to snack on. Before we landed, a breakfast of eggs and croissants completed the experience.

After we'd landed, my bladder threatened to explode as we made our way through customs. I spotted a restroom in the baggage hall and ran over. That's when I noticed a group of women in traditional attire enter the lavatory ahead of me. I almost forgot my need to go as I watched them strip off their long, black chadors to reveal western-style clothes of satin pants and sequined shirts underneath. They fixed their hair, makeup, and spruced up after the long flight. When done, they put their chadors back on over their other clothes. There was so much disparity between their outerwear and the things underneath. My jeans and multicolored blouse made me stand out as an American.

When I finally regained my senses, I did what I had come to do, then rejoined Sam.

The gleaming newness of the airport surprised me as well, even though I hadn't been sure what to expect. Men in white, flowing robes stood out against those in western attire while more women followed in their chadors.

After collecting our luggage, we left the secure area and saw a man holding a sign that read "Mr. and Mrs. Johnson." Putting away his sign, he took our luggage and motioned for us to follow him. We stepped into the brilliant sunlight, and the heat hit us. The temperature sat at a sweltering ninety-five degrees, even at this early morning hour.

The awaiting BMW's darkened windows and cold A/C blasting helped to protect us from the outside heat. We also found two cold water bottles waiting for us in the backseat. The coolness of the car drove away the sweat dripping down my forehead.

I plastered my face to the window while we made our way through the city en route to the hotel. I asked Sam to pinch me to make sure all of this was real.

"What are you smiling about?" Sam asked as I gawped at the modern architecture passing our luxurious car—another extravagance Sam's company had spared no expense on.

"I feel like royalty." I giggled. "Should I practice my wave for my adoring fans?"

"You're so silly, honey. And I love you for it. Now behave, so they don't kick us out before I finish my job here."

I sneaked in a quick royal wave, and Sam laughed.

Stunning high-rises sat next to desolate patches of sandy desert. This was no old-world style-type place, I mused, as I looked around at the shiny glass and chrome world. The creativity of architecture here differed from many of the buildings back home. One building looked like a pencil made of steel. Another twisted and turned its way toward the massive clear blue sky. I spotted one that looked like a replica of the Big Ben clock tower in London but was much taller.

How do they create such incredible structures?

Everywhere around us, buildings reached heavenward. Signs along the freeway announced plans for newer buildings to be built soon. A roadside billboard announced an upcoming housing development of homes with bedrooms built underwater while the rest sat above the waterline. Every luxury car dealership in the world lined the freeways. Money did not seem to be an issue for the Arabs living in the UAE.

The entire city looked spectacular until we reached our hotel, which made the rest of the place look shabby. Sam's company had used my travel agent number to snag a great deal at the Ritz-Carlton, so I had expected luxury, but this place far surpassed my expectations.

The hotel glistened like a palace sitting in an oasis of green. I didn't know such grandiose places existed in the world. My higher-end clients would relish such a place. Palm trees, swaying effortlessly in the slight breeze, surrounded the circular driveway leading up to the entrance. The driver opened the door for me, and a blast of heat stopped me in my tracks. It took me a second to catch my breath before stepping from the car.

The jet lag I started to feel in the car ride disappeared as Sam and I walked into the lobby adorned with a white marble floor gleaming in the morning light. The scene beckoned me to come in, relax, and enjoy. Beyond the massive windows in the lobby, the waters of the Persian Gulf shimmered like beautiful sapphires. Nearer to the lobby, the beautiful aqua water of the pool sparkled.

Laughter rose through the open doors from the guests splashing in the pool in the relentless desert sun. Several beach umbrellas lined the pool and gulf areas, which delighted this fair-skinned tourist. My fears evaporated, and I breathed an enormous sigh of relief. Everything on my required list of amenities would be ticked off easily here.

Sam took my hand and smiled. "I told you this would be a great place. I'm glad you're with me."

After checking in, the concierge walked us to the room. When he opened the door, my thoughts went immediately to the Royal Palace we had visited in Spain. This place was just as ostentatious. Well, almost.

Once the concierge left, I scoped out every corner while Sam placed our luggage on the racks and checked out the mini fridge. I found two luxury terrycloth robes and slippers in the bathroom where an oversized rain shower head and an enormous bathtub offered to take me away to a dreamy world of relaxation. Even the high-end toiletries added to the first-class feel of the place. Finally, I returned to the main living space and hugged Sam.

The long, overnight flight and time change caught up with us and caused our eyelids to grow heavy. I stripped off my sweaty clothes and stood in front of the A/C unit for a long time. Finally, we collapsed onto the feather bed and sank into the softness, vowing never to leave the room again.

Soon, I fell into a deep sleep and dreamed of lush gardens surrounding turquoise waters.

I awoke with a start and did not know where I was. Dazed, I sat up quickly, trying to comprehend what my eyes saw. Sam sat up next to me and tried to rub the sleep from his eyes. Slowly, the fog lifted. *Dubai.* The luxury of the room eased the slight fear arising within me at the realization of my location.

I lay back down and closed my eyes to calm myself just as Sam jumped out of bed and ran to the window. He threw back the curtains, and brilliant sunlight filled the room. Squinting, I fumbled my way out of bed.

Sam plopped down again to read about the activities offered by the hotel. The brochure showed tourist sites for every taste and budget. Some nearby, like the traditional souks, offered traditional shopping that had remained the same for hundreds of years. Other options included shopping malls with real ski slopes, museums, and parks inside the building. If we ventured farther, we could enjoy tours of desert areas on camels—something I thought might be better suited for braver souls. I preferred to stay put and enjoy all the things the resort offered. Being out beyond this oasis scared me as I worried about kidnappings or terrorist attacks.

"What would you like to do first?" Sam asked.

"Let's explore the hotel inside and out," I suggested to hide my fears of venturing too far away from the safety of the hotel. "I'm tired from the jet lag, so I'd prefer to keep things low-key today. Remember our international travel routine. And since tomorrow is still a free day for you, we can explore after a good night's rest."

Sam nodded. "That sounds like a good plan. How 'bout we put on our bathing suits and check out the beach and pool?"

Loving how child-like his enthusiasm seemed, I agreed.

Soon, the heat hit me in the face like a wet sponge once more as we walked out through the lobby doors at the back of the hotel. Sweat dripped down my back almost instantly. We grabbed towels and headed toward the beach.

Good thing I packed flip-flops to protect our feet from the burning sand.

I selected chairs under an umbrella and placed my things under it in an orderly fashion. The sun reflecting off the water blinded me, so I grabbed my sunglasses, then we made our way to the water. I waded up to my waist and waited for the cooling to begin.

And I waited.

The steamy temperature made the water feel more like a hot tub than a refreshing dip in the ocean, so I didn't linger long. When I passed Sam on my way back to the beach, I told him, "I'm going to the pool in hopes of finding cooler water."

As I grabbed my towel from the chair, Sam emerged from the water and collapsed onto the chair next to mine.

"Okay, at least I can say I swam in the Persian Gulf." He chuckled. "I certainly didn't expect the water to be so warm."

We gathered our things and went to the pool instead, where I sat in a chair under the shade of an umbrella and several palm trees. After a few minutes of lounging, I decided to check out this water's temperature. I walked to the edge of the pool and tested the water with my foot A slight shiver ran up my leg. *A much better option.*

I sank deep into the cold water. After a few moments, I surfaced, refreshed. I smiled over at Sam who was just now testing the water with his foot.

"Much better." I sighed and floated on my back, enjoying the refreshing embrace of the water.

Noontime approached, and my stomach growled loudly, announcing my hunger to those nearby. I walked back to the seats to dry off before searching for food. A shadow passed over me, and I jumped as a voice spoke to me from out of the blue.

"Here is a menu if you would like to order some food or drinks," a heavily accented woman said. "I will also bring you some iced water bottles to help you keep cool in this heat." She nodded and walked off, leaving me with a wide grin on my face.

"What are you smiling at?" Sam asked as he dried off the water from the pool.

"They have waiter service here. A woman brought us a menu and went off to get us some bottled water. I think I love this place," I said, my grin growing wider.

Soon, a silver bucket of ice arrived with several submerged water bottles. The cold water sent a welcome chill down my dry throat as I drank deeply. Before the woman could walk off again, we ordered sandwiches, then waited for our food, while a cool breeze blew across our damp bodies.

When our sandwiches arrived, I savored the food, only stopping my chewing when some movement on the beach drew my attention. A man leading a pair of camels sauntered along the edge of the water. I gasped and pointed, unable to speak with a mouth full of food. I swallowed hard and yelled, "Camels," and Sam laughed at me.

Sounds of splashing and laughter arose from the pool. I glanced over as a woman wearing a burqa made of bathing suit material entered the pool. The suit covered every inch of her body except her face, hands, and feet. I tried not to stare but could not take my eyes off the woman.

"We're not in Kansas anymore," I said, discreetly pointing to the woman.

That night, we feasted on a fabulous fresh seafood dinner of scallops, shrimp, and crab while overlooking the Persian Gulf. A quick stroll around the property finished out our first day in this desert kingdom. We turned in early since neither of us had slept on the fourteen-hour plane ride, and with the ten-hour time difference, our bodies did not know time anymore. Over thirty-six hours had passed since the last time we'd slept a full night. I slipped into a deep, weary sleep even before my head hit the pillow.

CHAPTER TEN

After breakfast the next day, we asked about recommendations for the best sights in town. The pleasant lady behind the desk told us to take a trip to the Mall of the Emirates to experience the opulence. A visit to the traditional spice souk would be another great way to experience Dubai, she told us and then arranged transportation for us.

A day of adventure lay before us.

We made our first stop at the Mall of the Emirates. The driver dropped us off at one of the main doors and agreed to pick us up at the same spot in two hours. Wide-eyed, we entered the mall and found a strange, new type of world, unlike any mall in America. Men in traditional white dishdasha and kaffiyeh on their heads lingered in groups around the door. Their presence added to the exotic ambience of the place. Some women sported the traditional abaya and hijab while others wore veils over their faces with only their eyes showing.

My attire of khakis and short-sleeved, red blouse again shouted I did not belong here.

"Do you believe this place?" I said.

Sam and I walked to the end of the mall and marveled at the ski slopes.

"Look at that," Sam shouted. "A full-up ski area inside a mall. I can't believe my eyes. I wish we'd brought the right clothes so we could try it. Maybe next time."

Laughter erupted from the children plunging down the hill in a tube while adults skied down the other side of the artificial mountain. We stood watching as the cold air poured out from the area, the chill causing goose bumps to stand up on my arms.

After gawking for a while, we left to see the other sections. Each one contained impressive high-end stores, such as Ferrari and Nespresso. We grabbed a snack at the French bakery, Laudree, followed by a cup of espresso.

I'd never experienced such luxury in my life, and I felt my heart skip a beat. "I feel like a millionaire," I told Sam while he snacked on his patisserie.

He nodded, and we people watched for a while until our allotted time expired.

As we walked back toward the entrance where we'd been dropped off, I took one last look around with my eyes as wide as a frisbee. "Amazing."

The car sat waiting for us when we walked out of the mall and back into the soaring heat. When we stepped inside, the A/C blasting made me say, "Aaahh."

We settled into the coolness while the driver whisked us off to the spice souk in the Deira area. A forty-minute drive took us through some undeveloped city lands with sand-covered lots and no vegetation. When we approached the market area, I spotted a waterway across from the souk, something I did not expect this far inland from the gulf and out in the desert. Boats lined the docks for miles and were ladened down with spices, preparing to head off to faraway lands.

"I wonder if any of those boats go all the way to the US?" I asked.

"I don't think any are big enough for such a long journey," Sam said.

"Surely, some of these spices get shipped to the US. Maybe they go by planes, or these small boats meet up with larger boats in other ports."

Sam said we could look it up later, as the driver brought the car to a stop. Again, he designated a pickup spot for us to meet him in two hours, then informed us we should also visit the gold souk next to the spice market.

The location reminded me of something out of the 1942 movie *Casablanca*. The colorful sights of the spices and pungent smells assaulted my senses as many shops displayed their spices and dried fruits in a towering arrangement outside the doorways. These rainbow mounds of colored herbs drew me back to a simpler time of life, but how did this place survive amid the modern, gleaming steel high-rises all around the area? Aromas of frankincense and shisha filled the air. The smells became overwhelming, and I covered my nose. The noises, scents, and chaos of the market left me wanting to explore it even more.

"This place is incredible," I said. "But aren't the smells too much for you?"

"They're a little intense," Sam agreed. "But the spices intrigue me. I wish we could buy a ton to take home and experiment with them in various dishes. Let's pick out a few that aren't common back home."

I nodded. "I see a few things I want to get. I plan to take home some of the Turkish Delight candy too. Ohhhhh, look over there." I dragged Sam to one of the little shops. "Let's get some saffron. It's really hard to get at home." We spent a mere $30 for stuff that would cost us over $100 back home.

The glint from a store window caught my attention when we turned a corner.

"I guess we are now in the gold market," I said as we gaped at the window displays full of trays of golden bracelets and necklaces twinkling in the sunlight.

"How 'bout you buy me one of those gold bracelets?" I said as I poked Sam in the ribs.

He glared at me before laughing at my request. I smirked, and we continued down the rows.

Some windows displayed shirts and dresses made of pure gold. As a noisy tourist, a part of me wanted to go in just to ask about the prices of these golden clothes. But nothing here would ever fit within my budget.

"If you don't want to buy me a bracelet, then how about a scarf made of gold?"

"No."

"Oh, come on, Sam. Just one little scarf." I laughed. "I'm sure it's no more than $5,000."

I guessed some of these pieces weighed many pounds, which meant they would cost hundreds of thousands of dollars—not to mention the expense to get them home. I'd read the average store contained approximately twenty thousand pounds of gold. At current prices for an ounce of gold, each store's inventory was worth hundreds of millions of dollars.

"I hope they have great security," I said as we walked among the finery.

Tourists mulled around the gold market, snapping photos and pointing out the most absurd items to their friends. Unfortunately, most stores appeared void of customers buying anything, causing me to wonder who bought any of this stuff.

The afternoon wore on, and the oppressive heat rose higher as we stomped around the market.

"I don't think I've ever sweated this much in my life," I said, using a balled-up tissue from my pocket to wipe some sweat from my brow. But that did nothing to stop the rivers of sweat running down my back. I dug out my passport and fanned myself with it.

"Me either," Sam agreed.

We made our way back to the meeting point, and thankfully, the driver arrived right on time. Another smile formed when I slid into the well-air-conditioned vehicle with its cold water bottles waiting for us.

Even though I enjoyed seeing the sights, the oasis of the hotel called to me. I felt a bit of tension drain from my neck as I dragged myself out of the car and up to our room. After a few moments, I collapsed onto the bed to cool off and rest before dinner.

The following day, the alarm went off at 6:00 a.m.

"Good morning, sleepyhead," Sam said. "Are you ready for the next adventure?"

"No. I just want to sleep." I growled. "Why are we getting up so early?"

"Remember, this begins the work portion of the trip. We both have to work today."

"Fine, do we at least have time for breakfast first? I need some coffee too."

"You're not usually this grumpy in the morning? What's up?"

"I'm just worn out from all our adventures. And I never realized how much the heat could take out of a person. Sorry about the grumps. I'll try to do better tomorrow morning."

His broad grin soothed me, and I got out of bed and headed to the shower. "To save time, do you want to join me in the shower?"

"Not if you want us to get to work on time. And I'm hungry."

I stuck out my tongue at him, and we both laughed.

Monday began an unaccustomed experience for both of us. We now worked and were no longer just on vacation. Sam headed off to look for likely locations for his company's new offices, while I worked my magic of planning dream vacations for my clients. I planned to eat my lunch in the room each day because I did not enjoy dining alone in public.

Each night, Sam and I tried out the hotel's various restaurant offerings, and none of them disappointed us. The luxury still offered me a much better working environment than our house. Saturday morning, we packed up to start the next leg of our journey. A rising tide of fear gripped me at the thought of leaving my new sanctuary in Dubai.

What lies ahead for us on the drive to Abu Dhabi? Is the road safe for us to travel? Will I ever be free from these stupid fears? I reminded myself I could return to the safety and routine of my life after only one more week away.

I can do this. I think.

CHAPTER ELEVEN

The drive from Dubai to Abu Dhabi covered about ninety miles and took around an hour and a half. In some spots, the road ran alongside the gulf. I wanted to roll down my window to smell the salty air, but the heat outside made me think twice.

We passed several smaller towns just outside of Dubai city limits, but before long, we reached areas of desolation, and I wondered how any people lived in such harsh conditions. These lonely desert regions offered nothing to see except sand for miles in every direction.

Where did they get their food? Nothing seems to grow in this area.

The road appeared modern enough and made for a peaceful drive. I hoped to see signs for camel crossings, but never did. Finally, a building appeared in the distance, and I let out a deep sigh of relief. *Now, if something happens to us, we can at least get some help.* I didn't realize my body had tensed up so much. The thoughts of becoming stranded in such an isolated area scared me. Did I drip sweat from the fear or the heat? I felt disappointed in myself.

Will I ever be able to enjoy venturing into the unknown?

"How do these people survive in this harsh climate?" I asked Sam, trying to take my mind off my fears.

"I thought the same thing. What do the locals do for a living out here? Where do they get their groceries or their water? I can't imagine a life like this at all."

"No matter how much your company offers you, I don't want to move here, please. Promise me." I grasped his hand and looked at him with wide eyes. "Please. I'm enjoying the visit but can't imagine living somewhere so different."

Sam's nod and a smile reassured me. "I know you well enough to understand how you think. I'd never expect you to move here. Just promise me you'll keep traveling with me and expanding your horizons a little at a time."

"Deal." I turned back to the view just in time to see our hotel.

We'd be staying at another Ritz-Carlton with their modern and up-to-date amenities for this stay. This one sat on the Grand Canal. Again, the hotel did not disappoint. The same incredible level of luxury greeted us when we arrived at the entrance to the hotel.

Sam let out a whistle when he looked across the driveway at the sprawling complex of the majestic Sheikh Zayed Grand Mosque. "Look at that place," he said.

I turned to look. "Wow."

The beauty of the mosque robbed me of words. Nothing I said would convey the amazing beauty. The mosque stood out against the brilliant blue sky and resembled something more than a mere building. This masterpiece of architecture captivated our attention with its eighty-two sparkling white domes and shimmering blue reflecting pools. Sunshine made the building appear to sparkle against the azure sky of the mid-morning light. I almost tripped over the curb when I entered the hotel because my gaze remained glued to the Grand Mosque. The impressive structure and amazing beauty took my breath away.

I joked, "How'd you like to stay there?"

"Nope, but I sure would like to see the inside. Can we tour it?" Sam asked.

"I'll ask at the front desk to see if tours are available. If so, we can get one scheduled."

Inside the lobby, an ornately decorated coffee shop and bar area caught my attention. Taupe walls with golden accents contributed to the place's warm and welcoming feeling. I wandered over to look at the menu while Sam checked us in.

Traditional teas and coffees, along with fluffy pastries, filled the menu. *Yum, I might have to sample each one of those.* They even offered a coffee made with camel's milk. I raised my eyebrows. *Maybe I can talk Sam into ordering one, and I can taste his.*

In the room, Sam studied the brochures on things to do in Abu Dhabi. This resort sat farther away from the city center and offered few sightseeing options other than the Grand Mosque. However, the hotel provided us with a number of other things to do, including a beautiful pool and a modern spa. We planned to spend some time at both because we wanted a break from the heat for the rest of the weekend. The extreme temperatures had sapped all the energy from my body, so my skin thanked me at the idea of a quiet weekend.

We went to the pool first to lower our body temperatures before trying anything else. Abu Dhabi also sat on the same Persian Gulf, so the water, including that of the Grand Canal, would be just as warm as the water in Dubai. After the cooling dip, we headed inside to the lobby lounge for a light lunch and coffee. Bravely, I ordered the coffee with camel's milk, but the café was sold out. *So much for bravery.*

"At least I tried," I said, shrugging.

"Maybe you can get one tomorrow or one of the other days we're here. Maybe you can even learn to milk a camel," Sam said.

"Ha, ha, ha," I said. "Just for that comment, I'm going to the spa to spend some of your hard-earned money."

"Actually, that sounds wonderful. Mind if I join you?" Sam said with a gleam in his eye. "A nice, refreshing massage would do us a world of good."

At the spa, I continued with my new-found bravery and tried something different. The Oasis Ritual intrigued me and included a stimulating Hammam exfoliation scrub. The brochure explained the attendant used eucalyptus soap and wore a traditional kessa glove. A massage with warm oils followed the scrub. Captivated by the description, I tried it.

Two hours later, I emerged a new, relaxed person and made my way back to the room where I collapsed onto the bed in a state of bliss. Within moments, I drifted off to dreamland and awoke to the hushed sounds of the TV.

Sam had returned from his massage feeling refreshed and relaxed too, and we lay quietly and unwound in the air conditioning while a sense of serenity wrapped around me. This level of luxury overwhelmed after a time and I longed for the simpler style of living back home in Texas, but today, I had enjoyed the opulence. I tried to sit up on the bed, but my body drooped like a rag doll. The only remaining question for the evening was what we wanted for dinner.

The next day, we spent a quiet Sunday lounging around the resort.

"The mosque and the Grand Prix racing track nearby might be exciting to explore," Sam suggested, "but I'm exhausted in all this heat."

"Oh, good. I'm feeling the same way. Of course, I'd like to see those things, but I'd agree to hanging out here."

"Maybe the next time we come, we can do those tourist things. Let's just relax before we work again tomorrow."

I whispered, "Or maybe there won't be a next time."

We enjoyed our day at the pool and reading for pleasure. I loved the time away from work. We opted for a light meal of chicken skewers and salad at one of the outdoor areas, then sat sipping glasses of wine after the meal until a funny slurping noise made its way to my ears.

The more I tried to ignore it, the more the sound grew in frequency and volume. Finally, curiosity got the better of me, and I turned to look for the culprit. Several local women puffed on hookahs at a nearby table. People used them in movies or on TV, but I had never witnessed one in real life. The process piqued my interest. I stared intently for a few minutes until one lady looked up and smiled. I blushed when they stared back. Still, the process fascinated me.

The lady asked with a heavy accent, "Would you like to try?"

I smiled but shook my head. "No, thank you."

"You should try it," Sam said.

I whispered to my husband, "I read that smoking one is like smoking an entire pack of cigarettes. No, thank you." Then I said to the woman, "Would you mind if I took some photos and watch to see how it works without trying it?" I could use the information for my clients who might want to indulge.

"Yes, yes. Come over," one of the other ladies said.

They explained the process to me in their broken English. "Okay, first we order pipe. Then a staff member lights the pipe for us. The staff person puffs on pipe until the ember start glowing. Once started, the man delivers the hookah to me. Then we smoke. The staff member keep checking our coals to ensure they stayed lighted and bring more when needed."

Laughter and the sweet, fruity aroma from the pipes rose to the heavens all around me, and a smile spread across my lips as I observed the scene. *Friends improve our lives.*

"Thank you," I said after I snapped the last photo and returned to my table.

"Good job, Kathleen," said Sam, patting my hand. "I'm proud of you for making new friends in a strange country."

I shrugged. "It might provide me some great expert knowledge to share with my clients who visit this area."

The next day, the stifling heat greeted us again. We headed for breakfast to start another day of our remote work week. The past two mornings, we had eaten a leisurely breakfast in the room but today, picked the dining room.

My mouth dropped open as we entered the breakfast area. Every breakfast food imaginable stood before us, and the options stretched over many counters in every corner of the enormous room. American options included omelets or Eggs Benedict made fresh to order. Fresh fruits, figs, and dates provided a rainbow of colors in the center of the room. One station even presented fresh, whole coconuts with straws stuck into the middle so the diner could enjoy the milk of paradise. The smorgasbord of options delighted us as we feasted like royalty. I ate enough to keep myself satisfied until dinner time.

With a full belly, I took up residence in the grandiose, Mediterranean-inspired lobby to do some work and people watch. With Sam off looking at potential sites for the new office, this gave me a better option than sitting alone in my room all day. I sipped espresso from a demitasse cup, even raising my pinky to blend in with my royal surroundings. These luxurious places allowed me to pretend I was somebody different than in my everyday life, and I enjoyed doing it too. After a while, something unusual moved outside the window. I stood up to inspect it.

After sitting in the same position for so long, I stretched my back and legs when I stood, then moved toward the window, which helped relieve the stiffness.

A tiny waif of a child stood among the bushes. The unexpected sight caused me to jump back. My heart pounded in my chest, and I glanced around to see if anyone might be the child's parents. I moved to another window for a different view, wondering if I had only imagined the child.

Dark, scared eyes stared pleadingly back at me. My heart sank. This poor child, clothed in dirty rags and without shoes. Questions ran through my mind. *Where did this child come from, and where are its parents?* I wanted to ask the child, but the window stopped me.

Again, I glanced around to see if anyone reacted to the situation. When I turned back to the window, the child still stood there. I hoped the poor thing would be gone, so I didn't have to figure out the whys of their presence.

Unfortunately, the child's size or clothing made the sex undiscernible. I pressed my hand to the glass, and the child responded in kind.

A large hand touched my shoulder, and I gasped, spinning to see a large man in a waiter's uniform smiling at me.

"I'm sorry that child is bothering you," he said. "We will have it removed from the premises immediately."

Shaking my head, I turned back to the window. The child had disappeared, but the image of the destitute juvenile burned into my memory.

The waiter escorted me back to my table and pulled out my chair so I could sit. Before turning away, he said, "Let me retrieve you another cup of coffee."

After some time, I went to the front desk to inquire about the child, and the clerk just kept apologizing for the interruption to my stay. I tried to explain to the gentleman that the child's well-being concerned me, but he assured me that "it" would not bother me again.

Why did they keep referring to the child as "it"?

The muscles in my back and neck tightened. All the relaxation from yesterday's massage quickly evaporated. I tried harder to explain that I wanted to help the little one if I could, but the clerk met all my questions with polite rebuffs.

Obviously, the hotel did not want any guest to witness such despair and hopelessness in case it ruined their image. *Does all of this culture hold this kind of attitude toward the poor of their country? Or maybe they reacted this way because of their upper-class hotel attitude? Or maybe tourists really don't want poverty to disturb their fantasy world?*

I returned to my seat and found a fresh coffee waiting for me. Images of the rag-clad child filled my mind, and a tear escaped down my cheek. I brushed it away and returned to work on my computer, hoping to forget the whole ordeal.

Later that day, I arrived back to the room at the same time Sam returned from his day looking at office spaces. Sweat dripped down his face. He removed his jacket to reveal sweat on the back of his shirt and under his arms.

"What a sweltering day," he muttered, grabbing a bottle of water, which he drank in one long drag. "Ah, that helps," he said as he pulled out another bottle then plopped onto the couch. "How was your day?"

"It was ... interesting." I replayed the events of the afternoon.

"Was the child a boy or girl?" Sam asked.

"I'm not sure. The clothes hung in torn rags across the small body and were void of anything that revealed a gender. I guessed the child's age was about three or four." I wiped a tear away and said. "I keep thinking about the child and wondering if there's any way to help."

I saw a flash of anger pass through my husband's eyes before he said, "Like what? Do you think you could adopt such a child from a foreign country? Do you think that something like this will change my mind about adopting?" The heat had obviously worn Sam down. He'd rarely spoken to me this way. "I told you years ago that if we couldn't have children of our own, I didn't want someone else's castaways."

I sat next to him and quickly explained. "No, no. Nothing like that. I know how you feel. I just wondered if the child needed help to find their home or if they had one at all. Maybe there was somewhere we could take the child if it was alone in the world?"

This feeling of complete helplessness made my head pound. *All I wanted to do was make a difference. Not anger my husband.*

"I wonder what the staff did with the little one, is all. Did they just shoo him or her away? Back home, I'd know to call the police, and they'd help the child. But here, I don't know what to do to help lost children. I think that's why I'm concerned." I took Sam's hand in mine and felt him soften. "Do you understand?"

Sam nodded. "Well, I think there's nothing you can do now. So best to put it out of your mind. I'm sorry you experienced this situation, but I'm sure the child will be okay." He smiled at me then, looking contrite. "I'm sorry for snapping at you too. This heat makes me irritable."

I snuggled into his shoulder, accepting his apology but not able to let the moment go. I wish my thoughts about the lost child would dissipate as quickly as Sam's anger, but the thought of those big, dark eyes haunted me.

For the remainder of our trip, I searched behind every bush on the hotel property, hoping to see the little face again. But I wasn't sure what I'd do if the child did show up again. Yet that didn't stop me from looking. I think some of the staff thought I had lost my mind because of the way they just smiled at me when they caught me peering out the windows. I tried to search with no one noticing me, but the child never returned.

Like the contrast from the women in the bathroom at the beginning of this trip, the UAE outwardly displayed wealth and luxury, but the inside of the buildings and people hid an emptiness I did not understand.

CHAPTER TWELVE

Weeks after returning home, I still reflected on the lost child. I tried to focus on all the beautiful things that had happened during the two weeks in the UAE, but the face of that little child still overshadowed the memories. *What could I have done differently?* The correct answer eluded me, so I finally put it all away in hopes of never dealing with such a problem again.

Maybe getting back to church will help me sort out my thoughts.

We attended a medium-sized, non-denominational church in Arlington. They offered a modern service housed in an old, white building with a steeple and bell tower. One aisle ran down the middle of the church with pews on each side. A simple pulpit stood in the front, while the choir sat in the balcony at the back.

Each week, Pastor John preached wonderful, Bible-based sermons that challenged me to become a better Christian. Sam and I often shared our thoughts and feelings after each of the inspirational messages.

The following Sunday at church, the pastor based his sermon on the parable in the Bible of the lost sheep, found in Luke 15:3–7. A shepherd realizes one of his sheep is missing and searches desperately until he finds the sheep. Once safely home, he calls all his friends together to celebrate the finding of the one that was lost. The pastor said the parable showed us how Jesus is looking for those who lose their way of faith and how he celebrates when a lost one returns home.

Was I one of the lost lambs Jesus went in search of so he could bring me back again? Jesus had rescued me from my old job, showed me the way to a great new career, and brought us to a beautiful new church and new friends. I once had been lost, but now I was found.

I smiled, but then my mind flashed back to the little lost child from Abu Dhabi. *Was that child one of God's lost lambs? Why didn't I try harder to find him, to rescue him as Christ did for me?*

My heart sank at my lack of action. Maybe I should have left the comfort of the hotel and gone after the child to take them to safety. Instead, I had failed to act like Christ. I offered a quick prayer for the little lost lamb and vowed to figure out a better way to react if I ever encountered that situation again.

I wonder if Sam feels the same way as I do.

My mind snapped back to the present as the final song started. We joined the choir as they sang "Amazing Grace," one of my favorites, but one that always made me cry. Sam slipped his arm around my waist as the hymn ended, and we joined the line of people greeting Pastor John as they left the church.

"Great message, Pastor." Sam reached out and shook Pastor John's hand, then continued walking.

"Thanks, Pastor. As always, you gave me lots to think about," I told him.

"Well, if you ever need to talk about any of those thoughts, just call the office and schedule an appointment with me."

John turned to the next person in line, and I walked on. I wonder if he could ever me sort out my feelings.

I also asked God to forgive me for all the times I failed him. And I hoped the thoughts floating around in my brain proved to God I would do better the next time he provided me with an opportunity to show his love.

"Thank you, Jesus," I whispered, determined to do better next time.

CHAPTER THIRTEEN

ONE YEAR LATER

My daily routine returned to normal, and I put the terrible memories of the little waif behind me. Since I had survived my first scary trip outside of my comfort zone, I counted that as a win. And I continued to plan trips for my clients, while Sam managed the offices for his construction company.

I found success and satisfaction in my work. I no longer feared destinations in less-traveled parts of the world. The UAE taught me an excellent lesson for when I planned foreign travels in remote areas of the world. All this new knowledge made me more proficient in my work.

Sam and I traveled domestically many times over the past year, but we had not ventured outside the US since the trip to the Middle East. I longed for more adventures in a faraway land. One night, while we enjoyed a home-cooked meal together, I asked Sam about taking a vacation to some place new.

"Are you thinking somewhere in Europe?"

"Actually, I'm thinking of somewhere more exciting. Maybe something on the other side of the world," I said with a smile.

"Wow, I'm impressed. You've come a long way, baby, since your days in the accounting world." Sam gave me a high five. "Where're you thinking?"

"I'm not sure. I really feel like going on an adventure. Once we pick somewhere, I can do lots of research about the area. Is there anywhere you've always dreamed of visiting? Maybe some site or attraction on your bucket list?"

Sam tapped a finger to his chin. "Well, there's one place, but I'm not sure how you'll feel about it." He paused for effect. "I've always thought it'd be incredible to see the Taj Mahal. I know India may not be something you ever considered, so we could look at other options if you'd prefer."

"India?" I stammered. "That's a place I'd never considered. But the Taj Mahal seems like an incredible sight to see." I took a moment to consider his suggestion, then said, "I won't say no right now. Let me do some research first. I've not booked many trips to India, so I'll need to get up to speed on everything that's needed."

A slight fear rose within me. Again, I had stepped right into a situation without considering all the possibilities. India. A trip like that would undoubtedly stretch me and my capabilities.

"I'll start researching in the morning and let you know what I figure out."

The following day, I discovered the visa requirements for a US citizen to enter India. Some countries, like the UAE, allow a tourist to purchase their visa upon arrival at their airport. In the past, India required people to purchase visas before the trip, but now, a new electronic option allowed a quicker way, without the worry of the passports getting lost in the mail. Green light for the ease of this requirement on travel to India.

The next item to check on my list before I booked any flights or hotels involved finding options for travel insurance and evaluating the medical system in India in case of any emergencies. India had become a hotbed destination for "medical tourism" and many of the Indian doctors doing these treatments received their training and medical degrees at American universities. I guessed that meant their medical system passed my requirements, if we needed it—another green light to move forward with the trip.

This trip may be a possibility after all.

With all my usual fears now eased for the moment, I researched flights and hotels.

"I better not say anything to Sam yet," I said to the cat. "I don't want to get his hopes up if I find another reason not to go. And I've got to make sure Sophie can take care of you while we are gone too. You're an important member of our family."

Some airlines offered layovers stateside, while others laid over in London, Amsterdam, or Frankfort. A night in any of those towns would be a pleasant addition to the trip.

I twirled my hair between my fingers as my excitement rose. "I might go to India," I told Rex. He purred his reply, then jumped into my lap. "Do you want to go with us?" I teased while I rubbed his head.

Researching hotel information took many hours because of the sheer volume of options for places to stay. I also wanted to satisfy my list of requirements to feel safe. We needed a hotel for about five nights in Delhi before heading out to the area of the Taj Mahal. I liked the looks of one of the internationally recognized chains. The hotel sat a few miles from the airport and provided easy access to many of Delhi's sights. And based on its excellent reviews, the hotel sounded perfect.

Delhi remained hot most times of the year, so I ensured the hotel provided air conditioning in each room. Sleeping in sweat-drenched attire never appealed to me. The hotel also offered transfers to and from the airport, which I always appreciated. Picking an unknown taxi driver out of the hundreds clamoring for my attention made me apprehensive. I preferred to walk out of the customs hall to find someone holding a sign with my name on it, ready to whisk me away to the place I needed to go.

We also needed at least one night in the town of Agra, the home of the Taj Mahal.

I found a place called the Aman Homestay, a small inn just a little over a mile from the Taj. Not chain affiliated, but the reviews ranked it as one of the best places to stay in Agra.

My eyes widened as I continued reading. The guesthouse only charged a rate of $30 per night. My mind screamed "No." Anything that cheap must have something wrong with it, I reasoned. I flipped through the electronic photos, trying to find the problems. But the glowing reviews and rosy recommendations—especially the ones about the owner—made me more feel confident about staying there.

Maybe my fears can relax enough to be a little extra adventurous and stay in a non-chain hotel.

I decided to take a chance, reasoning that since we traveled off-season and most of the other hotels showed space available, we could switch to one of the other chains if the Aman did not live up to the reviews. Now I just needed to jot down all my ideas about this grand adventure to Sam when he got home.

I met Sam at the door that night and kissed him softly on the lips. He smiled, then drew back to ask, "What's up? Or should I ask what you did this time?"

"Nothing. Can't a girl just let her husband know how much she loves him?"

Sam pulled me closer and kissed me again. "What smells so good?"

"I cooked up a special dinner tonight. Chicken tikka masala served over rice with warm naan bread."

"What?" Sam let go of me and ventured into the kitchen where he lifted the lid off the pot. "What kind of food is that? Oh, wait, did I miss our anniversary again or some other special event?" He turned to me with a frown.

"No, honey. I found a recipe on the internet and thought it'd be a good way to prepare our stomachs for the trip to India."

"Yo ... wait, what? Did you just say *our trip to India*?" His cheeks flushed, and his eyes grew wide. "Do you really mean it? We're going to India?"

"Yes. After dinner, we can go over the plans. I'm so excited to share my ideas with you. I think this might be the trip of a lifetime."

Sam threw his arms around me, squeezed me in a bear hug, then swung me around the kitchen before kissing me again. "I love you, babe. You keep surprising me with all your willingness to try new things for me."

"I've already called Sophie, and she agreed to watch Rex. We're going to have a great time!"

I wish I felt as confident as I sound. Maybe I need to ask Sophie if she would keep Rex if we die in India. Here I go again, one step forward and two steps back trying to get rid of my ridiculous fears. God help me, please.

CHAPTER FOURTEEN

As we exited customs at the Delhi airport, Sam spotted the driver with our name plaque first. We loaded into the car—no BMW this time but an old beat-up Hyundai Venue. At least the inside was clean, I thought, as we drove off to the unknown. The Delhi smog and traffic made the drive to the hotel an absolute nightmare. The driver inched forward as the cacophony of car horns rose to a crescendo around us. Hours slipped past while we waded through the overcrowded city. The cars kicked up dust from the road that seeped into my lungs while the high levels of pollution shrouded the tops of tall buildings from view. I couldn't keep myself from coughing and wondered if I would need a mask to keep out the pollutants on our trip. Already, this trip was not meeting my basic luxury requirements.

"I'm not sure I'm going to like it here," I moaned to Sam. "Where's my luxury?"

"You're just overly tired." He patted my hand, his eyes never leaving the sight of the chaos outside our car. "Give the city some time. I'm sure we'll have fun."

"Maybe, if we don't die from all this smog." I coughed again. "I feel filthy from all this dust."

"Relax, honey. It'll be okay. We're here to have fun and sightsee." He turned to me with a frown. "Don't ruin the trip with a bunch of negativities."

My jaw tightened, and I crossed my arms as I turned to look out the window. I knew my irritability might come from the jet lag. These two flights had been the longest of any trip so far and my entire body screamed at me to collapse into a bed and sleep.

Finally, we got to our hotel and stumbled up to our room. When the bellman left, I got under the covers and pulled them up over my head to drown out the noises of the city below.

The next thing I knew, my alarm was going off—thank God I had set it in the car on the way here—and I heard Sam snoring next to me. I shook him awake.

"Wake up, sleepyhead. I want to make sure we sleep tonight. You know me and my neurotic routines."

The fog from traveling across almost twelve time zones settled over my brain and kept me from focusing on much of anything other than wanting to crawl back into bed, but I wanted to make the most of our time here.

We wandered around the hotel and snacked on samosas in the restaurant for lunch and dinner. I ventured outside at one point to snap a few photos of the area and the hotel. By 9:00 p.m., we both succumbed to the gnawing tiredness. *Tomorrow will be better.* I prayed this trip would not bring back the fears and doubts I had worked so hard to overcome.

We spent the next few days sampling a mixture of sights around Delhi. When we visited the Red Fort, I gazed in awe at the impressive construction dating back to the seventeenth century.

"Did you know the Red Fort served as the principal residence of the Mughal Emperors?" I asked.

"Nope." Sam shook his head. "It sure is impressive though."

A sign in front of the building explained it had become a UNESCO World Heritage Site in 2007. Sandstone walls surround the fort and stood seventy-five feet tall. Inside the walls were palaces, entertainment halls, a mosque, and the Hall of Audiences. The contrast of red sandstone outside and the white, jewel-inlaid marble walls and floors inside stunned my senses. The richness of the fort stood in stark contrast to the poverty of the surrounding area, and I thought again of the small child in Abu Dhabi.

"Who knew such magnificent places existed? I'm learning so much about the ancient Indian culture," I said, trying to keep my focus. "After that drive from the airport, I really expected to hate this place. In fact, I thought about getting back on a plane home. But this is really cool."

"And this is just the beginning," Sam said. "We've got so much more to explore."

And explore we did for the next two days. More extravagant places and even a crowded market similar to the souks from our Middle East trip.

But the noisy chaos and pollution began to wear on my nerves, and I couldn't wait to get out of the city and to the Taj Mahal.

Finally, the day arrived for us to head to the Taj Mahal, the pièce de résistance for this trip. The sun rose above the haze of the city as we headed off toward Agra.

The guidebooks told us the 145-mile drive would take an average of four hours if we started early in the morning to avoid traffic. However, the pamphlets also cautioned it could take almost six hours at the height of rush hour.

Two hours into the journey, Sam asked me, "Are you feeling any better about this trip?"

"A little," I said. "All the hustle and bustle and noise has unsettled my nerves, but the sights around Delhi thrilled me." I stared out the window for a minute before saying, "I'm not finding any of this trip relaxing at this point though."

"I understand. It's certainly nonstop and noisy. But this is what adventure is about, exploring new and different places. Some will be more relaxing than others. We wanted to see the world, and craziness comes with this part of the world." He grabbed my hand and kissed the back of it. "Don't give up your new spirit of adventure yet."

"I'm trying. And I'm keeping an open mind." I smiled but wondered if the butterflies in my stomach came from my fears or the erratic driving.

We entered a small town and soon sat at a stoplight. I turned to look over my shoulder and noticed a large gray shape behind our vehicle.

I squealed, grabbed Sam's arm, and yelled, "There's an elephant behind us!"

The driver slammed on the brakes as he turned to glare at me. "What wrong with you? You scare me half to death."

"I'm sorry." I rushed to apologize. "I just never expected to see an elephant lumbering down a city street with a rider on his back." I turned with Sam to look at the magnificent animal. "So cool." *Maybe India would be okay.*

After the driver recovered from my outburst, he asked us if we liked animals. We both nodded.

"Before we get to Agra," the driver said, "a place near here rescues dancing bears from their captors. The charity rescues them and cares for them for the rest of their lives. We can stop by the place if you'd like to see it. It's called Wildlife SOS, and it's not far out of our way."

"I'd love to see it," I said before Sam could get in a word. My stomach needed a break from the lurching car too.

"Okay, we go. But no photos of the bears. Many of them dance when they see a camera, even after all the years away from the trade. So no photos," he said.

We promised not even to sneak a picture. The organization that cared for the animals had also hired some of the previous bears' owners to care for the animals, so the family still made a small income from the situation.

"Well, that was cool," I said at the end of the tour. "A stop well worth making to learn about the dancing bears of India."

"That was neat and worth the detour," Sam agreed. "How much did you donate?"

"I threw a twenty into the donation jar. They're doing good work."

"Good. I'm glad you did. You should tell your clients about this attraction too."

"Already in my notes."

Back in the car, we made the final push to Agra. We rolled into the parking area of the Aman Homestay around four that afternoon. The place looked nice enough, but my former self still fretted, and I looked for anything that might offend my delicate tastes.

The owner, Aman, greeted us and led us to the room, explaining we could walk to the entrance to the Taj in about fifteen minutes. Our room held a king-sized bed which filled most of the space. A small chair and a desk were crammed on one side of the bed and a couch was crammed in on the other. A simple bathroom with a porcelain toilet sat behind a door and the whirring A/C unit filled the room with cold air. I breathed a sigh of relief. *I may be okay here.*

This place appeared better than I'd expected. *Maybe a future as a fearless, adventurous traveler is possible.*

Some of the Agra tour books had suggested a sunrise or sunset visit to the Taj for the best chance to see the monument when it glowed pink from the reflection of the sun. So Sam and I walked hand in hand down the dusty trail in the fading light of dusk to glimpse the exquisite building.

Little stalls selling all kinds of Taj trinkets—touristy coffee mugs, keyrings, and other items with photos of the Taj—and some with more traditional options like hand-woven rugs and items made from the same material as the Taj, lined the pathway, and hawkers cried out, trying to catch the attention of any passersby as their day was coming to an end.

I picked up a little marble elephant with an inlay of semi-precious stones. "Sophie will love this," I said to Sam. "And I'll tell her about the elephant we spotted on the drive here too."

After I paid, we continued our walk along with the locals conducting their daily business and children running around playing. I snapped a photo of a group of women in green, pink, blue, and gold saris with their matching scarves blowing in the breeze. The burst of color danced in the fading light of dusk.

About halfway to the Taj, a little girl poked her head out from behind a shop. I smiled at her, and she quickly disappeared. She reappeared a few minutes later and kept her distance as she walked behind us.

I looked back at her and guessed she was about four or five. She wore rags and her face was streaked with dirt. A cringe made its way down my back as I remembered the child from the United Arab Emirates. *Okay, Lord, why are you showing me this child?*

Maybe she just wanted to look at the tourists and see if they would give her a coin or two. I walked on and placed my arm in Sam's. He smiled at me and kissed the top of my head.

Soon the Taj came into view, and I stopped, awed by the enormous size of the attraction.

The gleaming white color glowed pink in the receding light and the marble twinkled. I sucked in a deep breath. Awestruck, I did not move for a moment while I tried to take it all in. I stared at the grandeur of this extraordinary monument millions of people visited and wondered if anyone would even remember me a hundred years from now.

Sam pulled at my arm, and we moved closer. Signs instructing us to remove our shoes before going up the steps to the building stopped us once more. We donned green booties and walked up close enough to touch the building. The marble floors, slippery under our booties, forced us to step purposefully to keep from falling. Inlaid colorful precious and semi-precious stones against the pure white marble added another dimension to the beauty. The magic of the Taj entranced me. I could not tear my eyes away.

Finally, the sun sank below the horizon and shrouded the monument in darkness. We pushed our way through the throng of people leaving and headed back to the hotel before it got too dark. The crowds of people bumped and pushed against us as walked along. Neither of us spoke for a while because words could not compare to the beauty we had experienced.

I snapped back to reality when I spotted the same little child following us again. Flesh barely covered the bones in her arms and made them appear more like twigs. The lack of light added to her haunting appearance and made me shudder.

This time, I nudged Sam and pointed out the girl to him. "I think she followed us. She walked behind us on the way to the Taj. I wonder where her family is, and if they know she's wandering the streets."

"Don't worry. She's probably just a beggar child, hoping to get some money from the tourists around here. I'm sure she has a family who loves her."

"I don't know. Maybe we should call someone. Maybe the child needs help."

"Here we go again." Sam frowned. "Who are you going to call in this country? Do you even know how to make a call in India?"

I stopped to confront Sam, but the crowd bumping into me kept me moving.

"India might be a developing country," Sam said as he pulled me along, "but that doesn't mean she's all alone in the world. We'll get a nice meal back at the hotel, and you'll forget all about her."

But the little girl's face burned itself into my memory and her face even filled my dreams that night as I tried to sleep. The answers of how to help her eluded me while I lay awake. I tossed and turned for hours before offering a prayer to God for help.

Finally, I fell into a restless sleep.

The following day, the same feeling hung over me as I continued to think about the child from the previous night. Sam tried his best to lighten my mood, but nothing worked. As we made the short stroll to the Taj Mahal before breakfast to catch it in the rising sun's light, Sam attempted to lighten my mood with sweet talk and jokes, but I couldn't get my mind from the little girl's haunted eyes.

When we made our way past the stalls, I spotted her again. She looked up, recognition dancing in her eyes. She offered a small smile. I waved to her, and she waved back.

Sam tugged me along while speculating how the light would affect the building compared to last night's setting sun. He talked about his ideas to find the best places to snap photos and capture the monument in the best light possible. He prattled on, oblivious to my distraction.

In front of us, I noticed a fire burning in front of an open stall selling fresh fruit. I stopped and purchased an apple. Sam stopped farther up the road but turned to see why I lagged behind.

"What are you doing?" he called to me.

I held up the apple to show him. We walked on, and I slowed my pace to allow the girl to catch up. I stopped and motioned for her to approach. The child appeared both shy and afraid, but slowly crept up to me as I held out the apple. Suddenly, she grabbed the fruit, then ran off behind another building.

I turned back to see Sam staring at me, his neck muscles quivering. We walked on in silence for a while, and I felt the tension radiating off my husband. But I did not care. I had done what I needed to do. The story of the lost lamb from the Bible popped into my head, and I smiled. I had done the right thing.

While Sam snapped countless photos of the monument and ignored me, my mind went back to the little girl. I sat down on a bench while Sam found the best angles for his pictures. Finally, he tore himself away from the camera long enough to notice I no longer stood beside him.

He wandered over to me. "Look," he said in a sharp tone, "just because we can't have children doesn't mean you need to save other children."

Instantly, my good mood fled as hot tears formed in my eyes. "This isn't about that."

"Then what is it?" Sam shot back at me.

I sighed. "A while back, the pastor preached on the story of the lost lamb and how God leaves the ninety-nine to rescue the one. I'm the one he rescued. And sometimes I feel like he's calling me to return the favor by helping to rescue other lost lambs."

"That's crazy. I think you're just feeling sorry for yourself, and you think helping someone will make you feel better. I came here on vacation, to see the Taj Mahal, not to help some lost child." He turned his back to me then, but soon turned back. "Look, maybe, when we get home, you can find some volunteer work to help you feel better. Till then, forget about her and enjoy your vacation." His pronouncement done, he turned on his heel again and began snapping more pictures.

"You want us to be just like every American tourist?" I said, making him stop and turn to me. "Ignore the poverty in a country and only focus on the pretty things instead. I don't want to be those people. Please." I reached out for his hand. "I can't enjoy myself when there are people in desperate poverty around me."

"I guess we won't be going on any more vacations then," Sam said in a huff.

I decided to let the moment drop, and soon, Sam's mood lightened as we neared the Taj.

"I'm looking forward to a freshly made breakfast after all this walking this morning. Once we eat, we should pack up to head back to the city."

He continued talking nonstop about the fantastic beauty of the glowing pink marble of the memorial built to honor love. He clasped my hand, and we strolled back along the now-familiar route. Our tense moment forgotten, we chatted and shared our feelings about seeing such an incredible building.

We were about half way to the Taj when Sam dropped my hand, halted, and gazed at something ahead of us. I followed his gaze to the little girl now standing directly in our path.

She offered a weary smile and waved slightly.

"Your new friend's waiting for you," Sam huffed as he continued his stride forward, side-stepping the little girl.

"What's wrong?" I yelled as I ran after him. "I'm just trying to help her." I grabbed his hand and forced him to stop.

He spun and glared down at me. As he opened his mouth to say something, Sam's eyes softened. I turned to follow his gaze and saw the little girl still followed us, but now she was crying. Sam dropped my hand and walked back to the girl.

"It's okay," he mumbled as he wiped away the big tears leaving streaks in the dirt down the child's face. "Maybe we should get her something to eat," he said over his shoulder to me.

I hurried to the nearest little kiosk and purchased some bread. When I returned, I found Sam crouching in front of the child, trying to convey a message to her using hand gestures.

Finally, he looked up at me with pleading eyes. "Okay, okay. Now you've got me feeling bad for her. What should we do?"

"I don't know what to do. How do you go about finding out if she has a family or not? Maybe we could talk with the owner of our hotel since she speaks English well," I suggested. "Maybe she'll have some ideas. The girl will most likely follow us and stay nearby because she can sense we want to help. We can find her once we figure out something."

We started back to the hotel, and I gestured to the girl to come along. I glanced back every few minutes to check on our little follower who walked about fifty feet behind us. At the hotel, we quickly located the owner and explained everything.

She shook her head and covered her mouth with a hand, her shoulders drooping. "Lost children are big problem in my country," she said in a monotone voice. "Poverty makes them lost because parents can't care for them. Parents just put them on the street. Is child nearby?"

"The little girl followed us several times, so I think she'd still be nearby," I said.

"We go look for her." Aman headed for the front door.

It didn't take us long to spot the child near the hotel.

"There she is," I shouted, as if finding a lost treasure.

Aman approached the child and spoke in their native tongue. There seemed to be a lot of questions. Head nods and a few tears followed. Finally, the pair hugged and walked back toward us.

"This child's alone." Aman looked down as the child clung to her leg. "Her parents both passed recently. She lived with old aunt, but she passed now too. She begs in streets for food and sleeps any place with a little warmth. Little girls like her at high risk of disappearing."

"Is there anything we can do or somewhere safe we could take her?" Sam asked as he plopped down at the table and begun stroking the girl's hair. "Now that we know her history, I feel we need to do something so nothing bad happens to her."

I smiled warmly at Sam for his concerns, thankful he seemed to have changed his attitude about the whole thing. My weak smile and watery eyes sought answers as I turned back to Aman.

"Have you heard of Mother Teresa?" Aman asked.

"Yes, but she's not alive anymore," I said.

Aman shook her head. "But charity she started still here. They care for street children and provide homes for orphans. Missionaries of Charity. I can phone to get ideas on how to help the girl."

Sam and I nodded. The child offered a nervous smile then walked over and held my hand.

When we returned to the inn, Aman offered the girl a plate of food then went to the phone in another room. The child wolfed down all the food provided, then looked around as if she might still be hungry, so I walked over to the counter and got her another piece of bread while we waited.

An awkwardness filled the air between us, since we could not speak her language and did not know what to say, but I tried to assure her with smiles and small pats on the hand or back.

"Good news," Aman said as she returned smiling. "They will be able to care for the little girl. The nuns send over a rickshaw to pick her up. I explain to the little girl now, so she will be happy."

Aman bent down to talk with the girl and explained the situation to her. Again, a few tears fell from the little girl's eyes. Once Aman finished talking, she hugged the youngster then stood to address us. "The girl's name is Prisha, and she understands what happens. She little sad not to go home with you, but I explain about the place where nuns care for her. I tell her she be happy with many children and enough food every day."

A few tears rolled down my cheek as I watched the poor child and worried about her future.

Sam took my hand. "It's not like we could take her home with us. This option is the best thing we can do to help Prisha."

Aman nodded.

We had made the right decision, but I still wondered what would happen to Prisha as she grew up and became a young woman in this society that did not value women. What would her future hold? Life was tough for most people in India, so would it be worse for an orphan? An unsettled feeling filled my heart. But Sam was right—what else could we do?

"I don't want to be here when they pick up Prisha," I said. "I think I might cry, and then, my tears might stress her out even more under the circumstances."

Aman agreed to tell the little girl, and the girl's eyes welled with more tears, which caused mine to leak as well. I hugged her tight. Her small arms squeezed me back. Then I gazed deep into her eyes and forced a broad smile to comfort her. She smiled back, and I wiped her cheek. *This way is the best, my little one*, I reasoned to myself. Then Aman took the girl into the lobby to wait. Once the nuns picked her up, Aman returned to say goodbye to us.

When the car service arrived, I hugged Aman and thanked her profusely for the wonderful time she provided and for the help with Prisha. Sam handed something to Aman, and we loaded into our ride without saying another word.

We rode back to Delhi in thoughtful silence for the first couple of hours of the journey. Finally, I broke the silence and asked Sam, "What did you give Aman back there?"

"I handed her some money to give to the nuns. I hope it'll help with caring for Prisha."

"Really?"

A lone tear ran down my cheek, and Sam brushed it away.

"I guess I'm learning to have a heart like you, babe. And maybe we can send some money occasionally to help her out. I don't think I can ever ignore the surrounding poverty again."

"I love you." Sam couldn't breathe for a second because I hugged him so tightly. "Thank you. We can make a difference."

A few weeks after returning home, Prisha weighed heavy on my mind. I emailed Aman and asked how the transfer went. She informed me that all had gone well. She had even followed up with the nuns, and they told her that Prisha had settled in nicely and enjoyed playing with all the other children.

A sense of relief swept over me. Aman sent us a note with the information on sending money to help the girl in the future. I shared this information with Sam once he got home from work.

He thanked me with his wonderful smile, and my heart skipped a beat. "I guess we're now official sponsors of an orphan girl in India. Only you could make these kinds of changes in my life, babe. Thanks."

What does all this mean? First, I encounter the kid in UAE and now Prisha. I don't know if my heart can handle any more of these encounters. Maybe I'm too much of a pushover. Do I just need to become hard-hearted and ignore these problems? God help me.

CHAPTER FIFTEEN

In the weeks and months after the trip, haunting memories of Prisha still impacted me. *Could I have done more?* One day, I headed up to the church to talk with someone about the lingering feelings.

I stopped at Helen's office and found her sitting behind her desk. She greeted me with a hug, then motioned for me to take a seat on the couch in her office. "Would you like a cup of coffee or something?"

"No, thanks. I hope I'm not interrupting your day too much?"

"Don't be silly. I love visiting with you and can't wait to hear all about your trip. Was it wonderful?"

"Well, I'm struggling with some feelings from something that happened on the trip to India. I thought maybe you could help me sort them out." I explained about Prisha and the arrangements we'd made for her to go to the orphanage.

"Wow," said Helen, "those types of situations are tough on the emotions. Unfortunately, the world is full of many needy people of all ages, and we can't help them all."

"I know, but the Bible story of the lost lamb from Matthew makes me feel like I should do more to help others. Jesus died to rescue me, so aren't I supposed to rescue others? Instead, I feel like I just handed off the kid to someone else to solve the problem." I dug out a tissue from my purse to wipe away the tears. "I even studied the parable of the lost lamb several times."

"Oh, honey. I'm so sorry for all these struggles. Here, let me get you some coffee, and then, we can continue to dive into this problem."

Helen headed down the hall and soon returned with two cups, handing one to me.

"Okay, tell me more about these feelings and how this Bible story plays into what you are going through."

"I found two other stories in the Bible that also emphasize what we should do. The story of the lost coin and the story of the prodigal son. In each parable, finding something or finding someone caused rejoicing for the one searching for the items." I took a long sip of coffee to gather my thoughts. "But how do I take these parables and apply them to my life and situations like the one with Prisha? Since I suffered through several miscarriages early in my marriage, I believe those losses affect my feelings toward these lost children. I failed at helping my own babies survive, so am I compensating by trying to help poor children like Prisha?"

Helen thought for a few moments before she spoke again. "Those are some deep thoughts. But I think you're only partially correct in your interpretation of the parables. They tell us how God rejoices over a lost soul coming home and how Christ is always pursuing us to come back to him. Jesus also wants us to follow his examples, so we should rescue the lost." Helen paused as she reached over and took my hand. "Rescuing the lost is more about bringing them into the family of faith and not about bringing them into your home. But I can understand your feelings. And what else could you do? You rescued that girl from the street and provided financial help for her future. Her life will be so much better, and you should rejoice over that result."

"I know, I know," I stammered. "But it doesn't feel like I did enough. I really don't know what else we should've done, but I feel that's an excuse for me not to do more. How do I know the place that took Prisha will take good care of her? I have no way to follow up with her and be assured she is okay. What will the nuns do with her, or any child, once they turn eighteen? Do they just turn them out on the street? Do they provide an education so the children can find jobs? I just have so many questions and no answers. I thought you might help me sort through all this."

"What about developing a list of resources for helping kids in countries where your clients travel or where you go? That way, you'd have wonderful sources of information to use if this type of situation ever occurs again. Or you could think about setting up a charity to help these kids by building orphanages to house them until they grow up." Helen frowned. "The problem with that idea is that you don't have the money to set up an orphanage in every country. Also, how do you find reliable people to run the orphanages if you're not there full time? And setting up a charity comes with many issues, too, and requires money from donations. Do you really want to go down that road? It might not fix everything, but you should start with the list to get your feet wet."

"Good thoughts, Helen. I really like the idea of the list of acceptable places in various countries. I agree I don't want to consider orphanages or a charity right now." Helen nodded, and I continued, "I think I should spend some time researching this idea. What'd you think?"

Helen and I went back and forth for a while longer and finally settled on her idea of a thoroughly researched reference list. I planned to make a list available through my travel website and to any teams that went on a mission trip with the church. I shared the ideas with Sam that night over dinner. He agreed this would be a suitable solution and offered his help in any way possible.

Over the next few days, I worked on a list. I coordinated my efforts with Helen to see if she agreed with the direction I took with the information or if she wanted any specific countries added. The nagging feeling of being unprepared for third-world problems like the one we experienced faded away. I sat back and smiled. *What a great friend Helen has become. I love all her wonderful ideas. I'm blessed.*

Because of my experience with Prisha, I started building my list with India first. All the research took several days of digging and making phone calls to find acceptable places. I realized this project would take many months or even years to complete if I wanted the list to be useful. Also, I needed to update the information regularly to account for changes in orphanage status or to add alternative places.

After many months of work, the index covered about ten countries. Most were places with high incidents of human trafficking and child slavery problems. I published the findings on various websites and asked for feedback from anyone who used them.

I prayed the listing would make a difference to someone somewhere in the world and offered a quick prayer of thanks to God for giving me the wisdom to get started.

CHAPTER SIXTEEN

Leaning forward to stare at the computer screen, my pulse quickened when some information about safaris burst forth. Although my work on the index would be ongoing, the initial phase was done, and I wanted to plan another trip for Sam and me to visit some of the countries I had researched for my list. A safari might be a fun adventure to try as a trip for us.

"Have you ever wanted to go on a safari?" I asked Sam while we sipped coffee one Saturday morning.

He almost spit his out.

"Sounds incredible," Sam said, wiping his chin. "Do you think you're ready for such an adventure? If you're serious, I'd love to see some of the big cats in the wild. What did you have in mind?"

"I thought Kenya might be a good option. It appears to be one of the more stable countries in Africa. Nairobi has many modern hotels, and the tented camps in the game reserve offer first-class amenities, including porcelain toilets. The medical system in town is not horrible. And I can find better deals for Kenya versus South Africa, so I think Kenya would be the best option for the money. If you agree, I can start planning. What do you think?"

Sam nodded vigorously in response to my questions, and I soon set out to make all the arrangements. I found several options for our flights from Dallas/Fort Worth to Nairobi. Several choices appeared as choices for the route, including the cities of London, Amsterdam, or Frankfort. Other possibilities allowed travel through several places in the Middle East.

I found it best to avoid layovers at Heathrow Airport because of the tremendous crowds, making it difficult to move between terminals in a reasonable amount of time. Some of my clients had almost missed their connecting flights more than once because of the time to change terminals. Considering that, the route through Amsterdam jumped to the top of the list. I booked the flights and turned to researching hotel options.

I prayed a quick prayer as I began looking for a place to stay. A gem of a place—the Fairview Hotel—popped up on the first page of my search. *Thank you, God, for guiding me in my search.* This hotel sat on the edge of downtown but off the main roads, so I hoped it would be peaceful and have less of the city traffic noises to keep me awake at night. The photos of the hotel showed old-world luxury but with extremely reasonable prices. And the descriptions and reviews made the hotel sound like something from the movie *Out of Africa*, which told the story of Karen Blixen's life in Kenya.

Other hotels did not meet my expectations, so I picked the Fairview as my first choice. Then another great place called Giraffe Manor caught my attention. This one also piqued my interest because the hotel sat in the middle of a huge giraffe reserve. The giraffes used their long, spotted necks to look into the windows while the guest ate in the second-floor dining room.

Who could resist eating with a giraffe watching you? The nearby park also allowed visitors to feed the giraffes by hand from a treehouse near the hotel. My heart wanted to stay there, but my brain didn't like the outrageous prices. Maybe Sam would agree to stay there for only one night before we headed home. We would stay at the Fairview for the rest of our time in Nairobi.

"How'd you feel about spending a huge amount of money to eat breakfast with a giraffe?" I said to Sam as he walked into the kitchen one night after work.

"How much is huge?"

"Over $1,500 for one night."

Sam whistled, then said, "I don't think so, but it sounds cool. Can we go there just to eat a meal without staying there?"

"No, but we can visit the giraffe center and feed them. That would be fun too." I closed my computer and headed into the kitchen to start dinner.

"Okay, I think we should do that. Do you have other options for places to stay?"

I told Sam all about the Fairview Hotel, and the description impressed him.

"Any luck on the safari part of the trip?" he asked.

"I found one fascinating place called Kiboko Bay Resort on the shores of Lake Victoria. They have permanent luxury tents with king-sized beds and full American-styled bathrooms inside. The view of the setting sun over the famous lake is visible from the rooms. The hotel derives its name from the pod of hippos the lived near the resort. Kiboko means hippo in Swahili." I stirred the taco meat in the skillet and placed the tortillas in the microwave to warm them. "This lake area offers a variety of activities, including guided fishing trips and an impala wildlife sanctuary. The sanctuary also houses lions and many other animals besides impala. I think it would be a great option for our adventure."

"Sounds wonderful to me. I'll need to get some extra SD cards for my camera. I bet I'll take thousands of pictures.

Can I use your computer for a minute?" Sam grabbed my laptop and ordered the items he needed from his favorite website.

"If we drive from Nairobi to Kisumu," I continued, "we'll pass a lake called Naivasha. It's home to more than a thousand pink flamingos. One tourist review said that the lake's surface looks pink from all the birds resting on it. The only problem is the driving conditions. The road's full of potholes, and it could take us over eight hours to drive the 164 miles. Or we could take a one-hour flight to Kisumu and skip the flamingos."

"Wow," he said, looking up from the laptop. "Sounds cool, but I like the idea of flying better. Maybe we could see the flamingos from the plane or on another visit. What other things can we do?"

I explained about the other places to visit in Nairobi which included a wildlife park where the animals roamed freely inside a fenced in area, a baby elephant rescue center where we could see and touch orphaned baby elephants, and a separate baby animal orphanage with a variety of other orphaned animals.

Sam nodded so I added these places to our want-to-do list.

"Now, back to this giraffe place," Sam said. "How many chances do you get to stay and dine with giraffes? Maybe we should revisit that idea."

"Agreed. But I think we should stay there just for one night." I walked back to the table to get my computer. "I'll check to see if I can get a reduced rate as a travel agent to help offset the cost." When I pressed the button to make the reservation, I squealed. "I can't wait for this next adventure and all the magnificent animals we might see." A wide smile spread across my face.

"We might get one more adventure too," Sam said.

"What does that mean?" I turned to look at him.

"Well, remember my project back in the UAE? They are moving forward with the property I saw in Dubai, so I might have to go there for another visit so I can finalize the paperwork. Maybe we can make it a stopover on the way to Kenya?" Sam said.

I stared in disbelief. "No."

Sam walked over next to me and kissed me on the forehead. "If we do this, my company will pay for part of the trip and that will help to offset the cost of our stay at the Giraffe Manor. It would only be for one additional night. And we can stay at the Ritz again. I know you loved it." He looked down at me and smiled. "Please, it would make my life easier."

"Fine," I said as I snapped my computer shut. "But only for one night. Now, let's enjoy these tacos before they get cold."

I didn't like the way Sam had manipulated me into spending another night in Dubai. *What if I see the child again or other needy children? I don't think I'm ready for anymore of those kinds of encounters. Maybe I should just cancel the entire trip. I keep trying to be more adventurous and stepping out of my comfort zone to please him, but he always wants more from me. But then when I try to do something to help others, he dismisses them because they are not his ideas. What am I going to do?*

CHAPTER SEVENTEEN

After the two months of preparations, we disembarked the plane in Nairobi and stepped into the early morning sun to wait for the vehicle from the Fairview to arrive. The smell of wood-burning wafted through the area and tourists hustled around as they looked for friends or taxis to start their vacations.

The hotel shuttle picked us up and headed toward town as the entire city woke to the new day with the sounds of unfamiliar nature hanging in the stillness. A cool breeze added a slight chill to the air but disappeared when the sun reached higher into the sky.

Horns honked, and rush hour traffic crept along Kenyatta Avenue while the sun glistened off the gleaming high-rise buildings. Traffic circles added to the chaos of the traffic as everyone tried to push in front of each other. My heart raced along with all the surrounding hustle. A colossal nest sat atop the light standard and caught my attention while we waited at one intersection.

"What's that?" I asked the driver.

In a thick Kenyan accent, he explained the nest belonged to the storks, and they built their nest high up so no other wild animals could reach them.

I finally caught a glimpse of a stork gliding across the skyline as we wound the way to the hotel. My heart rate slowed and my body relaxed while savoring all the natural beauty within the city center. Eventually, we turned off the main road and away from the city's noise. We passed a large Anglican cathedral, All Saints, and the road continued to climb. The route meandered through an area of government buildings before finally turning into our hotel.

The natural setting of the Fairview took my breath away. Lush green gardens hid the entrance to a lovely outdoor café at the front of the property. Dark wood desks and counters surrounded by African artwork and handicrafts made it feel like something out of a safari movie. Even though slightly older, the luxury might match what we experienced in UAE. But temperatures only averaged in the mid-70s here, so I had no worries about sweating too much on this trip.

On the second floor of the original building, our room looked out toward the west. A small balcony looked down on the gardens and offered a great place to sip drinks while watching the sun dip below the city skyline.

"I can't wait to see a Kenyan sunset," I said as I checked out the spacious bathroom. A therapeutic rain shower and a large soaking tub with spa-like bath products greeted me. I walked back out to the king-sized bed to sit for a few minutes to figure out what to do next. But before long, I fell back and drifted off to sleep as my body relaxed into the comfort of the bed.

After the jet-lag nap, Sam suggested we explore the hotel and grounds like we did each time in a new place. At least Sam allowed this part of my routine to stay intact.

We relaxed in the lobby while drinking a cup of traditional African tea with its hints of cinnamon, cardamon, and ginger. The tea helped refresh us before we walked around. A tinkle, tinkle, tinkle sang out behind me while I sipped my drink.

A young man in a starched white uniform walked by with a chalkboard affixed with a chime on top. The sign announced a message for some guests. I stepped back into the early days of colonial Africa in my mind. I even imagined Ernest Hemingway sitting in a corner, smoking a pipe nearby. Kenya surprised me with its tranquility instead of the bleak, rustic environment I had expected to find.

After our refreshing tea, we found a sparkling pool in the center of our serene oasis. A casual restaurant sat on one side of the pool with colorful umbrella-covered tables. Upstairs from the lobby, a stone-walled bar area welcomed guests. The barrel-shaped dark leather chairs formed little conversation pits. Several other restaurants offered many options, ranging from casual to formal meals. The main restaurant downstairs served a breakfast buffet each morning.

What an amazing hidden gem in the center of a bustling city. I seriously contemplated spending the rest of my life in this place.

The following day, we visited the tantalizing display at the breakfast buffet, which included African options and traditional American breakfast items. Fresh tropical fruits of every variety imaginable sat waiting for me to sample.

"I'm tasting fruits I've never tried before," I told Sam as he filled his plate. "So far, I think the passion fruit's my new favorite. The tartness of it makes my tongue tingle."

"Mmmmm," Sam said, stuffing another piece of papaya into his mouth.

"At least wait till we're back at the table to eat." We both laughed.

"I couldn't help it. The fruit all looks amazing. I might just eat produce each morning to get my fill of all these unique fruits. I wish we could find a place to buy them back home. Yum," Sam said as he shoved another piece into his mouth. "You've got to try these bananas. They are sweeter than our bananas back home."

We gorged ourselves before setting off to do some sightseeing. "At this rate, I don't think we'll need to eat lunch today," I said, patting my belly.

Still a little jet-lagged, we planned to explore the nearest attraction—Nairobi National Park. We hired a pop-top vehicle, as I liked to call it, to transport us around the park. The tour also came with a driver who knew the best places to see the animals. With the park's vast size, we set aside the entire day to drive through as much of it as possible.

While we waited for the driver, I bounced up and down in my seat. "I can't believe we're really doing this. What animals do you think we'll see?"

"I hope we see lots of animals. I brought all my backup supplies for my camera, just in case I need to take a thousand pictures today."

"Are you ready to go?" asked the driver.

We both nodded and smiled.

Before long, the driver pointed out a pride of lions lounging by a small water hole to escape the rising heat of the morning. We drove within a few yards of them, and they never looked up at us.

"They've hunted all night and have full bellies, so they're not interested in us," the driver said.

Next, we spotted water buffalo, gazelles, and giraffes. They relaxed near each other, below the shade of one of the acacia trees covering the open savanna.

"Look!" the driver yelled and stopped our pop-top. He pointed behind us, and we turned in time to spot a white rhino trot across the trail. "Seeing a white rhino is not very common anymore. Poachers have hunted them to near extinction."

"It doesn't look white to me," I said.

"They're not white. The Afrikaans word for the animal is *weit* which means wide. People thought the locals were saying white, so that's what stuck as their name. They're much larger than the black rhino, and they have square lips instead of a pointy lip like the black ones."

We drove for long periods without seeing any animals. When the driver spotted something moving on the horizon, he would race off after it. We did see zebras, giraffes, lions, and so many other amazing herd animals. In one area, a troop of baboons howled at us from their gathering spot. A strong urine odor came from the troop when we passed, forcing me to hold my nose.

We continued onward in search of more of God's beautiful creatures. Soon, the driver pointed to a park ranger standing out of his vehicle and staring into the grass at something. We pulled alongside him, and they spoke in their native tongue about the situation. The driver hopped out quickly and motioned for us to follow.

He whispered over his shoulder while we trailed behind. "You're lucky. You're going to get to see something most people don't."

I whispered back. "What's going on?"

"In the grass over there," he gestured, "a python just finished eating an impala. The snake won't move for a long time. He'll lay there until he fully digests the animal. That could take up to six months. The park rangers will now watch over the python to make sure nothing eats it until it can move again."

I stood mouth agape, flabbergasted. I pulled out my phone to capture the swollen belly of the snake because something like this could only happen out in the wild and not in zoos. My skin tingled at the sight of the motionless beast while Sam snapped photos of his own.

By the time we finished the drive, the sun had sunk low over the grasslands. After all the day's excitement, a quiet evening back at the hotel allowed us time to relive all the amazing African sights from this grand adventure of a lifetime.

The elephant reserve and baby animal orphanage topped the agenda for our second morning. In the taxi, Sam and I chattered while the traffic flowed past us. My skin tingled, and my smile widened as I thought about the day's activities.

Something outside my window caught my attention. An enormous area of ransacked little buildings stood on one side of the road. I pointed it out to Sam and asked our driver about it. "What's that area over there?"

The driver shrugged. "Kibera slums. The area's largest slum and home to many people. I think it's an estimated population of somewhere between five hundred thousand to one million people. Those people live in extreme poverty, with most earning less than one dollar per day."

"Can we drive through the area?" I asked.

Sam glared at me. "Looking to save someone in there too?"

"Stop it. You know I'm trying to figure out a purpose for my life. I want to help others and maybe someone in there could use my help."

"You have a purpose in your travel business. Why can't that be enough for you?"

"That's a job, not a purpose. I thought you understood. There is more to life than just working. God has something more for me. Why can't you accept that and help me?"

Sam snorted as he turned to look out the window. A hot tear ran down my cheek. *Why is this so hard for Sam to understand? Please Lord, I need your help to move Sam's heart to help others in need.*

"Don't worry, we won't go there," the driver said. "It's not safe. Crime's extremely high. AIDS is rampant. The locals won't even go into the slums, and there's no police there either."

I stared at the slums as we passed. The area appeared alive with activity as the residents moved among the trash piles and derelict buildings. Small children played in the dirty water on the littered trails that pretended to be streets. My heart fell within my chest. How many lost children might live within the area's boundaries who needed help to survive? Another tear rolled down my cheek, but I wiped it away before anyone noticed.

"Are there any schools in Kibera?" I asked, trying to understand their world a bit.

"A few, but most teachers won't work there. Rapes and high crime rates keep qualified people from wanting to help in the area. Clean water is also scarce, so schools don't have any water for drinking or cleaning. All schools require children to wear uniforms and pay school fees, so most people in Kibera could not afford to send them to school," the driver told us.

Kenya lost some of its luster as I looked at all the poverty visible around us. The reality of extreme scarcity settled over me like a pall. *How could visitors to Kenya drive past a place like the Kibera slums without wanting to help?*

I tried to put the slums out of my mind by focusing on the next sightseeing activity—the baby elephant's sanctuary and orphaned animals' area. Sheldrick Wildlife Trust operated the orphan elephant rescue and rehabilitation program where keepers paraded the elephants around the visitor area and fed them from large baby bottles.

As the show began, one of the workers said, "Every orphan in our care will ultimately get reintegrated back into the wild. For this reason, we carefully limit their exposure to humans, and only keepers may feed and directly interact with them. However, some of the more mischievous elephants may choose to extend a trunk in greeting."

And sure enough, one little guy stretched out his trunk to touch me before the keeper pulled him away.

"Please tell me you got a picture of that?" I said to Sam.

"Yup. What a keepsake."

"Ya know, these orphans aren't much different from the ones I want to help," I said.

Sam turned away without answering me.

How can I make Sam understand what I want to do for the orphans of the world? How do I convince him we can have fun and help those in need also? I dropped my shoulders and walked after my husband.

At our last stop for the day at the animal orphanage, the guide took us over to see the three resident cheetahs. These animals looked majestic in the way they frolicked around their enclosure. While we admired them, the guide asked if we wanted to go in and pet them.

I laughed and asked, "Are you short of food and need to feed the cats?"

Our guide assured us he did not kid us. "Cheetahs are the only large cat species that, once domesticated, never reverts to being wild again."

I glanced sideways at him, and a shudder ran down my spine when he unlocked the gate for us to enter. I stepped aside to allow Sam to enter the cage ahead of me so he would get eaten first. But Sam grabbed my arm and pulled me into the enclosure with him.

I held my breath when one of the cats approached us. A loud purring sound arose from the beast, and a furry ear brushed against my hand. I jumped back to see the cheetah had laid down and rolled over, obviously wanting her belly rubbed. Pulling out my cell phone, I recorded the moment, then bent down and petted the cat. She purred even more when I rubbed her stomach. We played with the trio of cats for about fifteen minutes before the guide walked over to us and announced we needed to move on so we could finish up the tour.

The excitement of these experiences helped me focus on something else besides the heaviness in my chest of seeing the slums earlier in the day. But those feelings flooded back when we passed Kibera on the way back to the hotel.

I bit my lip and said, "I'll be glad to leave this area tomorrow, so I don't have to see those slums again."

Sam nodded. "Traveling to underprivileged countries has its downsides for sure. I'm sorry for my poor attitude toward your ideas. I do see the need and will try to do better and be more supportive."

I put my arm through his and leaned my head against his shoulder. "Thanks. I can't find my purpose without you. I had an idea. Maybe we could get the church to bring a mission team here to do some kind of work to help."

"I think that's a good idea, babe. Maybe God's going to use you to scout out areas needing help so you can organize groups to make a difference."

"I like that idea. Maybe I can be a gypsy for God by traveling around the world while bringing his hands and feet to those that need help. Once we find places that need help, I can go speak to civic or church groups and ask them to volunteer. You might be on to something, honey."

CHAPTER EIGHTEEN

The next part of the journey took us west toward Lake Victoria and the stay in a luxury tent resort on its shores. Instead of driving on the questionable roads, we opted for an hour-long flight on an equally questionable airline. All the bouncing on the plane and the water that dripped from the top made me question if this was really a better option than driving. But the flight finally landed safely in the town of Kisumu. I wanted to kiss the ground when we exited the plane onto the tarmac.

A short taxi ride brought us to the entrance to Kiboko Bay. When we walked inside the main building, I held my breath, unsure of what to expect.

Looking beyond the lobby, through the windows, the largest freshwater lake in Africa greeted us. The lake, widely acknowledged as the famed source of the Nile River, glistened in the brilliant sunlight. Soon, a tiny *dhow*, a handmade dugout boat with handsewn sails flapping in the breeze, glided past. I grabbed Sam so he could take a photo of the picturesque scene. Despite the initial beauty we encountered, I fretted the rooms would not hold up to my strict standards.

When a staff member walked us to the assigned tent and pointed out all the features of the lodge, I began to feel more at ease. Even though they called them tents, the rooms appeared more like cabins on platforms with canvas siding. The screened-in porch and doorway provided protection from any animals roaming the area at night. The bathroom sat off to one side, and although very simple and small, contained a normal toilet. I smiled.

After settling in, we walked down to the water's edge to breathe in the fresh air and bask in the lake's calmness. We walked past the pool and the adjoining dining area as a refreshing breeze blew by. We were far enough away from the town that traffic noises did not disturb the tranquility of the area, and we could enjoy a meal within sight of the water.

I sighed when Sam placed an arm around my shoulders. "Another great find, honey. This place's incredible. I can't wait to see the sunset over the lake tonight."

Back inside, the staff pointed us to the area where the hippos came ashore to bask in the sun in the late afternoon. They also issued a dire warning.

"Don't approach the animals if you see them. The hippo is one of the deadliest creatures in Kenya."

"Good to know. We will make sure to stay clear of them," I said.

"I will only get close enough to take a few photos."

I rolled my eyes at Sam.

The hotel clerk also told us about other places or areas we should visit in the Kisumu region. "We have a small tourist market on the far side of town from the resort, and it offers many traditional items for sale, like carved wood and soapstone statues. We can order a taxi to take you there. Just ask at the front desk."

The staff showed us the restaurant where we could eat breakfast and any other meals we might want to enjoy at the hotel. "Or if you prefer, there are several fish places to eat which sit right on the banks of the lake near town."

I wanted to check out at least one of these during our stay. The front desk clerk also told us we could ride to town on the back of the bicycle taxi as the locals do. That idea did not appeal to my good senses.

Since we didn't have jet lag from the short one-hour flight, we headed into town for dinner by the lake. We planned to get there before nightfall to watch the sunset over the water. Another worker at the hotel recommended the tilapia, a fish native to Lake Victoria, which would be available on many local menus.

As we stepped out of the taxi at the restaurant, my eyes widened, and I let out a gasp. Dilapidated lean-tos formed an untidy row on the banks of the river next to the restaurant. Plastic tables and chairs sat haphazardly under covered areas. Two individuals, a family of four, and three groups of locals, sat in them, enjoying their evening meals.

"I'm not sure I can eat here," I told Sam.

"Why not?"

"These places don't look sanitary. I don't want to get food poisoning."

"Stop being silly. Where's your sense of adventure? Besides, the taxi driver won't be back for a while, so we might as well check it out. And I'm hungry."

"Fine," I snapped, grabbing hold of his hand. "Which one do you want to eat at?"

Several of the locals stared at us, but a sizable, friendly looking lady motioned for us to join her.

"I speak English," she said. "Please, come eat at my place. I can explain the menu to you and help you figure out what to get."

"I guess we'll pick her place." Sam pulled me toward the waiting table.

The lady pointed us toward an area where a group of young boys hung around the front of the shanties. They stumbled against each other and talked loudly, appearing drunk or high. I nudged Sam, then nodded my head in their direction. He shook his head and continued walking. I lingered a moment longer as the kids huffed on something in a bottle, making a mental note to ask the employees at our lodge about them.

We ordered fried tilapia for dinner, and I actually enjoyed it. The woman who waved us into her café fried the fish in hot oil, so I prayed that would kill off any bacteria.

The gang of boys weighed on my mind the whole time we ate. To take my mind off them, I shifted my focus to the glorious pinks, reds, and yellows reflecting against the calm waters on the lake as it sank beyond the horizon.

Back at the resort, I headed straight to the front desk to inquire about the kids at the lake.

A young man on staff told me, "In Kisumu, we have problems with street children. Such kids become hooked on sniffing glue to ease their bellies' hunger pains. Most of them are boys, but some girls became part of the gangs by the lake."

My eyes welled up with tears as I walked back to our tent.

Before bed, I pulled up my resource list on my computer, reviewing it for organizations in this area of Kenya. I found one group called Chance for Childhood. This organization helped kids get off the streets and gave them opportunities to clean up their lives. As part of their charter, Chance for Childhood tried to reunite these children with any remaining family members. Since this part of Kenya lacked reliable cell service, I put their contact information into my bag in case I needed it during the rest of our stay in the area.

A fitful night of sleep awaited me. I tossed and turned for a while before I finally fell into a deep slumber—my dreams filled with visions of street children. Eventually, the sun peeked through the tent opening, and I got up to fix some coffee in the room before breakfast was served.

I slipped outside the tent and onto the porch to watch the world come alive. The coolness of the early freshening of the air chilled me. A bird squawked and flew just above the waterline, probably looking for its breakfast. A strange noise emanated from somewhere down by the edge of the lake. A deep huffing or blowing sound rose and fell somewhere over by the water.

A staff member walked past me, and I asked about the unknown noises.

She whispered, "That's the hippos, madam," and continued on her way.

Part of me wanted to run over to look for them, but the warnings from the staff stuck in my brain. So I sat back and enjoyed hearing them for now.

More sounds soon joined the chorus, rising around me as all the animals and birds in the area awoke to a brilliant blue sky. Suddenly, a distant, inhuman laughter drowned out all the other noises. I guessed those sounds might be the hyenas at the impala reserve nearby.

Coffee and cooking bacon smells wafted down from the kitchen and my stomach grumbled. The smell roused Sam from his peaceful slumber, and he joined me to drink his coffee in the early morning stirrings.

"Good morning, darling," Sam said, then kissed me on the cheek.

"Good morning, sleepyhead," I returned with a smile. "How'd you sleep?"

"Great. The feather softness of that bed just lulled me to sleep. How about you?"

"Not great." I explained my night and dreams to Sam.

"I get it, honey, but you can't do anything until we get home. Let's enjoy the trip and then figure out how to help. I know you feel God's calling you to this kind of work, but he also wants you to enjoy the nature he's provided for us. You need to balance all of this, or it'll drive you crazy."

"You're right. Please pray for me. I'm trying to figure out this thing."

We sat in silence and enjoyed the sounds of nature before breakfast. After a while, we headed down the pathway to eat. We feasted on eggs and bacon and tons of coffee and discussed the plans for the day. I wanted to visit the tourist market to get souvenirs for me and something for Sophie. If time allowed, we could visit the impala sanctuary.

"I want to eat by the lake again tonight to see if I can help any kids while we visit the area."

Sam expressed his concern about my idea about the kids, but he also knew all about my stubborn personality and how unrelentingly I followed an idea once I got it stuck in my head, so he agreed.

"Maybe you can start some kind of charity to help rescue kids." He laughed.

"You know what? That's not a bad idea." At Sam's frown, I turned to head back toward our tent, calling over my shoulder, "Once we go back stateside, I might have to check that out." I stalked off toward the room.

Even though I didn't want to start a charity, the idea began to bounce around in my head.

After breakfast, we took a taxi to the market on the other side of town. All the colorful paintings and carved animals of every shape and size caused my heart to race in anticipation of what I would buy.

"Buy from me!" and "I give good price!" called out the shopkeepers in their Kenyan accents.

An enormous selection of trinkets spread across the kiosks offered something for everyone's taste and budget. I hovered over the beaded jewelry made by the Maasai tribe and woven baskets created by women in Kisumu with their incredible colors.

For nearly an hour, we walked between the stalls and talked easily with the owners. The smell of Kenyan tea made with milk and masala spices made my mouth water as I remembered the wonderful taste of the tea I had tried in Nairobi.

In the next stall, a six-foot carved wooden giraffe caught my attention and made me laugh. *Imagine trying to get that in my luggage.* I chuckled and kept walking.

"No," Sam said when I gazed back toward the large wooden giraffe.

"I know, but wouldn't it be a great conversation piece?"

"Just, no." He rolled his eyes.

I found a smaller wooden giraffe, only about a foot tall. "What do you think about this for Sophie?" I asked. "Or should I get her another elephant to go with the one from India?"

"I think the giraffe, so she can have a variety of animals."

"Okay. Giraffe it is," I said and handed over the money to the shopkeeper.

A movement behind the stall drew my attention away. A shoeless young boy wearing only a dirty pair of shorts stared back at me. His glassy-eyed look and unsteadiness as he stared into space left little to the imagination about the situation. A filthy, empty plastic soda bottle in his hand must be his instrument for getting high. The hotel staff had told us that street boys like this one relied on the goodness of the shop owners to provide them with handouts of food to keep them alive.

The shopkeeper noticed me looking at the boy. "It's difficult to see children in such dire situations. Poverty's a terrible disease, forcing kids to survive any way possible." He spoke with genuine concern. "Many of us try to help them, but once the huffing gets them, there's not much we can do. I give this one tea and a bit of food each day, but I need to feed my family too, so not much extra." His voice trailed off. "So many people would just look away."

I tried to offer encouragement to the man. "I'm so sorry there is not more help for these precious children. I will be praying for them." I knew God had showed me these situations to change my heart, but I didn't know what to do to help. "Would it help to take the young man to the center that helps street kids?" I asked the shopkeeper.

"Sometimes it helps, but many times they end up back on the streets," the man in the next stall said. "The glue calls them back to their old life, and they can't resist."

A small group of stall workers gathered around me then, and we discussed the plight of these kids for a while. I crossed my arms, holding onto my shoulders to comfort myself from all the issues in this world. The conversation taught me many things about the problems in Western Kenya and the problem of street children. When poverty increases, it always seems that the children suffer the most.

"Poverty causes much sickness too," said another stall worker in the group, "and little access to medicine causes many parents to die off and leave their children as orphans. Our government offers no help, so the orphans live on the streets and fend for themselves."

I shook my head, and my shoulders sagged with the weight of the issues of poverty, then I shared the information about the Chance for Children's charity. The group didn't think it would help long term, but one shopkeeper agreed to call and get the boy some help.

Sam and I exchanged a knowing glance.

"We'll tell people back home about this situation to see if we can do anything to help as well," I told the group.

But we might have better luck trying to tackle world peace. Because ending poverty will take more than just this discussion.

I closed my eyes and prayed as we walked away.

As we caught another taxi and continued with the rest of our sightseeing, I realized how little I had accomplished in the way of real help for the boy. Despite months of work on my list, the real solution seemed much more complicated.

I pretended to check my watch to hide the tear that ran down my face, praying the boy would get the help he needed while trying to push down the negative thoughts filling my head. Maybe visiting more animals would take my mind off these lost children, at least for now.

The impala sanctuary sat just down the road from our hotel. This small zoo-like place housed a large variety of species. Along with the impalas, lions, and hippos, I found the hyenas that had made so much noise earlier this morning. I made loud noises at them now to wake them up.

We wandered along the nature trail within the sanctuary and enjoyed a glass-bottom boat ride on the lake by the hotel. We could not see much because of the murky water, so we just enjoyed the time on the lake with the slight breeze to cool us off. Kisumu temperatures ran much hotter than Nairobi's because of the lower elevation.

Before we left the facility, we saw several primitive campgrounds with small tents dotting the park. I pointed them out to Sam. "Could you imagine staying in a tent here?"

"Well, at least they've got an incredible view of the lake, even if they don't have any amenities. But I don't want to stay there either. I'll miss this town when we leave because it's so peaceful. I think the lake makes me feel that way," he said.

CHAPTER NINETEEN

The next day, we flew back to Nairobi for one last night in Kenya without visiting Lake Naivasha or the flamingos. But we would crown our trip with a stay at the Giraffe Manor.

I clapped my hands and cheered as we drove down the long driveway to the hotel. "I can't believe we're really staying here. Although the cost per night might be a waste because the money could help so many people."

"True, but God doesn't require us to live in poverty," Sam reminded me. "You're doing your part to make a difference, like with the money for Prisha. I think God would be okay with us splurging a little."

"That's true. I'm determined to enjoy this place. I hope we'll see giraffes, a lot of them. But, oh man, now I wish I'd bought that six-foot wooden one back in Kisumu." I poked Sam in the side and laughed.

"Stop it. You know we couldn't get it home." But he laughed too. "I'm glad to see your excitement for life return. You can make a difference in the world and still find joy in it too. It's a balance you need to figure out."

The main building of the lodge resembled an old English manor house with ivy growing up the walls.

"I seem to gravitate toward these old-world places, don't I?" I asked Sam, and he nodded.

A staff member welcomed us to the inn with a glass of fresh juice and a damp towel to freshen up. I left Sam to check us in while I went in search of the giraffes.

The dark wooden staircase led up to the dining room, and I took them two at a time. Soon, I found myself face to face with one of the resident Rothschild giraffes. My pulse racing, I walked over to pet the majestic animal, and it bent down to check me out.

I'm sure he wanted me to offer him food, but I showed him my empty palm and moved slightly away. After a few minutes, Sam found me chatting with my new friend. "Our room's ready," he said, but then stopped in his tracks and stood with his eyes wide and mouth agape. Soon, he also petted the animal.

Although I didn't want to move, eventually Sam tugged on my arm. "We've got an entire evening and tomorrow morning to enjoy the animals. Let's get our stuff upstairs, then we can check out the whole place."

I nodded and backed away from the window without breaking eye contact with *my* giraffe.

An outside lounge area provided some shade to sit and enjoy the views across the 140 acres of reserve. We sipped wine and watched the giraffes lumber around the field. Several giraffes came over to check us out. The waiter told us the dishes on the table held kibble—treats made specifically for the animals—that we could feed to them.

"If you like, you can put the treat in your teeth, and the giraffe will take it from you, so it looks like the giraffe is kissing you if you take a photo." The waiter then placed one in his mouth to show us. After the giraffe had licked the treat from the man's teeth with his long tongue, the man said, "A giraffe's mouth is very clean, so it's safe to do. Be prepared, though, because their long, purple tongues are very sticky."

I stared wide-eyed, unable to move. Sam tired of waiting for me to act, so he tried the trick first. He laughed after completing his "kiss." Then I plucked up my courage and tried it too. I whooped and clapped after my kiss and tried not to scare away the giraffes. After we ran out of their snacks, the five gentle giants turned and wandered away.

After I sat back down, something bumped my chair. I looked down to see a giant, ugly beast glaring up at me, and I let out a yell. The waiter and Sam laughed at me.

"That's one of our resident warthogs, madam," the waiter said. "He's just looking for a snack too, and he's harmless."

I continued to stare, and the beast bumped my chair again. I finally threw down some of the same snacks as we fed to the giraffes.

"No way am I going to let that thing take it from my mouth."

Sam snickered at me as I tried to ignore the little monster. A few more appeared, and Sam shared some snacks with them before they headed off in another direction. I sighed when the remainder walked off.

At dinner, we sat at a table by the window. A long neck peeked in as the waiter set down at our meal. "Please don't feed them any of the human food. They're on special diets." The server left, and I reached up to pet this giraffe.

"Please take a picture of me with this guy. No one back at church will believe this without pictures." I laughed.

"Smile," Sam said as he snapped a picture, then handed me the camera. "Now my turn. Take my picture."

"Do you think one of these might fit into my suitcase?"

Sam raised his eyebrows. "Nope."

I also brought home my own non-six-foot wooden giraffe. I placed it on a shelf above the TV so I could see it often, and it could remind me of the trip. I closed my eyes and reminisced about the poverty we witnessed.

God, what do you want me to do?

As I prayed, I let the tears flow. I had racked my brain for solutions and felt useless. But then a thought occurred to me.

No, I need to let God figure this out and show me my part of his plan. This is not something I can do on my own. I can't help everyone in need, but I can help make a difference by following God's leading.

A peace settled over my spirit. "Thank you, Lord," I whispered. "I think I get it now. I'm not the rescuer of the lost lambs. That's your job. But I'll be your gypsy and go where you send me in order to help you. Lord, soften my heart to help those forgotten by the world."

CHAPTER TWENTY

I soon took back the reins of my problems, though, and began to think of ways I could find more lost lambs. When no solutions fell into my lap, I plopped down in front of my computer to figure it out on my own.

Why is it so hard for me to let God be in control?

Maybe I just needed to give God a helping hand.

How does one go about creating a charity organization?

I did some internet research on setting up a charity.

To become a legal 501C3 charity required the completion of a slew of forms, which looked long and complicated. If the IRS granted the status, people who donated to the charity could deduct the gift from their personal taxes. However, the process could take months and still not get approved by the IRS. This information did not help clear all the thoughts swirling in my head.

Confused and disheartened, I fell to my knees and pleaded with God about this situation again. "Tell me what I need to do to help these poor children, Lord." My eyes filled with tears, and I rested my head down on the floor. "I can't do this. I'm helping none of these kids. The problem's too big. God, please pick someone else for this job."

When my tears had dried, I gathered myself and stood, then moved to the computer and stared at the screen again, hoping God would show me the answers I wanted. I didn't want to give up, so I switched my search to look at other charities that helped children in poverty, hoping to get some more inspiration. The sites that popped up included many names I recognized, and all had done excellent work in this area.

"Do I want to compete with such giants of the charity world by creating my own little company?" I asked God.

Thoughts of trying to solicit donations to keep a charity running, filing taxes, and setting up websites made my stomach twist into knots. The problem of children living in poverty looked so enormous that no single person or organization could ever tackle it. Overwhelmed, I shut off the computer and made myself a cup of hot tea.

When Sam walked into the house later that evening, I didn't give him much of a chance to settle in before I shared about my day. Tears spilled again as I told Sam about the lack of results. He wiped my tears away and let out a brief chuckle. I pulled back and glared at him.

"Did you really think you could solve this problem all on your own?" he asked. "Poverty and orphans have been around since the Old Testament time. Somewhere in the Bible, it even says that there'll always be poor people. This problem's bigger than you. I know you want to do something, but you need to stop obsessing over it."

I stomped off to the couch and buried my head in a pillow.

"Come on, honey." Sam sat down beside me on the couch. "The problem's too big for any one person to change. I figured you'd understand that and not pursue this idea any further."

"I'm trying to make a difference here, and all you can do is laugh at me?" I huffed back as more tears threatened to break free.

"Honey, I didn't mean to hurt your feelings. I'm sorry. Let's talk about this because I'm not sure what you're trying to accomplish with all of this."

"I'm not sure either." I sat up and buried my face in his chest. "But I feel like I want to make a difference besides just donating money to someone else to do the work."

"Where's this all coming from?"

"Sometime back, after the incident with that child in Abu Dhabi, I wanted to use all our blessings to do more to help those less fortunate than me. When we got back from that trip, the sermon in church about the story of the lost sheep touched my heart." I stumbled through my explanation, hoping I could articulate what I felt inside. "The pastor spoke about how God will do anything to rescue us and bring us back to himself. The words of his sermon made me think of that child and that maybe I should do the same. I think God wants me to rescue children and provide for them." I rubbed the back of my neck. "I don't know. But something deep within me thinks I'm supposed to do *something*."

"What about the list you made and shared with the mission team at church?" Sam said.

"The list doesn't seem like enough." I shrugged. "The list's a good start to helping, but it still feels like a bandage on the problem and not something concrete." Fresh tears rolled down my face. "I want to make a real difference."

Sam thought for a bit before responding. "So, are you thinking you want to do this helping work full time and give up on the travel agent work?"

I shook my head. "No, I don't think so, but I'm not sure at this point. Mainly, because I cherish my travel agent work and planning all those great trips for people. I don't think I want to give that up, but I don't know if God wants me to. I'm just confused right now." I wiped a tear away from my cheek.

Sam held me tight and rubbed my back for reassurance. His comforting only fueled the tears more as I thought about the blessing of having such a loving husband.

We sat together on the couch for a long while and soon the room darkened as the sun slipped below the horizon. The security of Sam's embrace warmed me all over. Finally, I sat back a little and rubbed at my puffy eyes.

"Feeling better?" he asked.

"Yes and no. Yes, because you now understand how I'm feeling, and no, because I still don't know what to do about it all." I struggled to find the right words. "I think I just need more time to pray about these feelings and how I want to move forward."

"Do you think you want to spend time each trip trying to help kids in the local areas?" Sam leaned forward with raised eyebrows. "Because if that's what you want to do, maybe we can add some time to each trip for volunteering. You could pick out an organization that works with the local children in the towns we visit. At least that might be a good place to start to see how it feels. It might give you a clearer picture of how you want to help."

Maybe that would serve as a good starting point. Volunteering would allow us to try out different roles to see what we liked better than others. Working with other organizations would also help me learn the ropes of running a charity if I ever opened my own. I threw my arms around Sam's neck and hugged him tightly.

"You're the best husband in the world," I whispered. "I love you." Maybe God had planned something for me after all.

"I'm always here for you. Two heads solving a problem's always better than one," he whispered back. "I love you too, and we'll test out this new idea on our next trip."

The next day, I called Helen to discuss my thoughts with her. She always gave me such brilliant advice and guidance.

"Have you thought about praying about how God wants this to look?" she asked.

"See, this is why I call you. Praying about these situations is never my first thought. Instead, I want to take control and do it all myself." My shoulders slumped. "Thanks for pointing me in the right direction."

"Stop beating yourself up, Helen said. "God will also put people in your life to guide you, and I'm so thankful I get to help. You have really grown in your faith and relationship with God over the last year. Just let him guide you."

My mind raced as I hung up the phone, wondering where we should go next. *What country needs lots of help with children in poverty?* But before we moved forward, I needed to step back and seek God and his purposes because I wanted to get it right this time.

CHAPTER TWENTY-ONE

Helen had agreed to meet me for lunch that next week. I wanted to pick her brain about my dilemma of figuring out what God wanted from me. And with all Helen's experience working on missions, I knew she would have some ideas.

Since we only had an hour for our meeting, I got right to my problem.

"I feel like God's calling me to help children in other countries. But every time I do something, I feel it's wrong. I try and try, but nothing makes sense. I need your help or advice or something. I'm not even sure what I need," I told her over our sandwiches.

"Let me ask you, how or when did this all start?"

I thought back to the time Pastor John preached a sermon on the parables of the lost coin, the lost lamb, and the lost son. I remembered how those stories made me feel like maybe I was supposed to be rescuing the lost children as Christ rescued me. Am I trying to find a way to repay God for all he's done in my life? I wasn't sure.

Shaking my head, I refocused on Helen. "Sorry, I got lost in my thoughts. It started with the parables of the lost things."

"I remember you mentioning that before." She smiled. "My pulse races every time I think about doing God's work and coming up with ideas. I love this kind of stuff." A radiant glow lit up her face as she talked.

"I feel called to help children in need," I told her. "But I don't even know if that's the true calling or not. I feel lost, and I need God to rescue me again. I'm not sure what this would look like for me or how to figure out what role I need to play in the global issue."

Helen listened intently then said, "I think what you want to do is to discern the Lord's calling for your life. For example, you feel called to work with underprivileged children, and now you want to further define that calling. I believe God's put a call on your life, and the best way to understand and discern what that looks like is to spend time on your knees."

"This is so much more than I ever expected to do or learn." I let my face fall into my hands.

Helen patted my arm as she continued. "I also recommend you speak with Pastor John about the process. So many people, through the years, have thought God called them to do something, but some fell away again because it's not a straightforward task to figure out. There may even be a lot of trial and error, or the calling could change. But if you're serious about figuring this out, there're many of us who'll help you walk through the process. I can be here to bounce ideas against too. But in the end, it's Jesus who'll show you how he wants you to go."

I sat back and contemplated everything Helen said.

I did not fully understand anything about this kind of "discernment." *Do I want to follow such a calling?* As much as Helen's advice made sense, her words also muddied the waters for me. The enormity of what might come from this process made my hands shake and legs feel like lead. Helen continued to talk, but I stopped listening because of all the thoughts rattling around inside my head. Finally, after a few minutes, I think Helen figured out I wasn't listening and gently placed her hand over mine.

"If you're faithful in pursuing God's calling, he'll show it to you. The process could take years, but don't worry. I'll be there to help in any way I can." Helen smiled.

Her sincerity touched me. And I would need her help to understand and move through this process. Tears filled my eyes, and I dabbed at them before they fell. But a sense of peace settled over me, even with so many unanswered questions looming.

"I think," Helen said, picking up her sandwich, "you should set up a meeting with the pastor, and he can help you understand some ways to discern your feelings through books and prayers."

Sheepishly, I said, "Maybe we could meet regularly, so you can help keep me accountable during this process."

"Thank you, my friend. I'd appreciate the opportunity to meet regularly. And we can hold each other accountable for all aspects of our Christian walk."

Again, the warmth of Helen's smile settled the storm raging inside my head. I believed this might be the beginning of the next chapter in my life, and I bit my lip as she hugged me at the end of our lunch together.

I ambled back to my car while pondering everything Helen told me during our lunch visit. A lot of doubts still roamed through my head. *Does anyone else in the world feel like I do? Do I really think I am qualified to help anyone when I can't even figure out things in my own life? Maybe I should give up and just be happy with my life as a travel agent.*

"God, I'm lost. Please, please, help me." I sobbed in my car for several minutes before heading home.

Despite all my doubts, I followed Helen's advice and set up an appointment with the pastor.

"I will not cry. I will not cry," I repeated while sitting in the outer office.

Pastor John, a married man slightly younger than I, sat behind his large oak desk when I entered for the first meeting. His tall frame, graying hair, and round face made him look like a jolly person, and the ever-present smile added to that persona. If he worked in any other field, his features might make him more of an imposing figure. But John's gentle and humble nature added to his appeal as a real man of God. John's soothing baritone voice also calmed my nerves when he spoke, and I relaxed as I listened to his fatherly wisdom.

After I explained my dilemma, John launched into his explanation.

"The Holy Spirit works in us once we accept Christ. The Spirit nudges us and leads us throughout our life. Some people spend their entire lives trying to ignore the nudges in favor of pursuing careers or wealth or a certain lifestyle. But some people feel the nudging and start exploring what it means, just like you are doing today."

I took a deep breath and rubbed at my temples.

John continued as he made direct eye contact with me. "I believe your passion for helping children's a nudging from the Holy Spirit. I've got a few books that might help you understand the discernment process. But the meat to understanding this calling is through prayers and Bible reading. I suggest setting aside some dedicated time each day to pray and ask God to show you the details of this calling. Keep your Bible with you during this time of prayer and a prayer journal for jotting down your thoughts or feelings. But remember, this process will take time. You usually won't get an answer in one day."

I furiously wrote down all he said in a notebook I had purchased just for this purpose and also made mental notes of his brilliant advice.

"How will I know something's from God and not just my imagination or desires telling me things I think I want to hear?" I asked when I caught up on my notes.

"Great question." John leaned back in his chair and rubbed his chin. "Sometimes, you just have to have faith and take the first step. Sometimes things will happen that help to confirm the path. Examples of those confirmations might be a chance encounter that opens up a fresh path to explore. Or a verse or story from the Bible directs you."

I let out another deep breath. "How do I get into these situations and how will God confirm anything for me when I don't have any clue about what I'm doing?"

John laced his fingers together. "Sometimes opportunities will present themselves in events like those that happened in the places you visited. Those might point you on the way to go. And sometimes it might come through a thought, idea, or conversation that keeps playing in your head repeatedly, showing you something to try or a new way of thinking about the situation. Whatever the path, it might require you to follow it with faith alone. Later on, there will be confirmation along the way. In my walk, the confirmation came right about the time I wanted to give up on something," he added with a gleam in his eyes.

John handed me a few books to borrow from his library to help me learn more about the Holy Spirit and the discernment process. Our hour together flew by, and we agreed to meet again in a month. John encouraged me to set up a regular meeting with Helen to help keep me moving forward in this new process. We prayed together, and I left his office feeling lighter than when I had entered.

I'd spend time later that evening explaining all I learned to Sam and set about putting a discernment plan into place.

Each morning after my meeting with the pastor, after Sam left for work and before I started mine for the day, I spent at least thirty minutes reading my Bible or books from Pastor John and praying. A sense of excitement pushed me forward to keep this schedule. Each evening, I read another chapter from the books on discernment before bed.

I determined to make this a habit for a long time, if nothing else. I would not stop even if I got confirmation that I walked on the right path God planned for me. Helen and I planned to meet for lunch every other Monday to discuss our walk with God and hold each other accountable for reaching our goals.

The weeks flew by with a new sense of purpose. After the initial dread that filled my mind regarding the drudgery of daily readings and prayer, I began to enjoy the process. I looked forward to my time with God each day. I had heard people talk about discernment for years but had never understood or wanted to explore it. But now, I wondered how I'd made it this far in life without it.

The answers did not come as quickly as I wanted, though, but I promised myself not to give up or wrestle with God to control the situation. I soon learned that undertaking these new disciplines might be the goal as much as figuring out the calling.

God wanted every person to spend dedicated time with him daily. So maybe that was part of what God wanted to show me. He wanted a deeper relationship with me.

Establishing that connection became a priority more critical than discovering my mission in life because I needed to make Jesus the mission. That one thing made all my other goals less critical and provided me with a great sense of relief.

I no longer needed to struggle to figure out life. He freed me with that knowledge. Now I understood that God just wanted me to follow him. He also didn't expect me to figure it all out on my own.

At my next meeting with Pastor John, we delved deeper into my calling.

"Now that you understand the discernment process, let's look back at how this all began for you. When or what made you think God called you to something?" he asked me.

I bit my lip as I recalled my first experience with seeing the lost child on the trip to the UAE. My mind then wandered back to that sermon about the parables of the lost things and how it made me feel like I was lost and God searched me out to bring me home to him. Then I remembered how God had rescued me after I'd retired and didn't know what to do with my life.

I looked up and saw the pastor waiting for me to speak. "God searching for the lost me makes me feel like I owe him something. I think I need to rescue others."

Pastor John nodded. "I can understand your feelings, but I think you might miss the point a little."

"How?"

"First, when we love God, we want to do things for him, which pleases God. So that part's correct. But the parable of the lost lamb is about God rescuing sinners from their sins. It's a spiritual rescue of the heart and not always a physical rescue, although both happen sometimes."

"So, what am I missing here? Aren't we supposed to try to save people?" My head drooped and my shoulders sagged under the weight of this process. "I'm not cut out for this. I think I've wasted everyone's time." I stood to leave.

John came around his desk and put his arm around my shoulders, gently leading me back to my chair. "You have learned so much already. I'm sure it will only get better. So let's keep going."

The warmth of his smile encouraged me, and I nodded as I dropped back into the chair.

"Okay, to start, only God can save." John paused for a moment so I could absorb that truth. "Our jobs are to point people toward God so he can do his part. In your desire to thank God for helping you, you're now trying to do his job. So maybe he's calling you to help children, but that call is for you to help them find Jesus. They might still live in poverty, but with Jesus, they'll have eternal life and spend eternity in heaven. That's the best rescue of all."

It felt as if a weight had been lifted from my shoulders. "That makes so much more sense. And it certainly takes a lot of the pressure off me. I need to spend some time in thought and prayer with this new information."

"I think you're on the right path," John assured me. "God seems to be calling you to this kind of work. I think you just need to figure out how that should look, considering this new knowledge. Don't give up. Stay connected with God by prayer and study, and the answers will come. But no matter what, remember that God loves you. You don't need to earn his love, and you can't lose that love either." John stood to signal the end of our meeting. "It'll always be there for you, no matter what you do."

Later that evening, I sat at my computer in the dining room and blew out a long breath and smiled as I contemplated how God used my yearning to travel and my desire to help others to craft a mission just for me. He wanted me to use my passions to accomplish his will for me and others.

Soon a new way of life emerged. Sam jumped in with both feet in the new direction and became more focused on our relationship and trying to understand what I needed. He even scheduled time to pray and read the Bible each morning before heading off to work, wanting to discern his role in all of this too.

We agreed we would select our future travel destinations based on prayers and not randomly as we had in the past. We prayed for God to show us where he needed us to work, not just where we wanted to explore. When we found a country or area to visit, we would research Christian organizations that needed volunteers there.

Praise the Lord for showing me the way. I will become a gypsy for God and go where he sends me.

CHAPTER TWENTY-TWO

After months of discerning God's call for me, I decided it was time for another travel adventure with Sam to test out my new-found confidence. But where to go? Between booking trips for clients throughout the day, I prayed about options for the next godly assignment, but nothing screamed out at me to "come and visit." I decided I needed to talk with my husband about it over dinner.

That night, I made Caesar salad and spaghetti, one of Sam's favorite meals. I popped the garlic bread in the oven to heat just as Sam walked in the door.

"Something smells great," Sam said with his usual smile. "I'm hungry."

We sat down to savor my culinary creation, and the conversation flowed effortlessly after our many years of marriage—laughing and sharing stories about our day.

After Sam sopped up the last of the sauce with a piece of bread, he reached over and grabbed my hand. "So what place is God laying on your heart for our next trip, and what organization will we help?"

"Stop reading my mind," I said with a huge grin. "I thought of asking you the same thing. I've tried to think of places, but nothing rose to the top of my list. What are your prayers revealing about a destination?"

"Actually, after I prayed, I found an article the other day that sparked an interest," he said. "The article talked about Mount Everest and Nepal. The description of the area intrigued me. Of course, I don't want to climb the mountain, but I imagine it would be so cool to see the sights and maybe even catch a glimpse of Everest."

"Wow, not a place I'd have thought of, but it sounds interesting." I gave the idea a moment to sink in, then said, "Okay, now that I've got a viable location, let me work on options for volunteering. And I just need to find some place that fits with my needs for helping children." I beamed at the thought of going to Nepal. "I'll work on the details tomorrow. With that settled, how about we go out and get some ice cream?"

Later as we climbed into bed, I reminded Sam, "Keep praying about it to make sure we're on the right track."

The next day, I sat down to map out our plans. The routes included many options. Nepal sat almost half a world away from us, which meant we could fly east through Europe or the Middle East from Dallas. Or we could fly west through several Asian countries. Either option required about the same amount of travel time.

I preferred flying through the Middle East because of the ease of connections we'd already discovered. And I always kept the United Arab Emirates in mind when I booked tickets because of the great experience with their airline previously.

Who knew Kathmandu had so many options?

My mind spun as I tried to make sense of all the information. Apparently, we couldn't see Everest from the town, so we needed to find another place to stay in the foothills around the city for a few days. But in the city, I thought the centrally located Hyatt Regency might satisfy my crazy, neurotic comfort needs, even if they had lessened some.

Now, will I be able to find something in the mountains for a few days?

I uncovered many options outside of Kathmandu, but most required long hikes up steep inclines to reach them. And many of those inns offered little in the way of modern comforts. Visiting Everest Basecamp became a hard "no" for us because it took almost a week of hiking to reach it and only offered hostels along the way. Even though we both exercised regularly, hiking for days at high altitudes did not seem like something we could—or wanted—to do.

Finally, in the late afternoon, I discovered some information about several resorts on a ridge on the lower hills above the Kathmandu Valley. The rooms offered unobstructed views of the Himalayan range on a clear day. One inn—Club Himalaya, in a town named Nagarkot—rose to the top of my list.

The award-winning resort fit all my requirements and offered additional amenities like a spa and pool. The photos and reviews confirmed the details in their description and impressed me enough that I wanted to try it out. I sat back and smiled at all the information I had gathered already.

I planned to share all my findings with Sam later that night over dinner. Then I would book the trip after praying and discerning some more. All that was left to do was find somewhere for us to volunteer for the visit.

Sam squeezed my hand later when I presented the ideas to him. "You've outdone yourself once again, my dear."

"Thanks. With all my years of experience, I can usually dig up some gems."

"I don't know how you do it. We'd probably end up in fleabag motels every night if I tried." Sam took a huge bite of salad as he smiled at me, then swallowed before he continued. "I really hope the weather will be good so we can see the mountains."

"Me too, honey. It would be terrible to fly all that way and not see Everest. So let's pray for at least one sunny day." I pushed my own salad around my plate. "And that I can find us a place to volunteer."

The next day, I checked out tourist sites that Sam mentioned he'd read about in the article. I thought that several of the Buddhist stupas and Hindu temples looked promising, so I jotted them down. Dunbar Square, or Little Tibet as some called it, contained a large stupa and many stalls selling traditional Tibetan trinkets to tourists. I added it to the growing list.

Thamel, a section of town where most of the Everest climbing community hung out, made the list too. We also liked to keep some time open for adding places based on local hotel recommendations.

All the pictures of the Himalayas showed snowcapped peaks, so I checked out the average highs and lows for the winter months. I envisioned mountains of snow blocking streets and freezing temps forcing us to stay inside. But to my surprise, Kathmandu sat in a valley, which kept the temperatures mild even in winter.

The average high was fifty degrees for the month of January. *Yippee, we won't need to pack heavy winter parkas.* Nighttime low temperatures hovered around freezing so we could stay in at night.

Sweaters and light jackets could provide enough warmth during the day while we visited the sights. Pangs of excitement caused my heart to flutter with the thoughts of seeing Mount Everest. My heart skipped a beat, and a thrill of excitement coursed through my body. *Thank you, God, for all these fantastic places to see in our world. I just wish we could leave now.*

One more task remained on my to-do list for this trip—finding an organization in Kathmandu that needed volunteers to help with caring for needy kids. My search didn't take long to find Maiti Nepal, an organization that helped combat human trafficking in Nepal. Its programs helped protect Nepali girls and women from crimes like domestic violence, child prostitution, child labor, and other forms of abuse or exploitation. Unfortunately, the website did not offer any information about volunteer opportunities. I prepared an email to them that explained our desire to help while we visited their town.

I struggled with the fact that the organization was Buddhist-based and not Christian. *Will that fit in with God's plans?* They did amazing work though, and we might learn a lot from them.

Additionally, their website detailed information that might help me in the future if we worked with victims of trafficking.

"Please, Lord, let this be a possibility. It sounds like something I really want to learn about so I can help girls in these kinds of situations any place in the world," I whispered as I hit send.

With that done, I put it out of my mind while I waited to hear from them. I figured it would take several days to get a response because of the time differences and didn't want to get my hopes up too much.

A few days later, a response arrived. With the organization's sensitive nature of work, they did not offer any short-term volunteer opportunities. The words caused my heart to sink a little, but I read on. The message said it would welcome us to tour the facility in Kathmandu during our visit. Also, during the dates of our stay, Maiti Nepal offered a workshop to teach people how to spot victims of human trafficking and what to do if you think someone is a victim.

The person who wrote the email mentioned they would like us to attend the seminar to learn more about trafficking globally and in Nepal. My contentment grew, knowing God had answered my prayer. The opportunity allowed us to dip our toes into another type of work without drowning in information. That resonated with me.

The dates for the conference fell toward the end of the trip. I liked this situation because the tour and information would not overshadow the "fun" part of our trip if we learned something that disturbed our peace of minds.

Human trafficking sounded like an ugly trade, and I did not know what we might see or learn. I quickly responded to the email.

"Please count us in for the tour and conference, and thank you very much." I hit send before I could change my mind.

Lord, keep me on track with your needs.

I called Sam at work to tell him about my findings. "Guess what I found? In Nepal, we'll help an organization that deals with victims of human trafficking. We'll tour the place and attend a seminar about this terrible practice. I think the knowledge might help us down the road," I explained to Sam.

"Can we volunteer there?"

"No, they're very protective of the girls they rescue, so they just do tours and seminars. A Buddhist lady runs the place, and I think the information will be valuable to us."

"Okay. We prayed about what to do, and if this came as part of the answer, we should check it out."

"Our days at Maiti Nepal might not be fun, but the experience will indeed be educational."

One bright sunny morning a few weeks before our trip, I saw Sophie standing on her front porch next door, so I walked over to see. "Is your mom home? I haven't visited with her in a while."

"She is, hang on." Sophie walked inside the door and yelled. "Mom, Ms. Kathleen's here. She wanted to say hi."

Sue walked out, wiping her hands on a towel. "Hi, Kathleen, long time no see. Although I do hear about all your adventures from Sophie. How are you?"

"I'm good. I wanted to stop by and tell you I'm sorry I haven't visited more. Life has changed so much over the last few years. But that's no excuse. We need to get together for lunch or at least coffee sometime soon."

"I'd love that. All my time gets taken up with work and Sophie, so I would love a break. Sometimes, life gets a little lonely without friends to share my thoughts with."

"Now, I feel bad. Let's plan to get together right after I get back from this next trip. We can catch up on everything happening in our lives. I also want to let you know how much we love having Sophie around. Rex loves her, and she brings so much joy with her when she visits. You are doing a great job of raising her."

"Thanks. I appreciate it. She is special. I just need to figure out some plans for her if anything ever happens to me. You know, just in case."

"Hey, that's not something to worry about. You're young and healthy. I'm sure you will be around to love on all the grandkids Sophie will give you someday. Maybe once we get back, you guys can start coming to church with us. I found so much comfort and connection there and maybe it will help you find some new friendships, too."

"Maybe. Let me think about it. Thanks for stopping by to visit. I've got to get dinner started." Sue turned to go back into the house.

"Okay. Oh, and Sophie, can you sit for Rex again, please?" Sophie nodded, and I walked back to my house.

I hope Sue starts going to church with us. Maybe I can help her find my friend, Jesus. And I think we have a single parent's Bible study group. Maybe if she connects with them, she can find some connections with others in similar situations.

I offered a quick prayer for God to work on Sue's heart to join us.

CHAPTER TWENTY-THREE

After a fifteen hour flight and four-hour layover in Dubai—just enough to stretch our legs and get a coffee—we were on our way to Kathmandu, with just a "short" four-hour flight.

The flight path flew us over New Delhi, and I spotted the crowded city below on this crystal-clear day. *Maybe if I listen hard enough, I will hear all the horns honking below.* I laughed to myself as I remembered all the noise in India.

When the plane moved over an unpopulated area, mountains appeared in the distance. The plane banked sharply to the right and straightened out. The pilot then announced we could view the Himalayan range out the windows on the plane's left side.

All the snowcapped peaks looked the same to me, but one peak reached higher than any other around it—Mount Everest. The majesty of the entire range covered in snow astounded me, and I sat back in amazement.

"Incredible," I murmured. "Can you believe your eyes?"

Sam shook his head.

I saw the mountains drop away as an enormous city came into view right before we entered the clouds. I held my breath, and my head spun from the fast descent. A sprawling town emerged as we came out of the clouds. I grabbed Sam's arm and pointed out the shiny gold stupas towering above the town. The sheer size of the city surprised me as I continued to stare out the window at the many other unique types of buildings that came into view.

"I thought Kathmandu would be a quaint little hamlet," I said. "I guess I forgot to look at that information in my research."

Sam said he'd read the airplane magazine and learned the valley held about six million people. "It's the most populated area in Nepal. And only half a million tourists visit this republic each year."

"I guess we'll add two more names to that number with our visit today."

After obtaining our visas and clearing customs, we walked out of the small airport to find the hotel van waiting for us. The driver wound his way up, over, and through congested streets while avoiding the many hazards of animals, people, cars, and slow-moving carts. *I didn't expect so many hills within the city limits.*

Everywhere around the city, enormous crowds loomed, and buildings sat almost on top of each other. Buckles in the road and potholes made for a bumpy trip, and I held onto Sam's arm to keep from bouncing out of my seat. My stomach lurched with each bounce and turn.

"What have we gotten ourselves into this time?" I asked.

"It'll be fine. We're just tired from all the travel. Things will be better once we get some rest. You'll see."

A gate appeared on the right, and we turned in toward it. I moved closer to Sam and held his hand when I spotted the uniformed guards at the gate. They stopped us to check our documentation and the car's contents before permitting us to enter. Beyond them, a long, straight driveway led uphill to the front of the hotel.

I pushed the feeling of nausea down as I pointed out the casino on one side of the *porte-cochère*. We stepped out of the taxi, and I took a gulp of air, hoping to settle my stomach. We passed a fountain and Greek-style statues along the walkway into the lobby. A group of musicians played traditional Nepali music to welcome guests, and the sounds relaxed my tense shoulders. A welcoming conversation pit sat in the center of the large room with more fountains to one side.

Bubbling sounds reverberated through the lobby and further settled my jangled nerves. Near the back of the lobby sat a bar with large, plate-glass windows overlooking the pool and surrounding cityscape.

The hotel sat above the central city, with magnificent views in every direction. Another hotel oasis of peace and tranquility compared to the chaos out on the streets. And that same calmness carried over into our room. An unobstructed view of the Boudhanath Stupa in Dunbar Square filled our bedroom window. The room featured Tibetan carpets and handcrafted *objet d'art*, which contributed to the serene and peaceful atmosphere.

The soft bed swallowed me in a feathery softness when I lay down to rest after the long journey. Sam read in a chair near the window for a short while before finally succumbing to the intense jet lag.

After several hours of shuteye, we both woke, but still did not want to do much while the grogginess lingered. A light agenda, as always, was the best way to combat our out-of-it feeling. A nice cup of hot tea did the trick to refresh my soul, while we enjoyed the calming sounds of the music in the lobby.

"How're you feeling?" I asked my husband.

"Blah. But that'll pass by tomorrow." Sam yawned and stretched. "The tea is helping."

I took a long sip and studied the area around the lobby. The sun sat low in the sky, and the rays glinted off the golden dome of the stupa. The reflecting light cast an amber hue across the entire lobby. "This is so peaceful compared to the craziness just outside the door."

We sat in silence for a long time and took turns yawning. Between yawns, I stared off into the distance and jumped when Sam spoke again.

"Maybe we can just get something light for dinner. I think I'm too tired to eat."

"Sounds like a plan. Once I get some energy to get up from this chair, we can head down to see what the restaurant has to eat."

After eating sandwiches which more than satisfied, we went back upstairs to explore the shops in the lobby area.

A twinkling light from one window caught my attention—a vast variety of loose gems of every size and color filled one window. A sign explained the jewels had come from mines in the Kathmandu Valley area.

"This place looks expensive," I said. We walked to the next shop window and found all kinds of local handicrafts. "This shop looks more in line with my budget. But I bet we can buy many of these same items in the markets at a much better price." We continued to browse, trying to keep ourselves awake.

By nine, we were beat and returned to our room. With Sam soon snoring next to me, the bed lulled me into a deep sleep too.

Before long, my dreams became filled with snow, and Yetis, and women screaming for my help. I woke up with a jolt as fear grasped me and my heart reached.

What am I doing here and what nightmares will I learn about at Maiti Nepal? God help me.

CHAPTER TWENTY-FOUR

Beams of light peeked through the curtains and caused me to stir. I rolled over to face Sam. His beaming smile greeted me. I snuggled in close while I enjoyed the freedom of not being held hostage to an alarm clock.

Sam stretched and headed for the window to throw back the curtains. The sun bathed the room in warm light, and I took a deep breath. The aroma of fresh coffee brewing filled the room, so I got up and filled my cup and walked to the window to survey the city spread out below.

In the distance, snowcapped mountains peeked above a layer of brown smog that hung over the city. I read that a choking cloud of dirt and dust obscured most of the Himalayas from view except in the early mornings. So, I counted seeing them this morning as a blessing.

How many people before me have gazed up at them in amazement over the years? What secrets still lay buried beneath the enormous snow drifts?

I smiled and considered all the crazy people who had climbed Everest.

Who would ever want to do such a thing when you can just enjoy its view?

"So what's on the agenda for today, Ms. Tour Guide?" Sam asked as he joined me at the window.

"Since this is the first full day and jet lag will still catch up with us later this afternoon, I suggest we check out Boudhanath Stupa. We can walk since it's less than a mile away." I pursed my lips as I stared at the city below us. "We can do some shopping around the stupa. This area became known by the name Little Tibet because of those that fled persecution in Tibet. And because most shops carry Tibetan goods. I can't wait to check it all out."

We spent the entire week tromping around the sights in Kathmandu. At least once a day, Sam serenaded me with Bob Seger's song called "Kathmandu," and I laughed every time.

Buddha's eyes adorned many of the temples and stupas in the area. The hotel staff told us that Buddhists believed Buddha watched them through those eyes. The idea of Buddha watching me all the time sent a shiver down my spine. Troops of monkeys hung around many of the temples, but they liked to bite people, so we stayed far away.

We toured the old streets of Thamel, whose quirky little tourist spots reminded me of the hippie movement back in the seventies. Dozens of sporting goods stores stocked every type of climbing equipment made with many of the items at meager prices compared to those back home. We checked out several stores, hoping to find some great bargains, but bought nothing. Hawkers kept trying to sell us something called "Tiger Balm," promising the secret elixir could cure every pain and ache known to humanity. We laughed and rushed past them and their aggressive selling techniques.

After walking a few more blocks, we turned down another street and found some art galleries and high-end craft stores.

"This'll be a suitable area to find something for Sophie. What do you think?" I asked Sam.

"Sure, are we sticking with the animal theme as in other trips?"

"No, I like those singing bowls I keep seeing in the windows. Do you think she would like one of those?"

"What is it?"

"Well, it's kinda like a bell. You roll the wooden dowel around the inside of the bowl, and the vibrations cause it to ring with a deep baritone sound. The Tibetan people use them to promote relaxation as part of their meditation." I stepped into a yoga warrior pose to demonstrate.

Sam laughed at my crazy antics. "Works for me."

With the first week in the country as tourists wrapped up, we headed higher into the mountains to spend a few days at the resort called Club Himalaya in Nagarkot. The drive followed one of the city's busy roads for some time before we finally left the crowds behind and gained elevation.

The road curved sharply, back and forth, and the driver drove as fast as possible. My stomach lurched into my throat on several curves. When sharp drop-offs without guard rails appeared on the passenger side of the car, my heart raced a little faster. I glanced out the front window, trying to avoid the sight of the sheer cliffs.

Cars barreled down the road without leaving us much room to maneuver. The driver pulled in the side mirrors so they would not bump. Scooters and motorcycles passed us as if we stood still, even as the scenery flew by my window like we drove a hundred miles an hour.

One time, four people on one motorbike passed us, and I let out a small gasp when they zoomed past. One wrong move and all those people would end up in a pile at the bottom of the hill.

"You're hurting my hand," Sam said.

"Sorry, but this road's scaring me to death," I said, grabbing tighter as another vehicle forced us to swerve even closer to the drop-off. "Look out!"

The driver glared at me in his rearview mirror.

"I'm closing my eyes until we get there. I can't watch anymore," I said.

"Look, we're almost there. Stop overreacting." Sam said, pointing up.

I exited the car on shaky legs and breathed in the fresh air to calm my upset tummy. My eyes followed the curve of the valley down toward Kathmandu, and I forgot all about my nausea.

My lungs screamed for air as I reached the top of the steps. I stopped to take in the view in all directions and to catch my breath. Behind me, the valley led down to Kathmandu. In front of me, another valley stretched out. This one led to the mountains in the Himalayas range.

A uniformed employee led us down the long hallway to our room. The employee opened the door and stepped away to reveal a king bed surrounded by more Nepali crafts and a window beyond that faced to the east.

I walked over to see a balcony with two wooden chairs for watching the sunrise over the king of the mountains, Everest. Unfortunately, the current cloud cover prevented us from seeing the mountains. We hoped for better luck at least one day during the stay. The hotel also offered a rooftop viewing deck to give us more options to relax as we enjoyed the surrounding views.

A bar around the corner gave us another incredible view of the Himalayas. A colorful mural of people dressed in traditional Nepali attire covered one entire wall, adding to the exotic feel of the room.

Sam and I took a seat at the bar to enjoy a glass of wine while savoring the view. We chatted with others in the bar about the things to do in the area. One man informed us to watch out for the resident panther, who sometimes visited the nearby hillsides early in the mornings.

I laughed, thinking he joked, but soon overheard several other people talking about it.

"When did the animal last appear in this area?"

The bartender told us no one had reported any sightings in more than a week. I gulped and glanced over at Sam for reassurance about our safety. He squeezed my hand as if to say it would all be okay. I asked the group if the panther ate tourists for breakfast.

After the laughter subsided, they assured me the cat preferred to feast on other local wildlife of the nonhuman variety.

After dinner, we walked the grounds for a little while and discovered several stores on the edge of a cliff selling traditional crafts.

Finally, we stopped by the front desk on our way back to the room to get information about details about walking trails in the region. Some of the recommended hikes did not seem too strenuous, so we could check them out during our stay. The fresh air and views near the top of the world eased my stress, and my whole body relaxed. I still planned to have a massage while here.

The next morning we rose to the alarm we'd set for 6:00 a.m. to get up before the sunrise to see the mountain. On our balcony, a crisp wind caused a chill to spread across my skin, so I ducked back inside to grab one of the terry cloth robes from the bathroom. Stuffing my arms into the sleeves, I returned to the outside chair and sipped coffee as I tapped my foot and wrung my hands. I yawned again and again as my body cried for me to return to the comfort of a warm bed.

A sliver of light broke through the darkened sky. Birds began the morning rituals of singing songs in a variety of keys. The leaves of the trees below us quivered with movement and chirping sounds floated on the winds.

Brilliant rays of sunshine slipped above the lower hills and bathed the clouds in brilliant hues of pinks and purples. The sun continued its climb until it disappeared behind another peak for a time.

In a blink, the radiance of the sun popped into full view, and the stately mountains appeared from the shadows. A quickened pulse awakened my entire body, and I stood in awe of God's creation of the Himalayas range. The royal Mount Everest stood tallest and proudest while all the other mountains appeared lost in its shade.

A gasp caught in my throat, and I tried to express words that would explain the grandiose image before me. My eyes welled up, and I grabbed Sam's hand to enjoy the moment together. A lone tear ran down his cheek, and the same wonderment filled his heart. We stood still for a long moment without words.

After seeing the sunrise over Everest, my heart rate finally slowed, and I leaned back. "I'm not sure anything can ever top that experience," I said in a whisper.

Back inside, the warmth of the room chased away the chill of the early morning air. After finishing another cup of coffee, we both lay back down and pulled up the covers. Snuggling close, we drifted off with dreams of mountains filling our heads.

When we finally got up for good, we tried some of the hiking trails. The front desk pointed out the easy trails and handed us a map for the shortest option. We followed the main road for the first part of the route.

Soon, the road wound its way to sections of green fields with hay bales scattered around. I spotted something unusual about one haybale—something that looked like a doorway in it. Upon closer inspection, the stack of hay revealed that someone had hollowed out the bales and converted it into a house.

"Does someone live inside that hay bale?"

Sam just shook his head as we stared down in disbelief. *I don't understand what kind of poverty causes someone to live inside a hay bale.* A somberness settled over us as we walked onward. *Are we too focused on seeing the world and not helping others? How do I balance Sam's desire to travel and my yearning to help those living in the poverty we see?*

The road turned into a pathway of sorts. My mental struggles continued as we bounced along at an easy pace in the thin air. The path rose slowly and walking became more difficult. I pulled off my hoodie and wrapped it around my waist when I started sweating. My original good idea now left me second-guessing myself. The thinness of the air forced me to gulp just to breathe with each step. We stopped every ten minutes to catch our breath and then resumed our slow pace.

The front desk clerk had told us that this walk should take about forty-five minutes, but it took us more than twice that long. Finally, spotting the end of the trail ahead gave me the strength to continue.

It was all worthwhile because of the panoramic view of the entire Kathmandu Valley. The terraced fields, snowcapped peaks, and lush green grasses made this area much different from the hustle and bustle of Kathmandu.

The trek back to the hotel proved much more comfortable for our weary bones. My aching muscles reminded me to make a reservation for a massage the next morning. In the meantime, I filled the tub with a fragrant bubble bath scented with oils made from local herbs of rhododendron, juniper, spikenard, basil, and mint in the steaming hot water. This made a perfect remedy for a sore body.

"Don't take too long in there," Sam yelled. "I want to take a bath too."

"Sorry, I can't hear you," I yelled back while I slipped below the water.

A cool breeze blew in from the bedroom when Sam opened the door and came into the bathroom. "If you don't get out soon, I'm going to pour cold water all over you."

"Nope, I'm not leaving the comfort of this tub." The next moment, Sam climbed in with all his clothes.

"What are you doing?" I laughed.

"Joining my wife in the tub, since she won't get out."

We both laughed. He got out and stripped off his wet clothes while I got out and dried off. "I figured this outfit needed a good wash after all the sweating from our hike. I'll rinse them off and hang them in the shower to dry once I'm finished. Or maybe I'll be like you and never get out," he said.

Massages, shopping, and visiting the many incredible vistas around the resort filled our days and nights for the rest of the stay. But we limited our other hikes to the nearby town to save our lungs from exploding.

I didn't want to leave this place or the beauty of Mount Everest we had discovered in this little-known "hamlet." But a lightness in my chest propelled me toward the next chapter in the journey.

In a few more days, we would visit Maiti Nepal and learn about human trafficking. My excitement faded into nervousness about the things we might hear, but I needed to know how to help. So onward and upward, or in this case, downward, into the valley below.

CHAPTER TWENTY-FIVE

Again, the Hyatt in Kathmandu became our home for a few more days because Maiti Nepal did not have space for overnight guests.

The drive down from the mountain still brought my stomach up into my throat. I tried not to watch out the car side window to minimize the queasiness, but something would always catch my eye. Yet each time I looked, the uneasiness grew worse. Finally, I shut my eyes and clung to Sam.

Down in the valley, a farmer tilled his fields with an ox team, and I drew in a breath at the sight. "This simple way of life and the sceneries are amazing."

"You, okay? You look a little pale." Sam felt my forehead.

"The curves and bumpy roads are making me feel awful." I rested my head on his shoulder and closed my eyes again.

"We'll get to the valley floor soon. Once we get back to the hotel, you can rest a little. We don't need to do anything tonight other than dinner."

"It'll be nice to get a full night of rest before we start the volunteering section of the trip. I need it. And, hopefully, my head will stop spinning before tomorrow."

My thoughts tormented me as I watched the poverty pass my window on my way to a luxury hotel. *Am I a hypocrite?*

In the room, I rested for a few minutes to stop my stomach from churning. It helped. On the advice of the desk clerk, we wandered down to the main driveway and out the gate a little way to eat because the walk might clear my head. He recommended a little restaurant nearby with good food at reasonable prices.

The cleanliness and the presence of the locals spoke volumes about the place. Several staff members spoke decent English, making it easier to order. The locals welcomed us like one of their own with smiles and waves. We communicated with gestures and pointing at items on the menu or at dishes other people ate. Everyone ended up laughing a lot.

With full tummies, we began the walk back to the hotel. "What fun," I said.

"I enjoyed that. How's your head?" Sam answered.

"Much better. The fresh air ... never mind," I said, coughing from the smog. "I think the walk and good food helped though. And I cherish the time spent meeting locals when we travel, especially when they share about their lives. Their world is so much different from ours. Could you imagine walking everywhere in Arlington or shopping for our groceries daily?"

"And how'd you handle the lack of heat and A/C in the homes?" Sam laughed.

"No thanks. I'll enjoy the visit, but I'll be glad to get home again."

A belly full of rice and spicy beef stew slowed our walking pace. The nighttime brought out a few beggars near the gate of the hotel. Each wore rags that hung across their bodies and appeared many sizes too big.

Hunched over from years of poor health and aging, they looked desperately poor. So gaunt that a slight breeze might blow them over. A bony hand reached out to us as we strode past. I distrusted myself in this situation. *Do you or don't you give?*

Unlike back home, I didn't think these beggars just wanted a handout. These poor people needed our help to rescue them from the jaws of death. It saddened me to know that their government provided no aid for the poor.

I offered one some loose change, and he graciously took it. My heart grew heavy from seeing the state of these people. Our visit to Maiti Nepal would be even more depressing, but we needed to learn about it.

As usual with these trips to impoverished areas, sleep did not come easy for me. I tossed and turned late into the night as visions of people living in poverty filled my head. When the first rays of light hit the room, I was still awake. I rolled out of bed to brew coffee, and the aroma soon filled the room. Sam stirred to the sweet smell.

"Good morning," he said, rubbing sleep from his eyes. "Did you sleep well?"

"Not really," I said. "My mind kept going back to the people begging on the street last night. And if I wasn't thinking about them, then I was preparing my heart for the disturbing things we might see today."

"It'll be hard to see the work of Maiti Nepal today, but how else will we learn about trafficking and how poverty impacts it? With the information we gather, we'll share the stories with others so they can help too." Sam rubbed his chin, and my stomach churned as I nodded. "Maybe that'll be part of your calling. Maybe God wants you to lecture to groups about poverty and trafficking so you can convince them to help."

"I like that idea." I smiled at my husband. "Sometimes, I think God speaks through you. Many church and civic groups want to help fight poverty, but they don't know where to begin. Telling them about places like Maiti

Nepal or the slums in Nairobi might give them a starting point." Adrenaline coursed through my body as I thought about all the possibilities of things to do to help. *So many children need help and rescue in this world. Dear Lord, please provide more organizations like Maiti Nepal to make a difference. And please move people's hearts to help provide a better life for children in need.*

After breakfast, we met the taxi the charity had arranged to pick us up outside the hotel's lobby.

After yet another jolting ride, I jumped from the taxi and prayed he would not be driving us on the trip back to the hotel. *I might need to bring a larger bottle of Pepto Bismol on these trips if all the drivers are this bad. Okay, one upset stomach might be worth it if it can help a child in the future.*

A guard stopped us at the gate to check the list of allowed visitors. When he found our names, we entered. The administration building sat in the middle of a large, landscaped green yard area. Signs asked us not to take photos for the protection of the residents. After checking in at the next building, they handed us name tags and directed us upstairs. A large conference room displayed posters and photos of the work of Maiti Nepal. Some included statistics on human trafficking in Nepal and various other countries.

We took a seat along with all the other visitors just as a woman stepped up to the lectern. She introduced herself as Sanjiya from one of the rural areas of Nepal and told us she had worked for Maiti for many years.

Next, she explained the charity's history, sharing many statistics to show the charity's ever-increasing need to rescue the girls. Sanjiya described the extreme poverty in Nepal, especially that in the rural areas, and how it made the country a prime target for those looking for victims.

"Nepal and India are considered source countries for trafficking. The US and other developed nations are more on the consumer end of the transactions. Let's look at some slides that explain the ways people get trapped in the sex-trafficking trade. In rural areas, traffickers set up businesses to lure people into the trade with the promise of good-paying jobs. Or sometimes, a low-income family barely earning enough money to exist might experience a tragic event that causes even more financial hardships. The traffickers sweep in and offer to help the family by employing the children. However, in reality, they take them to India and sell them off to the brothels. In other situations, the possibility of starvation forces a family to sell one of their children to the traffickers with the same results."

Sanjiya then introduced several young women from Kathmandu who had applied for jobs as housemaids in India. When these girls reached the work location, they discovered a brothel instead. "They only escaped with the help of the charity."

She told us that not all traffic victims, however, end up in the sex trade. "Another form of trafficking comes from factories that accept families as indentured servants when they can no longer pay their debts. They work until they have paid off the money they owe."

My stomach knotted up as I pictured all these people stuck in this heartbreaking cycle of poverty.

"But the factories add the cost of the room and board to the amount owed, which means the victims can never pay off the debt. Many end up dying on the job without ever tasting freedom again. Another common practice involves employment brokers who advertise construction jobs in the Middle East. Once the workers arrive, they face living conditions much worse than those back home. Sometimes twenty men sleep on the bare floor of a single-room flat."

The room began to feel claustrophobic to me, and I thought about leaving the room to get away. *Maybe I could use the excuse that I need to go to the bathroom. But these people need my help.* I set my jaw, determined to hear all the ugly details.

"Again, the company deducts the cost of rent and food from their pay, leaving them barely anything to send back home to their loved ones. Some of these men never come home, and no one ever knows what happened to them."

The last type of trafficking she described involved the practice of taking child brides. "In this situation, girls as young as nine are married to much older men, some over fifty. These men pay a fee to the family for this privilege. The girls are often abused and beaten because they don't know how to be a wife. The husband usually forces the child to drop out of school. And, without an education, she has no hope of escaping poverty."

I thought about Sophie and tried to picture her being married to some horrible old man at her age. Someone should never force a child into such a marriage. I shuddered and tried to shake the image from my head.

"The country of Nepal had outlawed this practice, but it still exists in rural areas where the men believe it is their right to take a child as a bride." The speaker stopped and took a sip of water. She shuffled her notes and cleared her throat. "Depression and diseases are common among these girls. Many become mothers at very young ages, and their bodies are not ready for this, so they die in childbirth. These young girls should still be in school learning."

I turned away and covered my mouth with my hand to keep from screaming. *What kind of evil forced these children and young ladies into such a dark world?* All these situations appeared very complex, but each had one thing in common—poverty.

A shorter than average life expectancy awaited any female living in these conditions. The statistics showed that many would die within the first ten years of their imprisonment.

I shook my head at the thoughts of these innocent girls forced to live like that. My head pounded, and I rubbed my temples, trying to find relief for a developing headache.

Sanjiya took a moment to collect her thoughts before moving on to how Maiti Nepal worked to help in these situations. "Making people aware of the problem is the beginning of finding the solutions. We hold rallies and pass out petitions to get laws changed to protect the innocent. Maiti deploys teams around the country's borders to watch for victims as traffickers try to get them out of Nepal. They also perform rescue operations to save those caught in a world of darkness. Our record of success is impressive but still only touches the tip of the iceberg of this billion-dollar industry."

Near the end of the meeting, survivors rescued from their prisons shared their stories via video with blurred faces to protect their true identity. Each spoke of their fear, imprisonment, torture, and sexual abuse.

Maiti provided counseling services to help the survivors cope with the memories. One person explained how her captor set her on fire after she tried to escape. As a result, she bore deep scars, both physically and mentally. Maiti helped her feel human again.

When the presentation was over, our hostess beckoned us to follow, and we toured the rest of the facility. A pang of guilt fell over me. *Why do we need to see them? I hate they are put on display this way.*

Inside the medical ward, we found a brightly colored room. Here, the victims and residents received any necessary treatments such as pregnancy care or treatment for their physical injuries. As we walked past the dorms, women and children played, and their laughter echoed between the buildings. Our guide explained that rescued women who had children could bring them here to stay.

I tried not to stare. But a sense of hope and maybe even some happiness filled the compound. The work the organization did on behalf of so many women inspired me.

Several rescued women looked at us and smiled, and I smiled back.

"Can you believe such darkness exists in our world?" Sam's hand trembled as he grabbed mine.

"I didn't know. We both need to remember all the victims of trafficking in our prayers daily," I said. "I'm disgusted by it all. What kind of man does this to a child?"

"Not me, that's for sure. Even if I weren't married, I don't think I could ever have sex with a child. The size of this industry around the world really surprised me too. I'm shocked. If we could keep men from buying the girls in the first place, the business would dry up. But how?"

"No clue." I stared at the floor, hoping to find some answers. "But educating the public like Maiti Nepal is doing is a significant starting point."

At the end of the tour, we were told the remaining days of the conference would teach us about advocacy for victims, how to spot victims, and what signs to look for when traveling. They would also teach us how to help change laws in our own country to stop the money flow. And we would learn about other organizations working in trafficking and how to volunteer.

On the ride back to the hotel, Sam and I reflected on everything Maiti Nepal had taught us about trafficking. I prayed that tomorrow and the next day of the conference would inspire and teach us how to help make a difference.

Even though I struggled with the intensity of the problem, now I wanted to help somehow.

The idea of spending several days of every vacation doing some volunteer work appealed to me. However, all the new information made me to stop and think, *did I want to do more?*

The plane took off from Kathmandu airport a few days later. Sam and I had purchased books, videos, and brochures—almost enough to warrant an additional suitcase—to help us along our new journey. I planned to get with Helen and a few others from church to discern what I needed to do once we returned. I wanted to cover this whole situation in prayer. Feelings of eagerness and dread took turns racing through my mind, wondering how I could truly make a difference.

Because of the mountains surrounding the city, the aircraft had to make tight spirals to gain altitude. My mind made the same tight spirals while I pondered one nagging question: "God, what are you calling me to do? And will my stomach ever stop churning?"

CHAPTER TWENTY-SIX

One day several weeks after we had returned from our trip, I sat at my desk contemplating what we had now accomplished. After consulting with church friends, reading through the materials, and prayer, one item jumped out that Sam and I thought would be easy to implement—a workshop focused on spotting potential victims of trafficking while traveling through airports anywhere in the world.

I had used Maiti's material to create my own informational sheet and handed it out to all my clients and teams from the church who traveled internationally. This one sheet would not only make sure more people watched for victims but would also make people more aware of the problem.

The sheet included the seven common warning signs to look for and a list of phone numbers of trafficking hotlines and airline contacts that could assist if a traveler suspected someone might be a victim.

Sam and I had brainstormed other ways to make a difference, but nothing had come to mind. So now I searched through websites of nonprofit organizations that fought trafficking to see if they offered any ideas to try or ways to volunteer.

Many of the sites talked about simply donating money, but I wanted to do more than just give financial assistance. *Do I want to go out and physically rescue people?* Probably not. That could be some of the most dangerous work in the trafficking world. *And what about those children living in poverty?* I wanted to help children in all kinds of horrible situations.

Lunch time approached as I scratched my head and stared at the computer.

Suddenly, sirens, screeching brakes, and loud voices outside caused me to look up from my computer. Soon a police car with lights flashing pulled into our neighbor's driveway. *Sophie and Sue's house.* "I hope everything is okay," I said to Rex, who rubbed up against my leg.

I watched the action through our front window, trying to decide if I should butt in or not. Then I spotted Sophie on the front porch, crying. I grabbed my phone and ran out the door. One of the police officers stopped me as I approached.

"May I help you?" he asked.

"I'm Kathleen, and I live next door. I know Sophie and her mom." I pointed to the girl still sobbing on the porch. "They watch our cat, Rex, when we go out of town."

"Okay. There's been a terrible car wreck over on ..." His words trailed off as he looked back over his shoulder.

Sophie ran toward me tears flooding down her face. "Oh, Ms. Kathleen," she said, burying her face in my chest.

I held her tight as sobs shook her whole body.

The officer stepped away, and I tried to console the poor child. "What happened?"

A long time passed before she could speak. "They said there was a car wreck ... and Mom ..." Tears full of anguish began afresh as her voice trailed off.

I stared at the officer, and his look told me what I needed to know.

"Oh my gosh, Sophie, I'm so very sorry."

My heart broke as I held the sobbing child. Mere words would not help this poor girl after such an enormous loss. I stood holding her for ages and felt her little body shake from the depth of despair.

Finally, the officer walked back over to us and said, "Maybe it would be best to move inside to talk."

I steered Sophie into her home and to the couch. I covered her with a blanket and told her I was going to talk to the officer for a bit. She did not respond but only stared into space. Her sobs caused her to breathe in gulps.

I followed the policeman into the kitchen to talk. "What happened?"

"It's all being investigated at this point, so nothing official yet. I heard a witness say they thought a dog ran in front of the car. Then the driver swerved into the other lane to avoid it and hit Ms. Talbert's car. But that's unofficial. We'll need to investigate it more." He folded his arms across his chest. "Do you know if the girl has any relatives we could contact?"

"I don't think so. Sue's mom was an only child, so she had no siblings. Both of Sue's parents are gone now too."

"What about the father?" he asked.

"He left years ago." I glanced toward the living room to make sure Sophie had not heard me. "I think she's all alone in the world now."

The officer sighed, then took out a notepad from his pocket. "We'll have to call child protective services."

"What?" I stammered, "No ... no, wait. She can't. A home. No. No. No. That doesn't seem right." I clenched my hands into fists. "Are there any other options?"

"Not unless someone will take her and become her legal guardian."

The sight of Sophie lying on the couch tore at my heart. I would never let this lovely young lady go into foster care. "I'll take her, at least for tonight. Can I do that?"

The officer nodded. "Yes. I'll need your information and will let CPS know you are taking her. They'll get with you to figure out what needs to happen next." He pulled out a business card and said, "Here's my card, in case you have questions."

I nodded and gave the officer a small smile. When he left, I called Sam and explained everything to him. Sam agreed we couldn't let Sophie stay alone for at least tonight, but I could hear the uncertainty in his voice about what might come later.

Then, I sat with Sophie for hours. As I rocked her and let her cry, I wondered how a fifteen-year-old would cope with this kind of grief. Eventually, she dozed but woke up crying before falling asleep again. In the late afternoon, I helped her pack a little suitcase to bring over to our house. I figured it might help to get her away from all the memories for a while.

I half-walked, half-carried her to my house and laid her on the couch, then offered her something to eat and drink, but she remained lost in her world of despair. My own tears flowed too at the loss of my neighbor. We weren't very close, but my heart still hurt at such a senseless loss. I remembered how I'd told Sue we'd have lunch and how I'd invited her to church, but it had never happened. As the light faded, Sophie seemed to disappear into the darkness on the couch. I could hear her soft whimpers, and it broke my heart.

Around six, Sam came through the door and immediately pulled me into a hug. "How's she doing?"

"Hard to tell. She hasn't gotten up. She just cries." I clung to Sam and let out a deep breath. "I'm not sure what to do right now. I think we just reassure her and love on her until she's ready to talk or at least listen."

Sam pulled back a bit from our hug and said, "Seems like the best plan for now. What about the long term? What are we going to do with her?"

"I'm not sure. I hope and pray that maybe there is an old family friend or someone close to Sue. But I know for sure that I can't let Sophie go into foster care." I searched Sam's eyes for answers. "What do you think?"

He wiped a tear from my cheek. "Well, let's check out all the options first. But I agree that sending Sophie to foster care doesn't feel right since we know her and can help her. Maybe this is what God has been preparing you for all this time."

"I'd not thought of that, but maybe you're right." I looked up to the ceiling. "Lord, please guide us on how to best help this girl. Amen."

As I turned to start dinner, I heard the sofa squeak in the other room. Then Sophie appeared in the doorway, her eyes red and swollen from crying.

"Hi, honey," I said, moving toward her. "Can I get you something to drink? I'm making tacos for dinner, and they should be ready soon."

"May I have a glass of milk?" she said as she bent down to rub Rex's head. He purred and jumped up into her arms in his effort to comfort her.

Sam strode for the fridge to get the milk while she sat at the kitchen table.

"What happens to me now?" she asked.

I began breaking up the bits of beef cooking in the pan. "For tonight, you'll stay here with us. Tomorrow, we'll tackle that question and others as we work through all the options." I turned to offer her a smile. "But don't worry, we'll make sure you're well taken care of. One step at a time."

Sophie managed a slight smile as tears formed again.

Sam put the milk in front of her and rubbed her shoulder. "It's going to be okay. We'll make sure of it."

We all ate in silence. Sophie picked at her tacos but managed to eat a little. After dinner, Sam and Sophie moved to the couch while I cleaned up, then we watched TV in silence for the rest of the evening.

About nine, Sophie headed up to the guest bedroom. Rex followed her up the stairs as if he understood Sophie's grief.

I followed a few minutes later to check if she needed anything else. She didn't move or stir when I opened the door. I found Rex cuddled up in the middle of the bed with Sophie and rubbed his head as a bit of thanks. *Animals provide us with so much healing love. Thank you, God.*

Then I tucked the covers up under Sophie's chin and paused to say a quick prayer over her before heading back downstairs. Sam and I sat for a while longer with no lights on and did not speak. The air hung with grief, and when we could bear it no longer, we headed off to bed.

As I prepared for bed, I silently prayed.

Lord, we never know what the future brings. Help prepare our hearts for your plans. Be with Sophie and comfort her as only you can. Guide our paths. In Jesus's name. Amen.

CHAPTER TWENTY-SEVEN

The next few weeks flew by in a blur of activity. Funeral and burial arrangements. Meetings with lawyers about Sue's estate and getting legal guardianship of Sophie. I was determined to keep Sophie out of foster care.

The process ended up being much more of a nightmare than I expected, but we finally completed the most challenging parts. Sophie accepted the idea of moving in with us. She did not want to go into foster care either.

Sue had left some money in a meager life insurance policy. With that and any money earned from selling the house, Sophie might have enough to cover the cost of college someday. We opened a bank account for the funds. Sam and I would keep the account in our names until Sophie turned eighteen and then turn it over to her.

Sophie experienced a level of grief that threatened to overwhelm all of us. I finally got her to agree to talk with a professional about her feelings, which helped.

"Before your mother passed, I invited her to come to church with us. She was going to join us the next Sunday, but the wreck happened. Since I failed in my goal with your mom, I want to make sure I don't fail you. God is what will help you and all of us get through this fog of grief. And he is someone you will need for the rest of your life." I wiped away a tear from Sophie's chin as she nodded.

We attended church together as often as possible and signed her up for the Wednesday night youth events to provide her with more positive influences. I was grateful to God she could continue at the same school. At least she could keep her friends—some sense of normalcy.

All our other plans and activities came to a halt so we could focus our attention on Sophie. I thanked God often that we could be there to provide for her. And Rex loved having her around full time. He acted like a kitten again when she got home from school each day, rolling around on the floor at her feet and purring loudly.

One day, after Sophie got home from school, she came into my office area, and a slight smile hung on her lips.

"Hey, Ms. Kathleen."

"Hi, honey. How was your day? Oh, and by the way, you can just call me Kathleen now. We're family now, so you don't need to be that formal. This house is your home too."

"Thanks, Kathleen." Sophie tucked a stray blonde hair behind her ear as she stared at the floor. "My day was fine. I really appreciate everything you guys are doing for me. You know I'm lost without you. I hope I'm not too much of a burden."

"Not at all, dear. I'm going to start dinner in a while. Any thoughts on what you'd like tonight?"

"Anything's fine. Maybe you could start teaching me to cook. Mom worked so much that we usually ordered takeout for dinner or popped something in the microwave." Tears formed in the corner of her eyes.

"I'd love to teach you." A new kind of warmth filled my heart as I smiled at Sophie. "I'm no master chef, but I know my way around the kitchen pretty well. Just let me know when you think you're ready, but no rush."

Sophie turned and headed down the hall. Before long, sniffling sounds came from the guest room. My heart broke even more for this poor girl, lost in debilitating grief.

I followed the sounds of the sobs and soon leaned against the door jamb of the room. "Anything I can do to help?"

Sophie wiped her nose with a tissue and said, "No, you're doing a lot. I just miss my mom so much. And I'm just having a moment. But I'll be okay."

"Don't apologize. We're here to help you, and we understand it must be very hard. Just let us know if you want to talk about your mom or how you're feeling. The best way to deal with your emotions is to talk about them." I looked about the space she'd been sleeping in. Although clean and comfortable for any guest, the room didn't offer much for a teenaged girl. "How about we go shopping this weekend so we can decorate this room? I want you to feel like this is your home."

A small smile played across her face. "Really? That'd be fun. I loved when I decorated my room at Mom's house. Thanks, Ms. ... I mean Kathleen."

"Great. We'll go sometime this weekend," I said, heading off to fix dinner. *Small steps for now. One day, she'll feel like this is her home too.*

We fell into a new routine with Sophie in the house, and she adjusted as best as we could expect. One night, after dinner, after Sophie had gone to her room to study before bed, Sam and I talked about her upcoming sixteenth birthday.

"I think we need to make this birthday extra special for her, considering everything that's happened."

"I agree. But what are you thinking?" Sam walked over to the couch and sat down.

"We can ask Sophie about having some friends over, maybe go out to dinner and a birthday cake. How's that sound?"

"What about a party at a bowling alley or a pizza place?"

I laughed. "Oh, Sam. Sixteen-year-old girls don't want that kind of party. They're too grown up for that kind of stuff."

"How am I supposed to know?" He shrugged. "I guess I have a lot to learn about kids, especially teenage ones."

"I'll ask Sophie about it tomorrow. Now, what about a gift? Should we use some of the money from the life insurance policy to buy her a used car? I think she's responsible enough to handle it. But, of course, you'll need to teach her how to drive."

"Why me?" Sam stood, stuffed his hands into his pockets and stared at me.

"Because you always tell me you're the better driver." We both laughed. "Since a car would technically be a gift from her mom, what do you think about taking her with us on a trip somewhere this summer as our gift to her?"

"Great idea, but where?"

"I'm not sure. We need to pray about it. Maybe something will come up that will allow me to pick up where I left off with helping children in poverty. I feel like it might be time to get back into it. But we need to pray first and see what God wants us to do." I looked off toward Sophie's room to make sure she had not heard us. "And I need to check into getting a passport for Sophie. I don't think they ever traveled outside the US before, so I suspect she doesn't have one."

This first birthday without her mom would be full of difficult moments and tears, but I determined to make it as memorable as possible for her.

Sam worked with a used car chain to get something reliable, safe, and with good gas mileage.

Meanwhile, I worked on finding a suitable destination for our trip. But I couldn't decide on a location until I realized I should include Sophie in the planning. So I made a coupon explaining the gift of a trip: "Redeemable for one summer vacation to anywhere you want to go." And I smiled as I slipped it into an envelope for her to open on her birthday.

Thank you, Lord, for giving me this opportunity to share my life with someone in need.

On Sophie's birthday, after the movie and dinner, everyone came back to our house for cake and presents. Sophie smiled a lot more than recently, but the red eyes and splotchy skin around her eyes told a different story. A tear rolled down her cheek when she glanced over at her old house, but the smile reappeared when her friends sang a boisterous rendition of "Happy Birthday" around the dining room table.

After passing out the cake, Sam handed Sophie our card. She ripped it open, and her eyes lit up. "Really?"

Her friends gasped while they looked over her shoulder.

"Yes, we need to get a passport ordered for you, but we can start looking at the choices sometime next week." I smiled and gave her a thumbs up.

Sophie jumped up from the dining room chair and hugged both of us.

"We have one more gift," Sam said, as he handed her a small box.

She tore open the box, stopped, and stared inside.

"That's from your mom. We took some of the insurance money to buy it for you. We figured it's what she would have wanted for you for your birthday," Sam told her, and her tears began to flow again. "It's out back in the garage. Let's go look."

The group headed out to the garage to check out the Toyota Corolla Sam had acquired from the used car lot. Sophie smiled and cried simultaneously and hugged both of us again.

"Thank you," said Sophie. "I love it, and I'll be very careful with it. I don't want to end up in an accident like my mom." Her voice trailed off.

"Sam will give you driving lessons," I said, pulling my husband in close. "He's a skillful driver, so I know you'll learn to be one too."

"Can we go for a ride in it?" asked one of Sophie's friends.

"Sure," Sam said. "We can take a drive around the block, but I'm doing the driving."

The girls laughed.

While they giggled and drove away, I stayed behind to clean up. The group returned about fifteen minutes later. After Sophie waved bye to her friends, she joined me in the kitchen.

"You look tired. Why don't you go to bed?" I told her.

"Okay. This day has been an emotional one," said Sophie. "But in good ways. Thanks for everything. I love the car, and I think I'll dream about the possibility of places to visit. If I can't live with my mom, you guys are the ones I'd pick. Thank you."

CHAPTER TWENTY-EIGHT

The week after Sophie's birthday, I needed to speak at a gathering of churches for a conference in Memphis. They wanted me to talk about how poverty affects children around the world. The organizer displayed a genuine heart for helping those children lost in poverty, but my heart faltered at the thought of leaving Sophie.

"Do you think I should cancel my trip?" I asked Sam one morning over coffee.

"Why would you do that?"

"I think Sophie might feel abandoned again if I go now." I shrugged.

"She's a sixteen-year-old girl, and I think she'll understand. Besides, if you cancel, you might not get invited back to speak there or at any other conferences. This type of work is something you want to do, so go. We'll be okay without you."

"I know, I know. I just feel guilty for leaving Sophie during such a difficult time," I said. A noise behind me made me jump. "Oh, Sophie. I didn't hear you come in."

"Hi. I'm sorry, but I overheard your discussion. Please don't change your plans on my account. I feel sad and hurt all over, but I know everything will be different, but okay." Sophie stared down at her hands. "I'd feel awful if you canceled on my account."

"Okay, I'll not change the plans." I put my arm around her shoulder. "Thanks, Sophie. This situation is new for all of us, so we're trying to figure out the best way forward. I want you to always feel free to express your thoughts and opinions since you're part of our family now."

"Thanks. When is your trip?"

"Next week."

"That's my spring break, so maybe it would be okay if I went with you." She looked up at me with pleading eyes. "I'd love to learn more about the needs of these children. I won't get in your way."

"I hadn't thought of that option. Let me check with the organization that's putting on the event to make sure they don't have an issue with it, then I'll let you know."

"Hey, what about me?" Sam stood with his hands on his hips.

"You can come too if you want, honey," I said, and we all laughed. "We can make it a family event."

A week later, we all flew to the conference, and I was glad for the extra hands to carry all my stuff. The organization planned the conference to last three days and would have about two hundred people in attendance. I would speak at an afternoon session on the third day.

Our little family attended many of the other panel discussions to help learn more about God's work in the world. When Sophie helped me practice my talks and made some brilliant suggestions on ways to improve it, I knew I had made the right decision to allow her to come.

When it came time for my session, Sophie volunteered to run the slideshow presentation for me. My heart filled with pride.

"You're a blessing, Sophie," I told her as I gave her a hug.

My pulse quickened and my hands shook when I stepped up to the lectern. All around the room, faces smiled up at me. I had doubted this many people would attend, but my spirit rejoiced at seeing the great turnout.

As Sam and Sophie watched from the sidelines, I began with the story of the young child from the United Arab Emirates and how that event had impacted my life and my search for a purpose. I also shared statistics from UNICEF that Sophie put up on the screen behind me.

"In recent years," I said, "the world has made remarkable strides in advancing development. Yet, over seven hundred million people still live in extreme poverty. Children are disproportionately affected. Despite comprising one-third of the global population, they represent half of those struggling to survive on less than $1.90 a day. Children who grow up impoverished lack the food, sanitation, shelter, health care, and education they need to survive and thrive. Across the world, about one billion children are multidimensionally poor, meaning they lack necessities as basic as nutrition or clean water."

As Sophie clicked through pictures from our trips, like the house in a hollowed out haybale in Nepal and the street boys in Kenya, I explained about human trafficking and how poverty caused this practice to flourish.

I finished my presentation by explaining how poverty makes children the most vulnerable to many other problems, then ended with the Bible verse from Proverbs 14:31: "Whoever oppresses the poor shows contempt for their Maker, but whoever is kind to the needy honors God."

When I looked up from the last of my notes, I saw many people wiping away tears.

During the Q&A session, many women wanted to know how they could make a difference. I shared my list of organizations, but these women wanted ways to be the hands and feet on the ground in impoverished areas of the world. Sam walked around the room getting contact information so I could follow up with them as I identified ways they could help.

When we left the conference the next day, it was with a mixture of feelings. A heavy sigh escaped my lips as the weight of the world settled on my shoulders.

Back at home, I racked my brain trying to figure out how to connect Americans who wanted to work on actual projects in other countries instead of just referring those in need to a local charity. My spirit sank lower the longer I went without finding a solution.

One morning, Sophie came into my office before school and said, "I've been thinking about your talk at the conference. I know you're struggling with ways to connect people with project that helps those in need, so may I share an idea with you?"

I sat up straight in my chair. "What's your idea? I'm all ears."

"Well, I read about several organizations that form groups across the country to help them accomplish their goals. Couldn't you form some kind of groups, maybe in churches, that go and do the work to help kids in poverty? If a church displays an interest in Kenya, you could connect them with someone there, and they would be responsible for getting the work done. You would just get it all organized. What do you think?"

I nodded as I jotted down her idea. "I like the idea. I think it's a good starting point."

"And I thought of a name for the groups. 'Gypsies for God' and you could add in the city's name they live in. 'Dallas's Gypsies for God' or 'Memphis's Gypsies for God.'"

I stared at her in disbelief.

"Did I say something wrong?" she asked, a concerned look on her face.

"Not at all, honey. I just can't believe you used that name. One time, I told Helen that I'd love to be a gypsy for God. I think you just confirmed a dream that started a long time ago." I walked over and hugged Sophie as my eyes filled with tears of joy. "Did I tell you what a blessing you are to me today?"

When I pulled back from the hug, she just smiled up at me.

I returned to my desk as my mind raced with all the ways to make this dream happen.

"We could connect with all the churches in our denomination to start. We could ask the mission teams to report back to us if they see an immediate need among the children while on their trips and determine if one group could tackle it."

Sophie nodded and jotted down some ideas so we would not forget them. She smiled and gave me a thumbs up.

"And as you said, if a group from one seminar or from another church shows a heart for that area, we could send them the information. They would be responsible for completing the project and reporting the completion back to us." I tapped a pen against my chin. "I think this could work. First, we can share the ideas with Sam, then we can all pray about it. I think I'll also talk with Helen and Pastor John to get their input. I'm so proud of you, Sophie. Thank you."

"You're welcome. I really want to help like you do, so this will be a great way to get some experience."

"Once Sam gets home from work, you can update him with your great idea. I'm so proud of you, honey." I patted Sophie on the back.

I scheduled a meeting for the next Monday to discuss all our thoughts with Helen and Pastor John and to get their input, hoping they could offer thoughts on the best way to implement Sophie's idea or find problems in the process that we might have missed. I invited Sophie to join us since she came up with the idea. My heart warmed that she was finally finding something to excite her again.

"I love your idea, Sophie," Father John said as we sat together around a conference table at the church. "And Kathleen, I think this is one more confirmation of your calling. We can start small within our denomination and see if God wants to spread it out. In the meantime, everyone keeps praying about this idea and discerning how God wants it to work."

When the meeting was over, Helen walked us out of the office, talking a mile a minute as was her style.

"Praise the Lord for this answer to your prayers, Kathleen. I think you're narrowing down the calling God's placed on your life and all with the help of this wonderful young lady," Helen said, touching Sophie's shoulder.

"My heart's racing," I said, "and I can't stop smiling. I believe this is an answer to prayer. And Sophie is part of that answer too. God brought us together for such a time as this."

I put my arm around Sophie's shoulders as we headed out to the car.

CHAPTER TWENTY-NINE

One morning several weeks later, I was starting breakfast when Sophie walked in and greeted Sam and me with a broad smile.

"I was just getting ready to make some pancakes. Would you like some?" I reached down to get out my griddle.

"Sure. Sounds yummy. Would you prefer for me to call you Mom or something?"

I almost dropped the griddle on my foot. "Oh, Sophie, I don't expect that from you, but if you ever feel comfortable calling me that, I'd be honored." I looked at her and said, "But you don't have to. Ever. We'll be with you for the rest of our lives, but we don't expect to replace your mom." I hugged her, then decided to change subjects to keep us all from crying. "Any thoughts on where you'd like to go on your trip?"

"I'm not sure. If you didn't have me here, where would you go next?"

I looked at Sam as I returned to my pancake prep. "We didn't have anything planned. I think maybe God cleared our calendar so we could be ready to help you."

"Do you miss going to exotic places?" Sophie said as she moved to the fridge.

Sam smiled at her. "A little, but we'll get back to it soon enough."

"Maybe someday, I can go with you on one of those trips." Sophie poured a glass a milk and sat at the kitchen table. "The kind where you help others. I'd like to do that kind of work someday."

"I'd love that, and I think you would too. On this first international trip for you, I think it might be best to go somewhere like Europe. We can see what God brings our way. Okay?"

Sophie took a sip of her milk and remained quiet for a moment. Then said, "Did you know my mom's family's heritage is Irish? Maybe we could go to Ireland and learn a little about my family history."

My eyes widened as I turned to look at Sophie. "We haven't been there. That sounds like a good starting place for your first trip overseas. I'll do some research about it."

"Can I help research?" she asked.

"Another great idea," I said as I mixed the pancake batter. "We can do it together after school or on the weekends."

As I researched our trip, I let Sophie watch and even do some of the investigation. Having someone help felt unfamiliar to me and slowed the process down, but I enjoyed our time together.

Sophie had discovered that her mom's maiden name, Murphy, originated in the south of Ireland but also had some roots in Northern Ireland. Sue had kept her married name even after the divorce, so she had the same last name as Sophie. Visiting both parts of the island became part of the plan. And easy enough since the country measured only 170 miles wide by 300 miles long. We could visit almost the entire Emerald Isle during a two-week vacation.

I showed Sophie how to look up flights on various airline websites and why looking at different days of the week might lead to better pricing. I explained that getting the best price was not the only important option. Sometimes convenience and ease were worth the extra money.

"For example," I said, "there might be a cheap fare, but it comes with three or more stops and that makes for an extra-long trip. So we don't just pick the cheapest fare without evaluating all the other information."

I kept my fears and neurotic tendencies hidden as we researched, so as not to pass my ideas onto Sophie. And since Ireland belonged to the European Union, every place should be modern enough to meet my needs.

For Sophie's first trip overseas, I searched for nonstop flights to make the travel time shorter. Layovers along a route caused added tiredness and grumpiness for new travelers. I smiled at Sophie as I pointed at the screen.

"We can fly a direct flight from Dallas to Dublin. Yay!"

"That sounds like a good plan," she said.

"Yes, it's nice. Sitting around at more than one airport for hours and hours exhausts the mind and body more than just the flight alone. And if one flight is delayed, then you worry about making those connections. Sometimes direct flights are more expensive, but this one is about the same price, so we'll book it."

"How long is the flight?"

"It'll be about ten hours going but longer coming home because of the headwinds," I said. "Before we book anything else, maybe you could spend some time looking at what you'd like to do while we are there. And once we have that, we can figure out where to stay and for how long."

"I like that idea a lot. And I want to make sure you guys can do some fun things too." Her eyes sparkled as she bounced up and down. "I'll make a list, and maybe you can add some more ideas to it."

"Sounds like a plan. Let's discuss it all this weekend with Sam, and we can start firming things up. Does that work for you?"

Sophie nodded and ran off to her room. I looked at the clock. Time to prepare dinner. As I walked into the kitchen, Sophie came in with several sheets of paper in her hand.

"What's that?" I asked.

"Did you know they split Ireland into two countries, the north and the south?"

"Actually, I did," I said. "But we can do both countries, so don't limit yourself in making plans."

"Oh, don't worry. I didn't. I already searched the top tourist things to do in both countries. They all sound wonderful, but I don't think we can do them all." Her face beamed as she continued. "I printed up a list of the things I found interesting. I figured we could talk about it over dinner, and you guys can add places to the list. This trip will be a blast." She handed me the list, where she had split the attractions by country.

"Very impressive," I said as I read through the list. "Northern Ireland: Giant's Causeway—a cool rock formation, Titanic museum, Ballintoy Harbor from *Game of Thrones*, Dunluce Castle ruins, Carrick-a-Rede Rope Bridge—a scary bridge to try, Glens of Antrim for a pleasant hike, Bushmills Distillery—for Sam and Kathleen." I looked up at her and smiled. "Not sure about that one. Let's see, what else? Causeway Coastal Route—a beautiful drive. Those all sound great. Now let's see about Ireland."

I looked over the list before reading it off, "Guinness Tour in Dublin—for Sam and Kathleen, the Blarney Stone—for a kiss for good luck, Temple Bar in Dublin—for the music, Ring of Kerry Tour—a scenic drive, shopping on Grafton Street in Dublin, the Rock of Cashel—old castle ruins, Bunratty Castle and Folk Park—where they hold medieval-themed dinners, St. Michan's Church in Dublin—mummies, stay at Ashford Castle or Dromoland Castle—real castles. That's quite the list, Sophie." I sat back and clapped my hands. "Good job. We'll need to figure out if we can do it all or not in a two-week visit." I looked at the list again. "I don't see any art museums on your list, though. Do you like those?"

Sophie shrugged. "Not really. I think museums are kinda boring. But you can add some if you guys want to go."

"No, this is your graduation present, so no problem."

"I think most of the things will be doable on the trip," I told her. "I think we'll use the cities of Belfast and Dublin as a base of operation. A couple of the sites are far away from those cities, but maybe we can still work it all out." I consulted the list again. "Bunratty Castle and the Rock of Cashel might be too far, but I'll work up a plan."

We started to pinpoint the places on the map of Ireland. Sophie asked if we could stay in a castle for at least one night, and I jumped over the moon at that idea. I started our search by checking out the castles that listed hotels within.

Ashford Castle looked impressive, but so did its $800 a night price tag. *Just think of how many people I could help with that amount of money.* Plus, it sat a long distance from any of the other sights we wanted to visit. I eliminated it from the list.

Dromoland Castle looked beautiful, too, and only cost about $500 per night but with my agent discount would only cost us $200. With its proximity to Shannon Airport, we could stay there for a night or two to adjust to the time change. Bunratty Castle nearby offered a medieval-themed dinner event, so we could stay there as well. From Shannon, we could add a visit to the Rock of Cashel as part of one day, only an hour away by car.

Unlike our other trips, a rental car would become a must for this trip for all the scenic drives. The plans fell into place, and soon, our little family would jet-set off on a grand tour of Ireland.

The next morning, something occurred to me that we had not planned.

"Wait, wait, wait," I said as the three of us sat down at breakfast.

"What?" Sam looked up from his plate.

"Now that Sophie is part of the family and going on the trip with us, who'll watch Rex while we're away?"

Sophie looked at me wide-eyed. "I'm sorry. I'll stay here to watch him if that would be easier."

"Don't be silly, Sophie. This trip's a present for your birthday, so you have to go with us. Do you have any friends who might watch Rex for us?"

She thought for a moment, then said, "I think my friend Vicky might be able to watch him. I know she could always use a little extra money. Do you want me to call and check?"

"Great. Thanks." I got up to clear the breakfast dishes.

CHAPTER THIRTY

After a month of planning, the day of departure arrived. I don't think any of us slept a wink on the flight to Shannon, chattering nonstop instead about all the things we planned to see and do. We even discussed what we would buy Vicky as a gift for watching Rex for us. Seeing the beaming smile on Sophie's face throughout the whole plane ride made my heart radiate through my chest. Who knew something as simple as a trip to Ireland could bring so much joy after all the heartache?

Sophie sat by the window so she could look down on the world below. At long last, Sam spotted the first rays on sunlight through the window of the plane. Then the clouds parted, and the land came into view on our approach to Shannon Airport.

"The ground looks like a patchwork quilt of greens." Sophie pointed out the window as her eyes flashed with excitement.

"Wow, it does. That's amazing," I said, leaning across her to look out the window.

"Next plane ride, I get the window seat," Sam quipped as he squeezed my hand.

As we left the plane, I prepared for the usual long waits in international customs. But we made it through customs and out of the airport in a short amount of time.

As we exited the sterile area, I pointed out a man holding up a sign with Sophie's name on it. "I think that driver is here to pick you up for this new adventure," I whispered.

Her eyes widened, and her smile spread from ear to ear.

Sam and I had stayed at some very luxurious places but staying in an actual castle made me feel more like royalty than any other place. As we approached the hotel, we spotted a horse-drawn carriage sitting in the hotel's front driveway.

"Maybe we can go for a ride during our stay," I said to Sam and Sophie.

Sophie clapped her hands and walked over to pet the horse. She smiled from ear to ear and waved for me to come over to pet him too.

Once inside, Sophie and I ran around the lobby, oohing and awing at the grandeur of the place, while Sam checked us in for our three-night stay.

"Look, a suit of armor," I said.

"Look over there at that grand staircase," Sophie said. "I'm going over to stand by that enormous fireplace. Take a picture of me by it to show how big it is."

Sam came over, laughing. "You two need to relax. Everyone in the lobby can hear you." He put his fingers up to my lips for a second before telling us. "We're all checked in. Sophie, your room is right next to ours on the second floor, and we have a door that connects our rooms. Here is a key for you and a key to our room, in case of any emergencies."

"This is your first trip overseas," I said, "and none of us slept on the plane. I know you won't want to do this, but we all need to go for a nap to get adjusted to the time change. Believe me, it makes a world of difference. Set the alarm on your phone for three hours. Once we get up, we'll do some exploring around the place. And an early dinner and early to bed. That way, in the morning, you will feel ready for all the things we want to do."

We walked back down the hall to our room. Once inside, I paced the floor.

"Okay, what's wrong?" Sam said. "Most of the time, you're all tucked in and asleep by now. I often think this is the favorite part of your trip."

"Do you think Sophie will be okay all alone in that big room?"

Sam laughed. "You sound like a mom. She'll be fine. I bet she's exhausted and will be asleep as soon as her head hits the pillow. Go to sleep and stop worrying. She is a smart young lady. She'll come get us if she needs anything."

"Fine. I love a good snuggle in a fresh bed as we begin a trip. It feels like—"

"Like royalty."

"I wasn't going to say that, silly. It feels like a new start. I'll wake up in this new place, in a new country that I get to explore and enjoy. It holds so much potential, and it all begins after a nap."

"I think you're a little crazy." Sam smiled and got into bed. I joined him and returned his smile. He pulled the covers up to his chin. "See you soon to begin another adventure with the three of us."

A few hours later, I roused both Sam and Sophie and we went outside to check the grounds, each of us still groggy.

The gray skies outside did not help brighten our composure. The carriage still sat out front, so I went back inside to inquire about a ride.

With a beautiful Irish lilt, the desk manager quoted a price for a half-hour tour of the grounds.

As we started the carriage tour, the driver offered us a tartan lap throw to ward of the chill in the air. The horse and trap bounced along the trail through the woodlands of the hotel while the driver told of the myths and legends of the grand manor. The three of us snuggled close as we listened and learned about the history of the area.

What a perfect way to start our time in Ireland.

The next morning, we headed back to the airport to pick up our rental car. Sam did not want to rent one upon arrival because he thought he might be too tired to drive. In the car, I programmed the GPS to take us to the Rock of Cashel. The almost two-hour drive from the airport took us through the spectacular countryside.

Sophie showed the same excitement as I with her nonstop talking. We passed through the city of Limerick, and Sam started to recite some of his favorite limericks. Sophie and I groaned at his new-found "dad" humor.

As we approached the Rock of Cashel, I read the brochure information to my captive audience. "The Rock of Cashel once stood as the seat of the High Kings of Munster. Most of the buildings on the current site date from the twelfth and thirteenth centuries. The buildings represent both Hiberno-Romanesque and Germanic influences in their architecture. It's huge, complex, iconic, and there is nothing like it anywhere else in the world."

I held my breath when the Rock of Cashel came into view. The impressive medieval buildings sat on an outcrop of limestone. The gray stone towers stood tall, silhouetted against the sky, rising above the lush green fields of the surrounding countryside. We marveled at its size and magnificence, then spent the better part of the day exploring the halls, chapels, and turrets. My feet hurt by the time we loaded back into the car.

"So," Sam teased, "what's next, tour director?"

"The little pub back near the hotel might be a good place to eat dinner tonight. It's called Durty Nelly's. When I discovered it on the internet, the page said it opened over four hundred years ago. The place has a restaurant, a bar, and live traditional music most nights. The reviews exuded the idea of 'Irish' to me. I think we should try it." Sophie and Sam nodded. "I want to try some traditional fish and chips."

The pub ended up as the perfect ending to our first full day in Ireland. With full bellies and the effects of jet lag lingering, we opted for another early night.

While we said our goodnights, Sophie thanked us again and hugged us both extra tight.

In our room, I said, "I think she's enjoying our trip so far."

"I agree. How 'bout you? Are you enjoying it?"

"I am." I rolled over, switched off the lights to end this perfect day.

We spent the following day closer to the castle hotel, so no need to rush. After breakfast, we wanted to do some hiking. The trails crisscrossed the immaculate grounds of Dromoland. A visit to Bunratty Folk Park and the themed dinner at Bunratty Castle rounded out the day's plans.

The enchanting gardens didn't disappoint. The hotel front desk clerk told us they based them on designs by Andre Le Notre, who planned the Gardens at Versailles. We found surprising features at every turn, including the lily pond and sundial, a beautiful walled garden, and a dramatic yew tree gallery that dated back to 1740. We also scheduled an excursion at the hotel that included learning about and interacting with the falcons, hawks, and owls that live on the castle grounds.

Folk Park provided a replica village of over thirty buildings, built and furnished as they looked in the olden days. The park showcased several farmhouses from the early 1900s period and featured characters in period clothing.

"What do you want to do first?" I asked Sophie.

"Okay, no laughing. I know it sounds childish, but I want to go to the Fairy Trail area first. The idea of fairies lounging about along the trail sounded so cool. And I'm just a big kid at heart, I guess."

"I read about it. But I figured no one would want to explore a land of fairies with me. Count me in."

"Well," Sam said, "I guess you might need a powerful knight to protect you in this land."

Laughing, Sophie said, "This is 1900s Ireland, not Camelot."

The Fairy Trail transported us back to a magical era with displays of carved fairies on holiday. The enchanted woods trail led down to the fairy shopping village, all carved from local wood. We didn't see any actual fairies, but the place still gave off a magical feeling.

We wandered through the replicas of ancient farmhouses before heading over to the old city street area. The fair weather and soft breeze added to the enjoyment. Before dinner, we visited the animal area to see some of native Irish animals, including donkeys, sheep, deer, goats, ducks, and cows.

Sophie bounced around, petting one animal after another. Soon, dusk settled over the park, and we headed up to the castle for the banquet.

Entering the castle made us feel as if we'd stepped back in time. A character dressed as the Earl of Thomond welcomed each guest over eighteen with a mug of traditional mead.

I took a sip and gagged. "This is awful." The brew tasted like warm honey and herbs mixed with strong liquor that burned my throat. "Do you want the rest of mine?" I asked Sam.

"No thanks. I'm not a fan either." Sam pushed his cup away. "Sophie, do you want to try a little sip of it?"

"Sure." She grabbed Sam's mug and took a slow swig. Her facial expression told us what she thought about it as she handed the cup back to Sam.

Laughter filled the banquet hall as music, singers, and performers entertained us. We sang along and laughed the night away, and we enjoyed a wonderful four-course feast of parsnip soup, ribs, chicken, and an apple crumble for dessert. At the end of the meal, the staff offered snuff to the men, per the ancient custom of the period.

Sam followed the instructions and snorted a tiny amount "to clear his head." Unfortunately, he began sneezing almost immediately. Sophie and I laughed while he continued sneezing.

"Do you want to try it?" he asked, but we both shook our heads.

The Lord and Lady of the manor bid us good night, and we headed out of the castle. A lone bagpiper stood beneath a lighted torch and played a haunting tune as part of the farewell. The wailing sound made me think of all the world's lost children crying out for my help at once. A shiver ran up my spine. Sam and Sophie's clapping snapped me back to reality. *What a strange sensation.*

We lingered in the hotel's grand lobby, enjoying the ambience of the peat fire before retiring for the night. I stopped to look around one more time before climbing the stairs to our room. We would leave here in the morning, and the Dromoland grandeur enthralled me enough to put it on my list of recommendations for my clients.

"Goodnight, honey. Sleep well, and we'll see you in the morning for the next leg of this grand tour," I said to Sophie.

"Goodnight, Sam and Kathleen. This has been a blast so far. I wish my mom could have been here with us. But I'm glad I'm here." She hugged us both and then we headed down the hall to our room.

"You're so quiet tonight. Everything okay?" Sam asked me as we settled into bed.

"Yeah. It's just the sound from the bagpipes. It made me think of the sounds made by a large group of children calling out for to me my help. So that kind of freaked me out a little."

"Strange." Sam pulled me close and held me. "When we get back home, you can get back to helping kids. I think it'll all work out. Try to put it out of your mind for now and enjoy the rest of the trip."

CHAPTER THIRTY-ONE

Our journey continued up the western coast of Ireland. A few nights in the town of Bushmills would check off a few items from Sophie's list. A historic little inn that dated back to the 1600s called The Bushmills Inn's on the main street made it the perfect option for exploring this part of the country. So did the quaintness of the place.

But before we got there, hours of driving on twisty roads through picturesque scenery lay ahead of us. This part of the drive became the longest. So we needed to stop for lunch in some little town, along with potty stops. The goal was to reach Bushmills before dark.

We made it about halfway before Sophie asked, "Are we there yet?"

"Well, if all these sheep would stop wandering onto the road, we could make better time," Sam said during our third stop to allow another group to cross in front of us.

"I think it's picturesque to see them," I said. "Plus, the slower speeds keep my tummy calm. The pace of life feels so much simpler here. I'm enjoying the journey, but I can't wait to get to the hotel. It looked lovely on the website."

A section of the road passed along to the North Atlantic Ocean. The wind whipped the waves into a frothy frenzy, and the white caps stood in stark contrast to the gray skies above. The cool, damp air sent chills through the car windows. Sam gripped the wheel tight to keep steady on the road.

"I believe this is what the Irish call a blustery day," I said. "Look at the foam flying onto the beach as the waves crash. Amazing." To chase away the cold, I rolled up my window and turned on the heated seats. "I hope we get some better weather tomorrow. I don't mind this cold, but some sun would be nice."

Sam and Sophie nodded.

In Bushmills, we parked at the back of the charming, whitewashed hotel and walked in through the bar area. A welcoming fire roared in the lobby, and I stood by it while Sam checked us in. The warmth from the forked flames licked up from the hearth and warmed my weary soul.

Sophie rubbed her hands next to me. The light of the fire flickered gently across her face, as we watched the red and gold flames dance about.

Sam's voice broke through the serenity of the moment as he joined us at the fireplace. "Our rooms are ready. Let's get our stuff upstairs and meet back down here to go eat in the pub."

I stretched and rubbed my tired limbs as I pulled myself away from the fire. "I love the smell of these fires. It must be the peat they use."

After dropping off the luggage, we headed downstairs for dinner. I'd check out the room later on. My rumbling tummy made the food my first priority.

"I think I'll have the lamb for dinner to thank all the sheep who held up our drive today," Sam joked as he continued to study all the options on the menu.

"You're so funny. But that lamb sounds yummy. I think I'll get the duck. How about you, Sophie? What're you going to order?"

"Huh, oh sorry. I'm reading the menu for the afternoon tea. Maybe we can do one while we're here." Sophie picked up the dinner menu again. "I'm thinking of getting some barley soup and maybe one of those great sounding desserts, if it's okay with you guys."

"Sure, go for it," I said. "And if we don't get the afternoon tea here, we'll look for one at the other places we stay. I want to try it too."

Later, with the last bite of dessert consumed, I pushed back from the table, too full to move. The long drive and full bellies made each of us sleepy, so we retired to our connecting rooms. Sophie said she would read for a while. Sam and I planned to watch a little TV. I lay down on the four-poster bed in the center of the room. The glow of the TV cast the room in a blue haze of light. The warm atmosphere continued with the light color scheme and plush carpet.

"Give yourself another A-plus for finding a great place to stay," Sam said.

"Thanks. The room lacks a fireplace, so it's *almost* perfect. I think I'll sleep well snuggled under this down-filled duvet. I just hope I can stay awake long enough to catch some news or weather," I said, with my eyelids drooping.

In the morning, Sam arose first and decided he would follow my usual grand gesture by throwing back the curtains, only to reveal another drab day. But thankfully it was not raining. A faint knock rapped on the door. Sam opened it, and Sophie bounced in and plopped down on the bed.

"So, what's on the agenda for today? I'm ready to get going." I laughed as she pulled the covers off the bed. "Get up, lazybones. We have things to see and do."

I appreciated her enthusiasm for life, but I wasn't ready to get up. I pulled the covers back up over my head and laughed.

We had planned three things for the day—Dunluce Castle, Giant's Causeway, and Bushmills Distillery. At breakfast, we decided to visit Dunluce first.

"Enough talk. Let's get this show on the road," Sam said as he threw his napkin down. "I hope everyone has a warm sweater and rain gear with them. The weather looks like another blustery Irish day."

Dunluce Castle was a short five-minute drive from the hotel. And even the unexpected light drizzle did not dampen our spirits one bit. The magical beauty of the castle left me breathless when it came into view after turning a corner. The ruins sat perched on the edge of a cliff that dropped away to an angry sea below, and the stunning scenery left me flabbergasted. We stopped on the side of the road to take some photos of the impressive structure before proceeding.

A sign at the entrance explained there was evidence of a settlement from the first millennium, and the present castle ruins dated from the sixteenth and seventeenth centuries. I stood motionless at the entrance, trying to take it all in. More of the castle walls remained intact. We wandered around the site for over an hour.

A chill ran up my spine when I stared down from the former kitchen into the frothing sea below and tried to picture the night of the collapse. "The legend said that it fell into the ocean during a storm in 1639, and several of the staff were killed. It wasn't long after the event that the castle was abandoned." I turned to look back at both Sam and Sophie.

Sophie spotted a sign on one of the walls. "Oh cool, some of the scenes from the show *Game of Thrones* were filmed here. I loved that show."

"We will also see several other *Game of Thrones'* sites on this trip."

"I can't wait," said Sophie.

As we made our way out, Sophie spotted another sign. "Did you know a pirate ship crashed and sank on those rocks out there? They're buried in a cemetery across the road. Can we go see it?"

"Really?" I said. "Okay, sure. That would be kinda cool to see."

"The sign said they mark their headstones with skull and crossbones," Sam said.

We walked around the cemetery for only a few minutes because of the threatening weather. Then we made our way to the Giant's Causeway.

"I just hope there're no sheep on the road," Sam said. "Otherwise, it might take us an hour to get there."

"Sheep are better than the traffic jams we have in Dallas, so hush."

We did not encounter any sheep on the drive to the Giant's Causeway, so it only took us about twenty minutes. We grabbed a quick bite of lunch in the café before walking down the pathway to the interlocking basalt columns. As we descended, the landscape changed significantly.

I read the pamphlet as we walked. "The Causeway lies at the foot of the basalt cliffs along the sea coast. It comprises some forty thousand massive black basalt columns sticking out of the sea. The dramatic sight has inspired legends of giants striding over the sea to Scotland. Deriving its name from local folklore, it is fabled to be the work of giants, one named Finn MacCool, who built it as part of a causeway to the Scottish island of Staffa for motives of either love or war. I like the folklore story."

"That sounds pretty cool," Sam said. "Maybe we can see the giant while we're there," he added, nudging Sophie.

The black rock formation appeared to stretch on for miles. Tourists scrambled over the massive black basalt columns and down to the edge of the sea. A chilly wind blew off the Atlantic, and I shivered more.

Sophie ran ahead of us, and I snuggled against Sam to stay warm. A voice came out of my mouth reminiscent of my mom's warnings from my youth.

"Be careful!"

Sam grabbed my hand and kissed it. "You're a wonderful mom for Sophie. I'm sorry I ever doubted your decision."

A tear ran down my cheek, but I told Sam that the icy wind caused it. I don't think he believed me. "Thank you for allowing this all to happen. Getting Sophie is a true blessing for both of us. I love you."

He took off in a trot after our girl, and I laughed as I watched them both. *This is my perfect life. Thank you, Lord. I love you too. Now, I just need you to show me how you want to help the world's needy children.*

Our last stop for the day took us back to the town of Bushmills. "We'll return to the hotel to drop off the car and then make the five-minute walk to the Bushmills Distillery," I said.

"Yuck. I put that place on the list for you guys, but I don't think I'll like it." Sophie wrinkled up her nose and stuck out her tongue.

"It'll still be fun for you too, Sophie. I found out they received the license to distill whiskey in 1608, making Bushmills the oldest distillery in the world. And while we get a free sample, you get a free soda of your choice."

The tour of the Bushmills Distillery gave us a glimpse of the whiskey-making process. The best part of this outing was seeing the old buildings, but the history of the place impressed me more.

Sophie appeared a little bored with it all but remained a good sport. She really wanted to try a sip of the whiskey. *Did we do the right thing by letting Sophie try the mead at the castle? It was a honey-based liquor so not as strong as whiskey. Do you let a kid taste it or not? What's the best way to handle this choice? Can she handle the responsibility? What would her real mom do in the situation? Am I overthinking this?*

"Go ahead and let her try a tiny sip," Sam said, interrupting my thoughts. "She tried the mead and did okay. This will let her experience some of the stronger alcohol. Isn't it better she does it with us around?"

"Fine, okay. But only one little sip," I said and handed Sophie my glass.

She sniffed the contents first and made a face. She held her nose as she put the glass to her lips. As soon as the golden liquid touched her lips, she distorted her face even more. She acted like she might even spit it out.

"Ugh! I think I've been poisoned," she said. "How can you guys stomach this stuff?"

Sam and I burst out laughing.

"Well, I don't think we'll have to worry about Sophie developing a drinking problem any time soon," Sam said. "We drink nothing other than wine once in a while, but it's fun to try new things. Although not everything's good for us." He gave Sophie a serious face. "The Bible warns about drinking too much or getting drunk, so remember that for the future. Some of your friends will think it's cool to get drunk, but it's not worth it. Learn to do all things in moderation and control them instead of them controlling you."

I stared at Sam in disbelief. "Where did that come from?"

He shrugged. "My dad lectured me the same way back in the day. Although, he might've left out the faith part of the discussion. But since becoming a Christian, I now understand the biblical importance of it too."

On the way back to the hotel, the sun peeked through the clouds. I savored the warmth on my face, even though the air chilled me to the bone. Sam held my hand as we walked, and before long, another chilly hand grasped mine. I smiled at Sophie as my wonderful little family walked hand in hand back to the inn. A gigantic smile spread across my face. The warmth of the moment chased away the chill of the air. *Thank you, Lord.*

We headed up the coast and toward Belfast the following day. "The Coast Road," as some of the travel guides called it, offered more breathtaking scenery and stomach-churning curves.

We planned brief stops at two more of the *Game of Thrones* sites in this part of the country. These included a stunning little harbor area called Ballintoy Harbor at the end of the road with three switchback curves in a short distance. And a short section of roadway called the Meeting of the Trees.

We stopped at the infamous Carrick-a-Rede rope bridge, walking through a field with cows to get to the bridge. A warning sign at the ticket booth told us more information.

"This bridge links the mainland to the tiny island of Carrick-a-Rede. It spans twenty meters (about sixty-five feet) and is thirty meters (about ninety-eight feet) above the rocks below." My stomach lurched into my throat as I glimpsed the bridge. "If that bridge is over two hundred and fifty years old, I don't think I'll cross it."

"Oh, come on," Sophie said. "It'll be fun. Look how it bounces and sways as the people go across it."

I plucked up my courage and ventured out onto the platform for Sophie's sake but held my breath with each step and clung tightly to the ropes on each side. I dared not to look down for fear it would cause me to panic and stop. Once across, I wanted to fall to my knees and thank God for keeping me safe. But I needed to cross back over before we finished. I now wanted to cry.

I took a few more shaky steps onto the island and stopped. Looking around, we discovered the locals used the tiny island for drying their nets after fishing. Exploring the entire landmass took only about ten minutes to explore. Fear washed over me on the way back to the bridge. I whispered to myself, "This is something I can do. I can do this."

This time, I made the mistake of looking down when I stepped onto the swaying bridge, and my feet refused to move. Sam wrapped his arm around my waist, encouraged me to keep going, and held me each step of the way.

I fell to my knees and kissed the ground on the other side. "Thank you. Jesus."

Sam and Sophie laughed at me.

Onward to the next stops of Belfast and then Dublin. Time for the sights of the bigger cities.

I'm so glad we planned this trip. I really feel like we are becoming a family. I want Sophie to feel safe and secure as our daughter. I pray God helps her find her purpose too.

CHAPTER THIRTY-TWO

After numerous stops for photos of the breathtaking rugged scenery and some hiking to see the waterfalls in the picturesque Glens of Antrim, we arrived in Belfast. Two gigantic cranes dominated the skyline in the port area.

"I think those are part of the shipyard area where they built the Titanic," I said. "We'll tour that area in a few days."

We continued to the hotel. Another long driveway graced the entrance to the Culloden Estates. My heart cheered at the sight of another grand old manor. The tagline on their website first attracted me to the place: "Built for a Bishop, Fit for a King." *My kind of place.*

Sophie exited the car and stared wide-eyed at the impressive building. "Are we really staying here?" Sophie raised her eyebrows as she looked around the place. "I'm going to tell my friends back home that I became a princess in Ireland as I show them photos of the amazing places we stayed."

My smile spread at the sight of fanciful gardens and the Belfast Lough area beyond. Contentment filled me when I walked into the lobby. A grand staircase stood on one side of the room. I turned in circles to capture the area while Sam checked us in. "Wow," I whispered to Sam when I walked up behind him.

"Welcome," the receptionist said in her delightful accent. "We've got two rooms ready. The hotel bar and formal dining area are just down that hall. Another restaurant sits on the property, but it's a short walk down the hill and features traditional pub foods. A spa is available if you're interested, and we do offer a traditional afternoon tea service each day at 1:30 p.m. We recommend reservations. Last, we include breakfast with your stay, and we serve it each morning in the dining hall. We hope you enjoy your stay with us."

Sophie tugged on my arm, and I turned to see her beaming face. "Can we please do the afternoon tea here?"

"Sure, Sophie. This trip is to initiate you into your new family, so that can be our grand celebration." I turned back to the lady. "May we please make tea reservations for the day after tomorrow?" Once confirmed, we headed up to check out our rooms.

A visit to the *Titanic* Belfast museum began the next day. The city of Belfast had built the museum on the slip that launched the infamous ship. The building resembled the bow of the boat and stood the same height as the ship. The museum displays carried us from the boat's conception to the day they found it at the bottom of the sea.

Outside the building, we saw the SS *Nomadic*. Our tickets allowed us to tour this ship too. This small vessel was used to transfer people and things to and from the *Titanic* when it was in port. Once the *Nomadic* retired from service, they thought it would make a wonderful addition to the museum.

The enormity of the disaster came to life through the exhibitions, stories of passengers and items retrieved from the sunken ship.

"What did you guys think about the museum?" I asked while we grabbed a bit of lunch at a little café nearby.

"It's so eerie the way they placed the display screens on the floor so you looked down on the actual images of the *Titanic* resting on the ocean floor," said Sophie. "And it felt like I stood over the actual ship. It's hard to imagine the ship lying on the bottom of the ocean like that. So cool. I guess some people go through worse catastrophes than mine. It made me appreciate what I have."

"First," Sam said, "this shepherd's pie is great. Second, this is one of the best museums I've visited. It's so well done. I loved the ways we could interact with the displays." Sam gave us two thumbs up as he took another bite. "Thanks, babe."

"Sophie researched this one, so let's thank her for putting it on the list," I said.

Sophie blushed and stood up to take a bow. We all laughed. The warmth of the moment gave me an extra spring in my step and made my heart swell with pride. I pulled out my phone for a quick picture. They both rolled their eyes.

The time flew by, and before long, we'd made our way back to the hotel to partake in a traditional afternoon tea. The white tablecloths, formal place settings, and candelabras greeting us as we entered the dining room. Hushed tones added to the air of elegance.

"Look at all the glorious hats the women are wearing," I said. "I wish we'd planned ahead and bought hats."

"I don't think I'd look good in one of those," Sam said, and Sophie giggled.

"Hush," I said. "We need to be prim and proper today. Please don't embarrass me."

Sam and Sophie stifled more laughter while we strode to our table.

The restaurant offered a choice of flavored tea, or the adults could add a special gin cocktail or champagne to the tea. Sam and I tried the gin cocktail. The waitress described the drink as gin based with simple sugar syrup and cucumbers. It tasted extra yummy. We each selected the Earl Grey tea as well.

After a few minutes, the three-tiered serving dish arrived.

I spied a variety of finger sandwiches, scones, petit fours, and other little cakes. Each of us letting out an "ooooh" at the same time.

"This feels like something fit for a princess. But I'm not sure if I know how to use all these forks," I said.

"This is my princess tea," Sophie said.

"Okay, I don't think you can both be princesses," Sam said. "How about we promote you to Duchess Kathleen, and you can be Princess Sophie? And I guess that makes me the king of this new family."

"Okay, I like that idea," Sophie said.

"I guess I'm due for a promotion. And welcome to this new family, Sophie. I pray we can help you find your way and purpose in this world."

We all laughed, then dug into the delicacies.

The next morning, we checked out of the hotel to begin the two-hour drive to Dublin, the final push of the trip. I waved goodbye to the Culloden and promised to visit again someday.

Day after day of sightseeing exhausted me. I would be glad to get home to our routine in a few more days. Out the window, the green fields and rolling hills drifted past the car windows. About an hour into the drive, something colorful caught my eye. "What's that?" I said.

Sam and Sophie looked over. "Oh, I read about these," Sophie said. "Those are real Gypsies. They live in those colorful caravans and travel around the countryside living off the land and doing odd jobs to earn money."

"Gypsies? Interesting. That makes me think about your idea of naming the groups who help us with poor children in the world as Gypsies for God. Maybe this is a sign from God."

"I think you guys are on the right path," Sam said.

"Once we get home, I'll start working on the talking points for groups to stir up interest. It's a perfect idea to group people with similar interests to tackle some needs of the poor. Some groups could be 'doers' and others could be 'funders' of the needs. And some can be 'prayer warriors' for the work. I'm excited to get started, and I hope you'll both help me."

"I will. Maybe we can even be part of a group that goes out to help someday."

"I want to help too," said Sam.

"I think this work will need all of us."

All of us drifted off into our own thoughts as we made our way to our next stop.

What does the future hold for the Gypsies for God? Can this happen? After all my struggles, have I found my godly purpose?

"I hope someone snapped a photo of that caravan for us to use in the presentations," I said.

CHAPTER THIRTY-THREE

Another old-world hotel named The Gresham would be home for several days. The hotel had been recently renovated, and the fresh paint and new carpet contributed to the room's bright and welcoming feeling. But the place still appeared a little dated and not as luxurious as some of our other hotels.

The spacious rooms provided lots of modern amenities and a comfy bed, so I found it acceptable. And its central location allowed us to reach most of the things we wanted to see with a simple walk.

After depositing our bags in our rooms, we wandered down the street to the famous Temple Bar for a bite to eat and some traditional Irish Music.

The Temple Bar first opened in 1840 and was famous for its Irish whiskey collection. Each of us tried their "world famous toasties" sandwiches, which turned out to be a delicious grilled cheese-type sandwich with lots of other fillings. My sandwich contained beans. Sam opted for the pizza fillings. Sophie selected one with peanut butter and banana.

While we ate, a band with a fiddle played rousing Irish folk songs that sent feet to tapping. Later, we took a different route back to the hotel which led through a quirky area with cobblestoned streets and brightly colored buildings housing touristy shops.

"What a blast," said Sophie, as Sam grabbed her hand and twirled her to the distant music still rising from the bar. "I wish more bars back home acted like that, you know—kid and family-friendly."

"I know. Great food and even better company," I said. "I loved the music too. Maybe we'll go there again tomorrow night for dinner."

The festive mood continued the following day. The day's plans started with a trip to the Guinness Storehouse—a museum dedicated to the famous Irish dry stout. After lunch, we'd visit an old church called Saint Michan's for a unique tour.

After the brewery tour, we gazed out at the city from the Gravity Bar, a rooftop bar on the seventh floor of the Storehouse.

"This is Dublin's highest bar," Sam said as he snapped photos of the scenery. "We're facing southwest toward the Wicklow Mountains. It's hard to believe they are over twenty-five miles away." Sam clicked a few more photos. "Help me remember that, so I can note it on the photo."

"I'm impressed," I said.

"Me too," Sophie said. "Wait till I tell my friends about having a soda up here. I'll love telling them about the entire trip."

"I could sit here for hours just enjoying the view," Sam said.

"Well, we can't. We have a church to visit next."

"Booooo," Sam and Sophie said in unison. "Can't we stay a little longer?"

"Okay, but just ten more minutes. But here is the teaser to get you moving. St. Michan's Church has a secret. It has an eight-hundred-year-old mummy reaching out of his coffin as if to shake hands."

Both Sam and Sophie jumped up from their seats. "Why are you still sitting there? Let's go." Sam grabbed my hand and pulled me up.

Sophie trotted off and stopped to wait for us to catch up. "Can't you guys walk any faster?"

I laughed and said, "It's like you never shook a dead man's hand before." Despite my teasing, I still felt a shiver run down my spine as we entered the crypt a few minutes later. "The website said that one coffin is set apart from the others and belongs to an eight-hundred-year-old mummy called 'the crusader.' It's believed he's a soldier who either died on the crusades or returned and died soon after." My hand felt clammy as I thought about seeing a mummy.

As we descending beneath the church, the caretaker told us a young Bram Stoker once visited the crypt, and it inspired him to write some of his scary novels. "Does anyone want to shake the hand of a mummy?"

"That sounds creepy," Sophie said, but stepped forward. "I'm in. I think this will be the weirdest part of the trip and the part my friends won't believe."

We met six mummies and learned how something in the basement's air helped to preserve the bodies. Sam and Sophie both shook the hand of the one mummified body, but I did not. The whole thing creeped me out.

My shoulders relaxed when we moved back upstairs into the central part of the church. In the sanctuary, I saw a sign that told me another little-known fact about the St. Michan's amazing pipe organ.

"Hey, Sam, look at this." Sam came over and stood beside me. "The church installed this pipe organ in 1724, and the well-known musician Handel played his famous work, *Messiah*, on it in 1742."

Back in the sanctuary, I sat in a pew to pray. I thanked God for this trip and the opportunity to draw closer to

Sophie. I prayed for safe travels home and for what my future would hold with my additional work as a Gypsy for God.

As the daylight faded, we made our way back to the Temple Bar for another sumptuous meal, then headed back to our rooms. While packing after dinner, someone tapped on our door.

I opened, and Sophie asked, "Do you have a minute?"

"Sure, what's up, kiddo?"

She entered and sat on the edge of the bed. "I just wanted to thank you so very much for this trip. It's beyond anything I ever imagined. I don't think I'll ever forget it." A tear welled up in her eyes. "I think God knew what he was doing when he made you my parents. I love you, Mom and Dad." With the last words, her tears flowed.

I choked back my own tears. "We love you too, honey. You're a blessing to the two of us and you made us a family. So thank you."

Dawn broke over the city on the early morning drive to the airport. We checked in for our flight and made our way to the gate. "Ten hours till we return to regular, non-vacation mode. I'm tired, but happy," I said, smiling at Sam.

"What a wonderful trip, honey," he said. "We saw so much, and I think we gained a daughter too."

Before boarding, I asked for a group hug. Seeing Sophie's smile at the request made my heart sing. *I am blessed.*

CHAPTER THIRTY-FOUR

On our first day back, Rex purred at my feet, while Sophie got ready upstairs for a day at the mall with her friends so they could hear all about the trip, as they enjoyed the last few days of summer break from school. After Sophie left, the quiet in the house distracted me from my work, even though a ton of clients needed my help with their next trip.

The phone rang around ten, and I picked it up.

"Hi, Kathleen, it's Helen. I'm glad you're home. Did you have a wonderful trip?"

"Another glorious trip in the books, thanks," I said. "What can I do for you, Helen? I've got a ton of work to catch up on, so I don't have much time."

"Do you think you can meet me for coffee tomorrow? I want to update you on what has happened with the Gypsy for God project."

"I'll make time. Please tell me it's something good."

"I think you'll be pleased," Helen said.

The call and plans to meet Helen the next day made the day drag on even slower. My mind drifted off to helping the poor children of the world. *Lord, please make this all possible.*

I arrived at the coffeehouse about ten minutes before Helen, and I jumped up to greet her when she arrived. She waved before ordering a coffee. The bounce in her step spoke to me a message of hope.

"I've been busy during your absence," she said. "I called lots of my connections and friends. As a result, we set up an area-wide conference for all churches that might be interested in helping children in poverty. On the sixteenth of next month, our church will play host to this gathering. We want you to be the keynote speaker so you can roll out your idea of the Gypsies." Helen grinned from ear to ear.

"Seriously?"

"Seriously."

"That only gives me six weeks to prepare." I stood and paced around the coffee shop. "That's great, but now I might panic. Can I do this? Maybe this is too big for me. Oh, no. Is it too late to call it off? No, I don't mean that. Oh, Helen. How do I do this?" I stopped to catch my breath.

"Everything will be fine, Kathleen. You've got this. I've seen your passion for this topic, so I know you'll inspire others to join the cause. I set up a meeting with Pastor John tomorrow evening at the church so we can make more plans."

"Okay, okay. Sounds good. After my day job, I'll start working on pulling information together. Good idea to meet with Pastor John. What time?"

"Does seven work for you?"

"Okay, now I've got to run. I've got a million things to do." I hugged Helen and ran out the door.

As soon as I got in the car, I called Sam to let him know about the conference.

"Wonderful," he said. "You and God have this. Just breathe and pray. After dinner tonight, let's spend some time in prayer together, including Sophie, so we can all help you discern how this should play out."

"Perfect. You're a calming influence on me, so thanks. But in case you can't tell, I'm very excited and scared."

Sam laughed. "I'd have never guessed. See you at home, after work. Do you want me to pick up something home for dinner?"

"Sure, maybe a pizza. Easy to get and easy cleanup. That'd give us lots of time to talk and pray."

When Sophie got home from visiting some friends, I told her the news and asked for her help in preparing. She bubbled with enthusiasm while we talked. Just as we finished chatting, Sam walked in with our favorite pizza, one loaded with all the meats and all the vegetables.

After we ate and cleaned up, we moved to the living room to chat.

"Okay, let's pray for God's guidance for this event. We don't do this enough," I said, "so now would be a good time to start. I'll begin, then each of you can say something before we finish up. Sound like a plan?" Sam and Sophie nodded. "Dear Heavenly Father, I admit that sometimes I do feel confused and uncertain of what you're calling me to do. I lay awake at night, tossing and turning as I think about all the children living in poverty in our world. I now turn my worries over to you and ask you to show me my role in helping your people. Your Word promises all I need to do is call on you to help me and believe you have my best interest at heart. Forgive me for my doubts and little faith in this matter. Amen."

Sophie cleared her throat. "Thank you, Jesus, for bringing me this new family. Lord, I want to help others like the way you helped me. I want to help children that don't have someone to help them. Please guide me to how you want me to spend my life too. Amen."

I peeked over at Sophie and smiled.

Sam prayed next. "Lord, we seek the Holy Spirit's wise direction and clear guidance. There are many options and choices before us. Let us turn to your Word as we seek the answers, Father. Thank you for leaving your Word to instruct us in your ways. Please remind us to always turn to you first for guidance when we are unsure of the path. Help us trust you more and pray together more as a family. Forgive us when we doubt and draw us closer to your Spirit living in us every day. Amen."

I finished up our prayer time by saying, "And Father, help me remember to seek your wise counsel and trust in the ways you tell me to go. There are many voices in my head of those who think they know the best way forward. Please guide me to those who'll provide me the biblical perspective and direction. Like Solomon, my desire is for wisdom to make plans that are pleasing to you, Lord. Even when I don't understand, I trust and believe in you. Amen."

I opened my eyes and smiled at both Sam and Sophie. "I enjoyed praying together. Thanks, guys. Let me tell you this verse I found today which I think is appropriate for us." I pulled out a slip of paper from my Bible. "'Trust in the LORD with all your heart and lean not on your own understanding; in all your ways submit to him, and he will make your paths straight.' That verse came from Proverb 3:5–6."

"Wow, that fits," Sam said. "I know you're meeting with the church staff tomorrow to discuss more details. But how do you think you want us to proceed?"

"Maybe pulling stats on children in poverty all over the world," Sophie suggested. "I think that kind of perspective would help. I also think we need to come up with forms and spreadsheets to track those who attend and those that want to help."

My head swam with all the thoughts of what information to include in the talks. I took a deep breath as I sorted through all the details needed and grabbed a piece of paper and pencil to write down ideas.

"And we might need to think about setting up a website or app or something so people can get the information they need about helping others." I wrote this idea along with the others on my paper. "But that part might be down the road. At least that's what I thought about so far. What are your thoughts?"

"I can do some of the research for you, Mom."

That new name still stopped me in my tracks. I smiled over at Sophie, and she returned my smile.

"I can work on the forms and spreadsheet. Down the road, I can help with a website," Sam said.

"Perfect. I'll work on gathering photos from some of our trips to show actual kids and places in the speech. How long do you think I should speak?"

"No longer than an hour." Sam stood and stretched before rubbing his temples. "Maybe talk for thirty minutes and have a Q&A session at the end."

"That makes sense," I said, writing down the idea. "Okay, I think we've got an initial game plan. We'll see what Pastor John and Helen come up with at the meeting tomorrow, then we can talk again."

I awoke extra early the next day with thoughts pounding through my head. *Lord, this might be bigger than me, so I need you to take over. I need you to give me the right things to say and do. Please.*

I spent the next hour reading the Bible in the quietness of the early morning. Then I ended up reading the entire books of Romans and James and prayed for an extended period. I needed God's strength for projects like these because I would fail on my own.

At the church, I stopped by the chapel to offer a few more prayers. I found the pastor and Helen in his office, and I slipped into the open seat.

"You look like you just lost your best friend," John said.

"I'm feeling overwhelmed. I know I wanted this, but now I'm doubting my abilities to make this work."

John smiled. "You have spent so much time discerning this call. He's answered your prayers. Now, trust him with the work. He'll not leave you alone to do this task. Two Bible verses come to my mind that I think will help you. You should meditate on them as you prepare. The first verse is Proverbs 16:3. 'Commit to the LORD whatever you do, and he will establish your plans.' I think you are committing this work to him, so he will be there the whole way."

"That's perfect."

"The second verse is my personal favorite and also applies to this situation. Romans 8:28 says, 'And we know that in all things God works for the good of those who love him, who have been called according to his purpose.' So again, we all know that you're called to this task from all your discernment."

I scribbled down these verses to post them around the house to keep me encouraged during this time, and a small giggle escaped my lips.

"How's that funny?" Helen asked.

"Years ago, when I started thinking about this calling, Sam quoted Romans 8:28 to me. The fact he memorized a Bible verse by heart shocked me. God, bringing it up again, made me chuckle." I smiled up toward the heavens. "Now, what about logistics for the conference?"

Helen pulled out her notepad. "We'll set up the parish hall for about three hundred people. We also thought about setting aside two hours for the event. Does that work for you?"

"How about I speak for about thirty minutes and have time for Q&A. But what about the second hour?"

"We'll have coffee and snacks, and we can spend whatever time remaining just interacting with the guests," John said. "Maybe have a table where people can sign up to be on an initial email list. A second table could allow the attendees to give us their ideas for the project."

"I like that. Let's do it."

"I've got an idea," Helen said. "What if we serve a traditional meal from an underdeveloped country? That way, the guest could be part of a poverty experience. We can also have coffee, tea, and water."

"That might be good." I wrote down the idea on my paper. "I guess the meal would be some rice and beans since it's common in many parts of the world. We could put signs around the place with statistics about children in poverty. And maybe a bottle of dirty-looking water to show what some people drink just to survive."

"I think we've got a plan in place, ladies," John said, clapping his hands. "Since we have about six weeks until the actual event, let's plan to meet once a week to touch base and pray. I'll get the word out to other churches in the area and post it on all the church's social media accounts."

We wrapped up our meeting, and Helen hugged me when we left the building. "I'm so keyed up to be a small part of God's work here. You'll do wonderful. Just let me know if you need anything."

"I need prayer," I said without hesitation.

"You've got it."

Our family discussed the day's events and information over some pie à la mode that night. After Sophie and Sam helped clean up the dishes, we each set off to work on our part of the conference.

"Remember to pray for the Lord to guide you," I shouted after them as they headed off.

I stayed at the kitchen table to organize my thoughts. I wanted to start by telling the group why we came up with the name "Gypsy for God." So I did a little more checking on Gypsies. I discovered they believed they did not fit in with regular society and often felt like outsiders within their own countries of origin. Gypsies traveled or roamed from place to place, which is what this group of helpers would do.

A chieftain, who gets elected for life, leads each group of Gypsies. We have God as our chieftain in this endeavor and as our Savior forever. From all of this, I formed a mission statement for the work: "Gypsies for God. A group dedicated to following God to the ends of the earth so we can be his hands and feet to the poor children of the world."

Now on to preparing the speech.

CHAPTER THIRTY-FIVE

The auditorium filled to capacity, and the din of the clamor sent my nerves jangling. I headed over to the chapel to pray for a few minutes before everything started.

The coolness of the chapel, coupled with the silence and sweet smell from the lilies in the flower arrangements, settled my spirit. I sighed and offered a prayer for God to give me his words and wisdom for the day. I wrote a note to myself using Psalm 19:14: "May these words of my mouth and this meditation of my heart be pleasing in your sight, LORD, my Rock and my Redeemer."

A unique mixture of smells assaulted my nose when I passed the kitchen. A team had prepared coffee, sandwiches, and rice and beans as part of the food for the attendees. I also spied plates of sliced pies and brownies. Even if the talk failed to sway people to help, at least they will go away well-fed. Self-doubt threatened to stop me in my tracks, but I pushed the thoughts away as I made my way past the kitchen. Too much was at stake.

Someone grabbed my arm. "We've got a great turnout. Everything seems ready to go. How you feeling?" Helen asked.

"Nervous."

"You've got this. Plus, we've covered this event and you in prayer, so it's all good."

Sam and Sophie walked up, and she said, "Mom, did you see all the people? It's a full house. This is so exciting." Sophie's eyes twinkled as she held my hands. "Dad and I found seats near the back, so we can hear you talk, then sneak out to help them set up. Good luck." Both hugged me and headed off.

I paced and tried to interact with those in attendance, but anxiety made it impossible to focus. Shoes shuffled across the floor and chairs squeaked as those in attendance made their way to the seats when Pastor John stepped up to the lectern.

"Welcome, everyone," he said. "We're glad you're here and want to help us change the world. Before we begin, the bathrooms are outside this room and to the right. Our speaker will talk for about thirty minutes, followed by a time for Q&A. Also, we'd love you to join us for some snacks and a time of mingling in the community hall, which is just beyond the bathrooms."

I grabbed my notes to steady my shaking hands and took a deep breath to relax.

"Now, let's pray this prayer I found on World Vision's website: 'God, thank you for the abundance of life, relationships, health, comfort, and wealth you have provided, and thank you that even in times of need, despair, and brokenness, you are there. Please, put your arms around children and families in extreme poverty to feel comfort and hope; meet their needs both physically and spiritually. And, Lord, guide us so we can be your hands and feet pursuing justice for the poor and upholding the cause of the needy.' Thank you for all those willing to help and guide us daily. Amen. Now, please welcome our speaker, Kathleen Johnson."

I stepped onto the stage, and another hush fell over the crowd. "Welcome, my fellow Gypsies for God. To prepare for this meeting, I wrote a mission statement for this group. Here's what I came up with: 'A group dedicated to following God to the ends of the earth so we can be his hands and feet to the world's poor children.' We hope many of you and others will join our cause. I'll explain how that happens at the end of the talk. But for now, let's talk about the children."

I looked around the room to gauge the interest of the group as I began with the meat of the presentation. "Children are the most vulnerable population in our world. They suffer the most when bad things happen in the world around them, and they're powerless in those situations. There are many stats online, and I don't want to bog down this discussion with them, but I think we need to look at a few to understand the scope of the problem."

Sophie moved to the front of the room to help with the slide show. Once she was in place, I nodded to her to click onto the next slide of my presentation. "Across the world, about one billion children are multidimensionally poor, meaning they lack necessities as basic as nutrition or clean water. And about three hundred and fifty-six million children living in extreme poverty. These children are more than twice as likely to live in poverty than adults. Also, we find that children from the poorest households die at twice the rate of their better-off peers.

"And I would add, the Bible also talks about our responsibility toward the orphans and the poor. The verse that meant the most to me as I prepared this talk came from James 1:27 'Religion that God our Father accepts as pure and faultless is this: to look after orphans and widows in their distress and to keep oneself from being polluted by the world.'"

I told the stories of my encounters with poor children on some trips over the last few years, then stepped around the lectern to make better eye contact with the audience.

"You might think this problem is too big for us to solve. And you're correct. But that doesn't exempt us from trying to help children stuck in poverty. As Christians, God requires this kind of work. And that is where Gypsies for God came into play. Let me now explain how I envision this working. We're setting up a website that should be operational in the next month or so. Interested parties would sign up for an account. Once logged in, the user would see three tabs to begin with.

Sophie moved onto the next slide, and I began to talk about the lists of projects we envisioned, including the description of each, what would be needed to complete it, locations, number of people needed, and the total cost for each. Then I talked about how both prayer and financial partners would be needed and how people could help in both areas.

During this part of the talk, I noticed several people raise their hands, so I stopped to remind them I would answer questions at the end of the presentation, then continued.

"Churches, civic groups, or just a group of friends could sign up to volunteer for a project. In that situation, they take over the project with some oversight by my team. They can do the project themselves, hire someone to do it, or fundraise to pay for it. But the project is theirs until it reaches completion. All projects will be geared toward helping children in poverty anywhere in the world, including here in the US.

"Some groups might only want to be involved in praying for projects. Other groups may only want to raise the money to cover the project's cost. In either case, that additional information will show on the project. We'll list a funded project with that designation on the first tab. As we get this off the ground, we might set up other tabs as we deem necessary."

I wrapped up by asking the volunteers to hand out Bible verses to those in attendance so they could put them up as reminders of our purpose.

Each card contained three verses, Psalm 82:3 "Defend the weak and the fatherless; uphold the cause of the poor and the oppressed," Proverbs 19:17 "Whoever is kind to the poor lends to the LORD, and he will reward them for what they have done," and James 1:27 "Religion that God our Father accepts as pure and faultless is this: to look after orphans and widows in their distress and to keep oneself from being polluted by the world."

The Q&A session lasted about twenty-five minutes. When we finished, Pastor John wrapped up by reminding everyone about the refreshments and explained the purpose of the rice and beans. He also mentioned the tables where people could sign up to get more information as it became available. He offered a blessing over the food, and everyone moved down the hallway to the room with the food and sign-up tables.

A small crowd gathered around me to offer congratulations and shake my hand. My hands still shook some, but when I spotted Helen, Sam, and Sophie among the group, I sighed and smiled.

"You did great, Mom," Sophie said. "I think you stirred up some interest."

"Time will tell. Once we get a few projects started, I think it will be important to do these kinds of meetings in other areas. The more exposure, the better our chances of success," I said as Pastor John walked up.

"I agree. But remember to stay grounded. Even if we only ever complete a few projects, it will still be a success. God is in charge of this, not us."

We all nodded.

"I think you might need to remind me of that from time to time in the future," I said. "But I think we're off to a good start. I'll head down to the parish hall to mingle and answer any additional questions."

Sophie, Sam, and I walked down the hall to the community hall. A buzz of excitement filled the room, and it energized me.

"Thank you, Lord," I uttered under my breath and walked deeper into the room.

People called out my name from every corner, and I spun to see who to talk with first. Others tugged on my arm to join them. Before the crowd dispersed, I floated around the room, talking to everyone. I pressed my lips together to keep from smiling too much. I helped with the cleanup after the last attendee left.

"Did you see the sign-up sheets?" Helen asked.

I walked over to the table and could not believe my eyes. "There must be over a hundred names on the list. I can't believe it. This response is so amazing."

Pastor John joined us, and his face beamed as a broad smile formed. "I think you're on to something here, Kathleen, and I'm so glad I get to be a part of this work from the beginning."

"Me too," added Helen.

"It's so exciting," I said, "but scary too because now the actual work begins."

The buzz of excitement continued in the car on the drive home.

"What's next?" Sam asked.

"Well, I need the website as soon as possible. I think we should get at least one project out there right away. We don't want to lose momentum. People seem so eager to help, and they might lose interest if they to wait too long to get a project."

"Okay, I'll work on it tomorrow after church." Sam pulled into the garage and we all got out of the car. "Most of it's already done. You'll just need to figure out what project should go first."

"Maybe we should have two projects to start," Sophie said. "One big and one smaller so you can attract the most people."

"Oooh, I like that idea. The small project might not scare off a smaller group that doesn't think they can handle a larger one. Good idea, honey. Let's all pray about it and see what floats to the surface."

As usual, stress caused sleep to evade me. Ideas and thoughts swirled in my mind, but this time, all these thoughts made me breathless. God's good nature provided us with such a wonderful plan, and I dreamed of all the possibilities and what he would accomplish through this effort. Again, I offered thanks to God for staying faithful to me. I fell asleep, but I think the smile stayed on my face all night.

CHAPTER THIRTY-SIX

When Sam got the website up, we needed to decide on the first project to help. Overwhelmed by all the options, I sought Pastor John and Helen for their input.

At our Tuesday morning meeting, we reviewed the progress since the conference. "I think we start with just one project to see how it goes. This plan would also allow us to evaluate the systems we have in place. Sophie thought maybe start with one small and one big project, but now I've had second thoughts. What if we missed something in the process? What do you guys think?"

"I think one to start," said Pastor John. "But I think we need to have several more ready to go in case the response is larger than expected. Nothing drives away potential volunteers like not being fully prepared."

"I hadn't thought of that."

Helen added, "If you don't mind, I can be in charge of writing up the information for the projects as they come in, so it takes some of the burden off you. It also ensures consistency in the type of information shared. And I can use some of that same information to build a newsletter each month that highlights new projects and the status of ongoing ones."

"That would be so helpful. Thanks." I jotted down Helen's suggestion in my notes. "But back to the original question. What project should go first?"

Silence filled the room while we stared at each other.

Helen spoke first. "We get requests in from missionaries on the field all the time, and we could pick one of those. But Kathleen, this is your baby. So I think we should start with something to help the kids you discovered on your travels. This first project should be something that moves your heart. I think long term, we'll get overwhelmed with project requests, but this first one should be from you."

I nodded because I worried my voice might crack if I spoke at that moment, and a tear trickled down my cheek. John reached across the table and squeezed my hand for support.

"I think Helen is right," he said. "Kathleen, whom do you want to help first?"

More waterworks threatened to flow. I held up a finger to give myself a moment to compose myself.

"Well," I said, clearing my throat. "Let's look at some of the problems I've come across. In India, where we met Prisha, I'm sure the home she lives in could use some kind of help, like school supplies or building updates. I'll contact them to see if there is anything urgent they need. Seeing the enormous slums on the outskirts of Nairobi struck at my heartstrings too. They lacked schools and many of the basic necessities. I can envision lots of projects there. So much need." I shook my head. "Nepal, our next encounter, taught us all about human trafficking. Where do you start with it—rescuing, giving counseling, or housing the victims? So I think trafficking might be too big to start off with or ever."

Helen jumped in. "You mentioning human trafficking reminded me of something. Can Sam add a tab to the website? We could add information like the checklist you created on how to spot a victim of trafficking. And maybe list some resources like hotlines so people could use it if needed?"

"Good thinking, Helen." I added this task to my to-do list. Continuing with my train of thought, I said, "I'm leaning toward doing something in Kenya, like building a school in the slums. But that seems so big. Should we start smaller?"

"If we allow God to lead us on this," Pastor John said, "then nothing will be impossible. So starting big might be a good idea."

"Do we have any church contacts in Nairobi that can help us get cost information? And can they partner with us to make this project a reality?"

"I do," said Helen. "If that's the project we want to pursue first, I'll contact them. Then I can report back to everyone once I get more details. Is that the project you want to begin with, Kathleen?"

"I think so. Yes. Yes, it is. And maybe you could ask your contacts to include the cost of a water well too. That way, we can provide fresh water for the school and surrounding community."

"I think we're done for today." John stood, stretched, and gathered up his notes. "I'm feeling good about this. Thanks, ladies. Now, let's end today with a prayer to thank God for this first project and ask for his guidance to move forward."

Later, at home, the excitement continued to build. I paced the kitchen while I waited for Sam and Sophie to get home to share this morning's decisions. The garage door opened. Sam had picked up Sophie on his way home, so they arrived together.

"Someone's face is beaming," Sam said when he kissed me.

"We've got the first project," I blurted. All the details spilled out, with me talking a mile a minute.

"Slow down, Kathleen. I can't keep up," Sam said, smiling.

I started from the beginning and recounted the discussion and decision from the meeting at a slower pace. Both Sam and Sophie jumped up from their chairs and grabbed me in a bear hug.

"I'll add that tab on trafficking information after dinner," Sam said. "I can pull the details from the electronic copy of the flyer you sent me. Once you get more details about the project, I can add those too."

"I looked at the website during a break at school today and could not believe the amount of traffic it was getting already. It even looked like several groups signed up to be prayer partners. It's so cool to be a part of this work," said Sophie. "Maybe someday we can go to see a finished project. And I'd love to help with one some summer too. Good work, Mom."

"Now, we wait for the information to come from Kenya. Lots of waiting with this work."

The banter and laughter around the dinner table that night filled my heart with joy. After all the turmoil of my encounters with poverty, I believed we could impact the world. No, a better way to think—God could use as part of his plans. My heart overflowed with hope and joy.

CHAPTER THIRTY-SEVEN

With information pouring in from Kenya, the Gypsy team of Pastor John, Helen, and I met to discuss details. Through our network of churches and connections, many people provided their input into the feasibility of this idea.

But is this the right project and if so, where to begin?

After offering an opening prayer, we began the discussion.

"Well, have you and your family prayed over the first official project of the Gypsies for God?" Helen asked.

"We have," I said. "I think we each received the same message from God. Doing something in the slums of Nairobi is the best place to start. One group who contacted us mentioned how much they need a daycare center. If we built this, it would enable single moms to get jobs without worrying about the safety of their non-school-age children. The place needs to be safe, clean, and inexpensive. That might be simpler than building an entire school for the first project."

"I like it," said Pastor John. "We help the children and the moms at the same time. I think it's a win-win for the entire community."

"All in agreement, say aye," Helen said, and we all laughed.

"What's next?" Pastor John asked.

"I think we start the discussions with our contacts in Nairobi." I scratched my head as I organized my thoughts. "Maybe they could find an abandoned building that we can convert. I think this might be cheaper and easier than building a new building. We could ask them to gather other pricing information too. How much to rent a building, prepare it, and furnish it?" I looked from Helen to John to see if either had anything to add. "Also, we would need to know about ongoing expenses, at least to make sure the first few months of operations are covered. I think it might be two projects. One to set up the daycare and one to keep it running once it's built. After we have commitments for all the funds, we can put out a message asking if any of the teams wanted to go. If no group volunteers, we will use locals to make it all happen."

"I'll contact the church down there," Helen said. "Do we need a 'coming soon' notation on the website so we can keep people excited?"

"That's a good idea," Pastor John said. "Also, maybe write up a small blurb about the slums, the poverty and problems within them, and any other needs in the area. And we can ask people to pray with us as we figure out how to move forward and how they want to become involved."

"I think we've got our marching orders," I said.

After a final group prayer for more guidance, we headed off to do our parts, agreeing to meet again in a week. If we needed anything before then, we would exchange texts and emails when information became available to keep everything moving along.

The announcement of the Kenya project on the website garnered lots of interest, and a prayer team formed within the first few hours. The group, primarily ladies, started prayer chains across the US with the goal of praying for the work daily at a set time. What a blessing for us.

While things moved for us, nothing happens fast in less-developed countries. After more than a month, the information we needed arrived via email.

The Nairobi church had met with the local council department of the Kibera area. Buying a pre-existing building was one of the proposals put together by the elders. The structure sat on a prominent route through the slums and allowed easy access. And it contained two large rooms, a kitchen area, and a pit latrine out behind the structure.

The church in Kenya proposed one room for young children in cribs and a second room for children not yet of school age. The building needed painting on the inside, along with some roof repairs. The church sent us photos of the empty building and it seemed more than adequate for the needs of the area.

Summarizing the information, I told the committee, "The building cost is about $5,000. The repairs would run us another $150 and $200 for the furniture. Ongoing cost for the teacher and food would run about $250 per month. If we did want to put in a well to help the school and the whole community, it would cost about $8,000. The center will care for six infants in the baby room and ten older children in the other room."

Our little committee set the initial project budget at $20,000 for two reasons. Since this was the first project, we wanted to cover any forgotten costs along with a contingency plan for the underestimated cost of materials. Any leftover money would go back into the pool for future projects.

After we settled on all the details for the project, I said, "I like it. I think we should go with it. What do you guys think?"

"The cost appears reasonable," Pastor John said, "and the center will provide an enormous benefit. But once we complete the building, how will the locals decide which children to accept?"

"I think I read in the recommendation that they will pick using a lottery system. If successful, we can always look at doing a second center someday," Helen said. "Do we know how much they will charge per child? We want to make sure it's affordable to the locals."

"The council suggested no more than $10 per child," Pastor John said. "Unfortunately, that will not bring in enough money to cover the ongoing cost, but I think that is okay. And we'll need to ask a group to agree to cover the shortfalls as part of their ministry."

Everyone nodded, and we ironed out enough of the details for now. Next, Helen put all the information on the project section of the website. Now we just needed to wait to see if and when a group might claim this work.

The following day, I sat down at the kitchen table and checked the Gypsies for God website before beginning my travel work. A group out of Georgia had expressed an interest in claiming the project. Based on our recommendation regarding the lack of security for tourists in the slum area, this team would raise funds to cover the initial costs instead of going in-person. The Georgia group had also agreed to cover the first several months of operating costs. I knocked over my chair when I jumped up.

Sam ran out of the bedroom with his toothbrush in his hand. "What's wrong? Are you okay?"

I pointed at the screen and stared in disbelief, choking out a few words. "We ... we did it."

Sam stared at the screen and let out a yell that brought Sophie running next. Sam and I danced, shouted, and pointed at the screen.

It took her a minute to realize why we celebrated, but soon she hooted and hollered with us. We danced a jig around the living room. Sam twirled us both around and around.

"I can't wait to tell my friends at school." Sophie grabbed up Rex and spun with him in her arms. "This news is so awesome. I feel like I'm a small part of this work."

"You're more than a small part. We all share a part in it, so you should feel proud of yourself too," I said.

We danced and celebrated for a few more minutes before Sam and Sophie headed out to start their day. The house fell quiet after they left, so I took a few moments in the quiet and sank to my knees.

"Thank you, Lord. This work is all yours. Thank you for allowing us to take part. Bless the group from Georgia. Bless the work of their hands. Let this be the start of better lives in Kenya, and may we accomplish more for your kingdom. Amen."

Soon more requests than we could handle flowed into the Gypsies for God's website. My joy soon became despair at all the needs in the world.

I prayed constantly for God to shed light on how to proceed, and I shared my feelings with my family and the committee so they could pray as well.

"This is too much. I can't help this many people," I said to Helen and Pastor John at the next meeting.

Again, John's calming voice and reassurance helped me. "God doesn't expect you to do it all. He wants you to trust him with whom to help and for the results. We're all praying about this, and we'll succeed on God's terms, not the world's timing or way."

In my heart, I knew he was right. "I need to get more opportunities to speak to groups so we can get more help. The more help, the lighter the burden."

"We'll list the viable ones on the website as projects come in and trust God to provide for them," Helen said. "And if they don't receive support, we'll still trust God. The work of the Gypsies is bigger than us. We've got to come to grips with the fact that not all the requests will be doable. So focus on the good we are doing in his name. I think we need to go ahead and send the money to the church in Kenya so they can pay the workers for the project. Is everyone in agreement?"

John and I nodded in agreement.

"Okay, thanks, guys," I said. "Now, what are the latest requests for help?"

"I browsed my emails this morning and found the following." Helen clicked some keys on her keyboard. "One request for help in starting a sewing class in India to teach skills to girls, so they have future income earning potential. Another request asked for money to start a feeding program in Pakistan near some of the brick factories. Many families work there as indentured servants with little to eat. This program would give hot meals to them daily."

"Both of these projects seem straightforward to put into place and they would make a tremendous difference in the lives of those people in the area," John said.

Helen continued, "We also received several requests to help with supplies for vacation Bible school activities in several South American countries. For each one, I need to do a little more checking with our contacts to make sure they're genuine needs. But I think we can place them on the website right after the confirmation. These should get snapped up because of their smaller size."

"These are decent projects and easy to implement for a smaller group," I said. "It might be a good idea to offer lots of these smaller projects to feel like we are accomplishing more. Maybe do only one or two extensive projects a year. What are your thoughts?"

Helen and John nodded, and I left with a little more bounce in my step.

"How's the Kenya daycare center doing?" asked Sophie when she came home from school later that day.

Sam and I sat in the living room reading and I looked up. "It's moving along. The group in charge is doing a great job of sending us regular updates. They expect it to open in about a month. All the funding seems to flow in just liked we planned."

"If you forward some of those update emails, I can post some of the information on the website and Facebook group to help you out."

"That would be perfect, honey. Maybe you can also put together some kind of flyer to announce that I am available to speak to groups." I clasped Sophie's hand and smiled. "The more volunteers on this side of the projects, the more people we can help."

"Sure, I'll work on something this weekend. And maybe I can go with you on some of the speaking engagements too."

I smiled at Sophie. "You're a blessing."

Sam said with a smile, "Thanks. I think you're both a blessing."

"I'm talking to the kid, silly."

"So, I'm not a blessing?" He chuckled.

I stuck my tongue out at Sam, and I walked into the kitchen to start dinner.

We relished our Friday night dinnertime together as we shared about our day and week. These times warmed my heart even with all the challenges of Gypsies for God. Family time kept me grounded. Welling up, I smiled and recalled all the blessings in my life. I choked back tears while I listened to Sam and Sophie tell each other silly jokes. *Thank you, Lord.*

In bed that night, Sam and I cuddled with the lights out.

"What's that goofy grin for at the dinner table?" he asked.

"Just a moment of pure joy as I inventoried all the blessings in my life, and yes, you're a blessing." We snuggled deeper into the covers. "I love you."

"I love you too, darling. You're a blessing to this family too—and many people in this world. I thank God daily for you," he whispered as I drifted off to sleep.

CHAPTER THIRTY-EIGHT

It did not take long for trouble to show up with Gypsies for God's work. When I opened my email account on Monday, hundreds of new messages popped up in my personal account. "What's going on?" I said to myself.

Several were from Helen and marked urgent. I started with those, and my heart sank when I read her first message.

"Kathleen, we have a major problem. It seems like some of the money in the Nairobi daycare fund is missing. I've made calls and sent emails to get more information. This news is terrible and might affect the future work of the Gypsies. Please get in touch with me as soon as you get this message."

Instead of calling, I jumped in my car and headed to her office. I figured talking face to face would be better. I startled Helen when I burst into her office.

"What's going on, Helen? Start from the beginning."

"I got a call late last night from the project manager in Kenya. He told me that one of his employees didn't show up for work," said Helen. "But this man never missed work, so the manager went to do some checking. He found the employee's wife at home, crying. She explained the employee came into some money and ran off with another woman. Our PM went to the bank and found that about

$2,000 was missing from the account." Helen paused as the words caught in her throat. "The employee took it and disappeared. Now, they are short of funds to finish the project."

I paced around Helen's office. "What're we going to do?"

"We've got to let the group in Georgia know about the theft and see if they will raise more money for the project. If not, I think we have to drop it for lack of funds. Plus, we need to figure out some safeguards for the future to prevent these kinds of problems." Another long pause ensued as she processed the information. "And do we publish this problem to the rest of those involved with Gypsies? I'm at a loss."

Pastor John strode into the office. "I can't believe this happened. Because I believed no one would steal from church funds that helped others." He shook his head. "I'm in shock."

"I think we all are," I said.

We sat in silence for a while, contemplating the events. Finally, Helen broke the silence.

"First off, in the future, all funds need to stay here in our account and only get forwarded once we have receipts or invoices in hand. Even though we are working through local churches, it still must be an enormous temptation for some people to handle that money. Especially because some people we help think we can afford to replace it. And if, for some reason, money has to be in a local account, we need to require two signatures to access it."

We all agreed.

"I think we need to let the prayer team know about this issue so they can pray for the man and his family." Pastor John looked like he might shed a tear or two. "Anyone who would do such a thing needs our prayers. I feel sorry for the man, and we must still love and forgive him as Christ would do."

"That's hard to do, even though I know you are right. I'll try," I said. "Maybe we need to start a fund that covers this kind of situation in the future because if it happened once, it could happen again. I'm just not sure how to share this information with the other project teams."

"Honesty in this situation will be the best policy. We must be transparent at all times. If we lose people, then that is how it'll be for us." John bowed his hand and rubbed the back of his neck. "God will provide more. We need to add some information to the website and presentation that helps educate our volunteers about this possibility and how we need to remain Christlike. We can use the example that Christ washed the feet of the person who betrayed him. Let's keep praying, and I'll draft an email for each of us to review. Once we agree, we'll send it out to all those involved with Gypsies. Agreed?"

We all nodded again, and I left the church in shock and disbelief, but resolved to make this work, despite all the problems.

The next morning I found an email with a letter attached from John asking Helen and me to review before he sent it out to all the Gypsies. In the message, he described the situation and explained how we planned to move forward. He worded the message well with an even tone that went straight to the point, and I agreed he should send it out. Helen responded likewise. The message went out to the fifteen thousand people on our mailing list, and we waited for the chips to fall.

Relentless turmoil ensued for several days. Numerous people expressed their opinions about the steps we should follow, including shutting down the work. At times, the name-calling and finger-pointing threatened to send me running to hide under the covers.

I avoided responding by biting my lip when I read the comments, and I prayed instead. How some of the Christians reacted to this subject shocked me. *Maybe they forgot about the grace and forgiveness modeled by Christ. I wonder if this is why some people shy away from church people?* On the other hand, the civic groups offered much more support to move forward with the additional safeguards in place.

Pastor John responded to each message with the grace I wish they offered us, addressing each of their concerns with outstanding professionalism. Later on, he told us that he had sent several strongly worded messages to some people but did not copy us on those.

I guess even pastors have a breaking point once in a while.

Pastor John's continued support for our cause helped calm me down. By the end of the storm, we had lost one group of financial supporters, a few of our prayer warriors, and one team that wanted to help with a project in the future.

But one group had stepped up and replaced the missing funds.

I pressed my palms to my eyes and rubbed them. "Thank you, Lord." Now I could move on with adding new projects for to our website and trust God to do his work.

Skepticism and doubt became my alternative names. I doubted my abilities to do this work and even the calling on my life. *Why would God pick such an inept person to help poor children?* I cried myself to sleep a few times during that week. But before long, Sophie and Sam came to my rescue and talked me off the proverbial cliff before I gave up.

"Mom," Sophie said as she came into my bedroom toward the end of the week, "you know in your heart you're doing the right thing. You just need to get on the road again to do more group meetings. By getting more people involved, you'll feel a sense of accomplishment once again."

"She's right, you know," Sam said. "Add some smaller projects to the list and watch them take off. Nothing helps overcome doubt better than success."

I nodded as a few tears ran down my cheeks. Sam handed me a tissue. Rex even jumped up in my lap to offer his support.

"I know you're right. Maybe a few small project successes might help lift me from this despair."

"Let's work on adding them this weekend." Sam lifted my chin in his hand. "And please, stay off the group email for Gypsies. I suspect you'll keep rereading the mean messages and beating yourself up even more."

"You know me too well. I promise I won't."

"And if you can't, I'll ask Ms. Helen to remove your access until you feel better," Sophie said, wagging her finger at me.

The time came to put doubt behind me and move forward.

Maybe.

CHAPTER THIRTY-NINE

Sam, Sophie, and I came up with a game plan to keep me sane and moving forward in this work. I took all the ideas and notes to the next committee meeting to discuss with the team.

"We revisited some of the early submissions and came up with several minor projects that I think would be perfect to start this new phase," I said as I sat down with them the next week. "The request to set up a sewing class in a remote part of India could be a start. This one could help the community in two ways. First, moms could learn to make clothes, and that could earn money to buy food for their families. Also, some orphans or street children could learn the trade and make a better life for themselves."

Pastor John and Helen nodded, so I continued.

"The next request was for help to set up feeding programs in Pakistan near the brick factories in the north. Many of these workers are indentured, and enslaved people who did not have enough to eat. Children as young as ten also work in the factory. I think feeding them is an important issue, especially if we can't help them out of their current situations."

Again, they nodded.

"And last, I saw lots of requests for teams to come and help with summer vacation Bible school activities in many countries. This project would be a great opportunity for a church youth group. They could do it as a mission trip." I closed my notebook and looked at the other committee members for their responses.

"I think all of those are great ideas," Helen said. "Each of them seems straightforward. For example, we could do one sewing class, one feeding program, and one VBS. Afterward, we could evaluate the success. Plus, that would allow us time to figure out continuing costs if we kept the programs going."

"I agree. Great work." John scratched his head. "But where do you think we should start? The VBS?"

Helen jumped in on this one. "I think somewhere less remote might be a good place to start. Yesterday, a church on an Indian reservation in Oklahoma made such a request. I think it might be perfect for a youth trip. Even for our kids here."

"Perfect," the pastor and I said in unison.

"Now, on to the next topic," I said. "I think, considering our recent setbacks, I need to get out on the road again to get more groups to sign up to help this cause. Helen, would you be able to get me some contact information so I can call them and start planning?"

"Already have a list going for when you're ready," she said, handing me a sheet of paper with about fifty organizations on it.

"Wow, that's a lot." I stared down at the list. "Maybe if I can group them by city, I can combine a few. I have my regular job too."

"Whatever works best for you, Kathleen," Pastor John said. "We didn't expect you to meet with all of them in the next month. It's just a comprehensive list that we can work our way through over time."

After a few minutes of chit-chat, we broke up and went our separate ways.

Back at the kitchen table, I worked on the plans for conferences while Helen and John pulled together cost estimates and timing for the new projects. Helen put it under the website tab of Gypsies asking for volunteers.

Various groups signed up to complete each of the newly suggested projects. The ease of achieving these tasks and their small cost appealed to more people.

For the sewing class in India, we recommended three manual sewing machines for $40 each machine. And suggested manual machines because of the lack of electricity in some rural areas. Our research found fabric for about $5 per yard. With ten students, that would mean a cost of about $100 for fabric and patterns for one outfit per class. And last, the price of a teacher ran about $10 per class. The first sewing class cost ran about $250, but we recommended a budget of $300 for any unexpected items.

Alternatively, the group accountable could send a team to set up and teach the sewing class themselves. A group from Iowa selected this project and opted to send the money to India so the church could set up and run the course. The Iowa group agreed to fund one class and would consider other ones after seeing the reports and photos from this first one.

The project for the feeding program went to a civic group in Michigan. That group agreed to fund the program with one meal a week to evaluate the process. Research showed that a typical meal might include rotis with yogurt, raw onions, and chilies. The group opted to add some chicken for additional nourishment. They budgeted the cost at fifty cents a meal and started with one hundred meals per week totaling about $200. This group also added money for disposable plates and utensils and any unexpected costs, which added another $100. The local church in Pakistan provided the labor free as part of their mission. The group agreed to a six-month program and then would reevaluate the success of the program before continuing the work.

Several teams from different parts of the country signed up to help with the vacation Bible schools. The task detailed a one-week program from 9:00 a.m. to noon each day, with lunch for each child before sending them home. The church in Oklahoma estimated two hundred children and would split into two sessions. Two teams agreed to provide all the materials and food for the weeklong classes, while two groups wanted to send youth groups along to conduct the VBS. The suggested cost of the material came in at $1,000 per session, including the food. The teams going made all their plans for transportation and lodging, so we did not have to worry about that funding.

My sleeping patterns improved with each successful launch of a new program. One night, at dinner, my family and I talked about the upcoming conferences.

"Did you get any responses for the next set of conferences?" Sophie asked.

"Well, somewhat of an overwhelming response," I said. "I plan to schedule two a month for the summer months. I think that will be enough for now and allow me lots of time to prepare."

"Since they're during the summer, maybe Sophie and I could go with you." Sam shifted back and forth in his chair. "Any of them in fun places where we could extend our time and see the sights?"

"Sure. The meetings break down this way," I said. "In June, I'll speak at two in the Colorado area, and they're on back-to-back weekends. We could visit the mountains between meetings. The July events are both in Georgia since we already have a friendly response from them. The final ones are in North Carolina. These cities are more spread out, so I'm not sure if it would be a good fit for a family trip. In August, the groups are in Virginia and Maryland. These are also back-to-back weekends, so we might be able to do some stuff."

"Well," Sam said, "I'm not sure how much time I can get off work, so I think only one of them will work for me."

"For the June and August ones, I plan to stay in both areas the entire week because I can work remotely," I said. "If you guys join me for one of them, I will take some as vacation time."

"I'd love to go with you to all of them," Sophie said. "If it wouldn't cost too much for me to go."

"No problem. I'd enjoy the company." I leaned back and cocked my head. "Plus, we can share a room when Sam's not with us. Sam, what's your choice for vacation spots?"

"Since it'll get hot here in Texas for the summer," Sam said, "I opt for the coolness of the mountains, so that I'll be with you guys in Colorado. Can you make that happen, tour guide?"

"Okay, I will get to work."

Thank you, Lord, for all the support from my friends and family. I'm scared the groups I talk with might be hostile to our team because of the stolen funds, but I'm trusting you for whatever happens.

CHAPTER FORTY

First up, the trip to Colorado. Some quiet time in the mountains would help my soul. Where could we go with easy access to things that we all could enjoy?

The first conference occurred in Denver and the second in Boulder, but nothing appealed to me in those big city areas. But I found a great vacation rental near Colorado Springs in Manitou Springs.

From the photos, it looked just picture-perfect. The house sat nestled in a grove of aspens halfway up a hill. They sat alone with no neighbors in sight. The city was a twenty-minute drive away, and I expected it to offer a lot of tranquility. I booked the house without consulting the family, then investigated the entire area and came up with a list of fun things to do. I planned to present my case to the jury at just the right moment.

The phone rang, and I picked it up. Before I could say a word, Sophie blurted, "Mom, I've had a car wreck. The police and ambulance are here. And they're taking me to the hospital. They think my leg might be broken. Mom, I'm scared." Sophie gasped. "This intersection is the same spot my real mom had her accident. Do you think the same thing will happen to me? Please forgive me. I think I wrecked the car, so I won't blame you if you want to put me in foster care. Again, I'm sorry."

"It's okay, Sophie." Although my knees buckled and my hands shook, I fought to reassure my girl. "You'll be fine. I'll meet you at the hospital. This will all work out. Say a prayer as they transport you. I'll pray too. I'll call Sam, and we'll be there as soon as possible. Don't worry, honey, and no reason in the world would cause us to put you into the foster care system. We love you."

Sophie sniffled. "Okay."

I called Sam and explained everything while I headed out the door.

"Poor kid," he said. "I'm just finishing up a quick meeting, then I'll head that way. Let me know once you get there and how she's doing."

I sped out of the driveway but seemed to hit every red light on the way to the hospital. Why does that happen when a person is in a hurry? I'm not sure I have ever experienced such a scared and anxious feeling before. My heart thumped wildly in my chest. My sweaty hands made it hard to keep my hands on the steering wheel. I yelled at a few drivers to get out of the way. I'm sure they labeled me a madwoman.

But I also prayed while I drove, and thankfully, no police officers got in my way.

The next nightmare hit me when I tried to find a parking place at the emergency entrance. After my ninth pass through the parking lot, a car pulled out of a spot, and I pulled in. Halfway to the entrance, I realized I'd forgotten my purse. Back at the car, I discovered I had left the doors unlocked as well. I grabbed my bag, locked the doors, and ran off again.

I burst into the emergency room, out of breath, but blurted, "They just brought my daughter in from a car wreck. Her name is Sophie Johnson." I gulped for air.

"Are you a relative?" the nurse asked.

I almost blew my top. "I just said she's my daughter, so yeah, that makes me a relative."

"You'll need this armband," the nurse said. "Go through those double doors, and someone will direct you to her room."

I grabbed the band and pushed through the doors—bells, dings, loud voices, and crying noises overwhelmed my senses as I entered. A frazzled-looking nurse asked me if I needed help.

"I'm looking for my daughter, Sophie. She wrecked her car, and they brought her here."

"They just took her up to X-ray, so you can wait in the room till she gets back."

"How bad is it?"

"The doctor will meet with you to give you all the details, but we think she broke her leg." She checked one of the monitors. "She's banged up quite a bit. But nothing that time won't heal, I think. She should be back down soon."

The nurse left me alone with my thoughts. I paced and watched the clock. It seemed to stop moving a few times just to frustrate me more. After all the waiting, Sam's voice floated in from the nurses' station out in the main area of the ER. Someone brought him over to the room.

"Have you seen her yet?" Sam asked.

"No, she's been in X-ray since I got here." Sam held me in a tight embrace. "This waiting is excruciating. I just want to see her to know that she's okay. The nurse said they think she broke her leg, but the doctor would meet with us with all the details."

Sam plopped down in a chair and held his face in his hands. "Poor kid."

We sat in silence until a wheel squeaked in the hallway, and the door opened. A male aide wheeled Sophie in, and

I tried not to cry. "Oh, baby, I'm so sorry. Are you in much pain?"

Sophie grimaced, and the aide helped her move from the wheelchair to the bed. "I hurt all over. I keep hoping the pain medicine will kick in soon."

"The doctor should be in soon," the aide said as he turned and left us.

"I'm sorry," Sophie said. Between the pain and the drugs, she appeared out of it.

I studied her face and noticed a gash below her left eye, and both eyes blackened. She looked pale and so small in the hospital bed. I tried to hold her hand, but the IV got in the way. I walked around to the opposite side and grabbed her other hand tightly. She grimaced, so I relaxed my grip. A burn mark on her arm probably came from the airbags inflating. Tears ran down my cheeks while I stroked her hair.

Sam lifted the sheets to look at her legs and mouthed, "I think it's broken. Yuck, it looks crooked."

Finally, after a wait longer than we liked, the doctor came in.

He introduced himself as Dr. Conrady, then said, "I've reviewed Sophie's X-rays. She has a fracture in her femur and a clean break in her fibula. She's lucky. I don't think she'll need surgery for either. But she'll need to be in a cast for at least six weeks."

"What about other injuries?" I asked.

"Most are superficial, bumps and bruises. I think we'll put a few stitches in the cut on her cheek. We gave her a thorough checkup and nothing else showed up." He looked down at her chart again. "She will be very sore for a while, but she'll heal nicely. I'll give you a prescription for pain meds, but only use them when necessary. I'll get the nurses to come in and cast it and stitch the cut." Dr.

Conrady stopped before he walked out the door. "Do you have any other questions?"

We both shook our heads, and he left. After several long hours while the leg was set and paperwork completed, we left the hospital with a doped-up Sophie in tow.

At home, we tucked her into bed, and Rex curled up at her feet. She rubbed his head. "I'm okay, little buddy," she murmured, and he purred.

Early the next day, Sophie's groaning woke me, and I rushed to her room. She looked pitiful. Swollen cheek. Two black eyes. Pain all over her face. I eased onto the bed and touched her arm.

"Good morning, honey. How're you feeling?"

"Not well. I hurt all over. I feel like a Mack truck ran over me. But, no, wait, it was only a pickup truck," she said with a slight smile.

"At least you still have your sense of humor. What happened?"

"From what I remember, I think I stopped." Sophie swallowed hard. "The light turned green, and I went. The next thing some policeman talked to me and asked me if I was okay." She winced. "The truck hit me in the rear door. I was so scared." Sophie paused to catch her breath. "The cops said the pickup truck ran the red light and T-boned me." She rubbed Rex's head. "Are they okay, the other driver?"

"Sam will call the station later this morning to get a copy of the report, and he'll ask them. I'm so sorry you had to go through this, honey."

"I'm going to be okay, so that's good. But I kept thinking about my mom while I sat there, stuck in the car. Do you think she suffered from any pain before she died?"

"I don't think so. The officer said your mom died instantly from the impact, from what I remember. I don't think she ever knew what happened."

Sophie's whole body shook as she wailed then. She clutched her pillow to her chest and buried her head into it. The episode lasted about ten minutes.

"I feel terrible. You guys bought me a car for my birthday, and I wrecked it. You must hate me for all the trouble I cause." Sophie sobbed.

"It's okay. The car wreck was an accident and not your fault." I stroked Sophie's hair and brushed away her tears. "The insurance will fix or replace the car. Remember the car is only a thing, and we can replace it. You're irreplaceable. We love you like our own. So stop this fussing about hating you. These things happen, and families pull together in the tough times."

"Here, here. I agree," Sam said from the doorway. He walked over to Sophie and hugged her gingerly while she sobbed into his shoulder. "Stop worrying about anything other than getting better."

"How long will I be in this cast? Will it ruin our Colorado trip?" she asked.

"Six weeks at least is what the doctor told us last night. We'll follow up with a specialist in a few days." I smoothed the covers on the bed and smiled at Sophie. "As far as Colorado, we're still on. The trip is seven weeks away. By then, you might be out of that thing, and if not, you'll be a pro on the crutches. So, I say we still go. We might have to limit our hikes or other activities, but we'll still find fun things to do."

Sophie's chin trembled, and a weak smile appeared. "Thanks. I wish Mom was here to see the wonderful life you've given me. Maybe she's watching over me from heaven." Sophie blew her nose and wiped at the tears. "I think I'm going to go back to sleep now. Thanks."

I tucked her in and kissed her on the top of her head.

Back in the living room, Sam said, "I'll call and get the police report this morning and call the insurance company to see what needs to happen next. Will you call the orthopedic doctor to schedule the follow-up appointment?"

"Sure, after I call the school to let them know Sophie will miss at least a few days of classes. And I'll call the church and get her added to the prayer list."

"Yup. I'll pick up some flowers for Sophie on my way home from work."

"And maybe a stuffed animal. Something she can cuddle to help her feel better emotionally." I kissed Sam before he headed out the door to work. *I'm so glad I work from home so I can monitor Sophie. It's going to be a rough few days.*

When I called the church, Helen answered. I explained what happened and asked her to put Sophie on the prayer list. I cried about the troubles over the last few years but knew I could trust Helen. She listened so well and always offered incredible support, and today appeared no different.

"We'll pray for a speedy recovery for Sophie," Helen said. "Always remember that the Bible tells us there will be tough times. The passage in Ecclesiastes 3 always helps me when I feel overwhelmed by events. Let me read it to you before we hang up. 'There is a time for everything, and a season for every activity under the heavens. A time to be born and a time to die, a time to plant and a time to uproot, a time to kill and a time to heal, a time to tear down and a time to build, a time to weep and a time to laugh, a time to mourn and a time to dance, a time to scatter stones and a time to gather them, a time to embrace and a time to refrain from embracing, a time to search and a time to give up, a time to keep and a time to throw away, a time to tear and a time to mend, a time to be silent and a time to speak, a time to love and a time to hate, a time for war and a time for peace.'

"These tough times for Sophie and your family will pass too. Keep trusting in God, and someday, you'll look back and see how the hand of God guided and kept you."

Her words encouraged me, like always.

Later, I shared the passage with Sophie and Sam at the dinner table. We sat quietly and pondered the words. As I lay in bed that night, I told myself that God was in control and that this would all work itself out.

But I feel a little like Job. Why do these things keep happening? And what will happen next?

CHAPTER FORTY-ONE

The first few weeks of Sophie's recovery were difficult—her learning to use crutches and deal with the constant pain took their toll. But she weathered the storm like a champ and ended up only missing three days of school. With the school year winding down, Sophie's excitement rose while she looked forward to our time in Colorado and a complete recovery.

The accident caused us to change our vacation trip somewhat. I combined the two Colorado conferences into one meeting. With the date set, we planned out the twelve-hour drive to Colorado for the week before the conferences. Sam would fly home from Denver over the weekend before the meeting, and Sophie would stay with me throughout the conference. The two of us would drive back to Arlington. This drive time would give us time to talk about life, blessings, Gypsies, and anything else.

About a week before we headed to the mountains, the doctor removed the cast.

The doctor told us, "Her leg looks great, but you need to remember to take it easy for a few more weeks. You might continue to experience some swelling and pain for another month or so. If you have any additional problems, make sure to contact our office again."

Sophie skipped out of the office, ready for life to return to normal. "I feel at least twenty pounds lighter without that cast on my leg. I'm ready to explore Colorado."

"Me too."

"Now that the trip is on for sure, we need to call Vicky to make sure she can watch Rex while we're away."

"Yes, we don't want to forget about my favorite little fur ball. And we can continue with the tradition of finding a souvenir for Vicky."

Once I had called Vicky, and she agreed to watch Rex, I told Sophie, "We're all set. Now we can relax and enjoy our trip."

On to our grand adventure. But conflicting thoughts filled my mind. *Lord, are you calling me to be a mom or a missionary? Can I do both things successfully? What is my real purpose, Lord?*

Even with the cast removed and Sophie healing so well, we decided to break up the long drive. We would drive for about five hours at a time with stops along the way to allow us to stretch our legs. We left Arlington early enough to see some things around the city before continuing onward to Manitou Springs. The long ribbon of a road shimmered before us as the day's heat kicked in.

"What's that?" Sophie asked pointing into the distance.

"Oh. Pullover, Sam," I yelled. "That's the Cadillac Ranch. Some guy buried those ten Cadillacs standing up like that. People who stop at them like to sign their names on the cars. Isn't that cool?"

"Can we do it?" Sophie asked.

"You'll need to walk through that field to get to the cars," Sam said, "and it will be very uneven ground. Do you think your leg feels up to it?"

"Well, I'm willing to try."

Sam did a U-turn to get us on the correct side of the road and found a spot to park near about twenty other vehicles. The heat baked the ground hard, which made the walking easier for Sophie. But it also caused sweat to run down my back. We did not have any spray paint with us to record our visit, but God provided as someone had left a partial can near one of the cars.

Sophie got busy adding her memento. Such a touristy thing to do, but the moment was better than I expected. Even the unrelenting heat did not dampen the experience. The feel of the A/C cooled my skin and dried my sweat when we got back into the car.

Back on the road, we planned to check into a hotel in Amarillo, Texas, before heading south to Palo Duro Canyon State Park for some adventure. This "Grand Canyon of Texas" is the second largest canyon in the country. I had read the canyon floor sometimes reached temperatures of 115 degrees this time of year, so we opted for the sixteen-mile scenic drive around the park.

"I think we can get out and see things if we like and Sophie is up for it," I said.

After leaving the hotel, we made our way south for about twenty-five miles before seeing the sign to the park. We descended from the grasslands down to the canyon floor. I gawked and pointed out the impressive, multicolored layers of sandstone. The hues of yellow and orange blazed in the bright sunlight, and the walls rose dramatically all around us. Rock formations, called hoodoos, jutted up from the ground like ancient sentinels of the park. We stopped at several spots to snap photos.

"I can't believe the beauty of this place," I said. "I'm at a loss for words."

"Me too," Sam said.

"I never knew such places existed." Sophie pulled out her cell phone and took several photos. "I love seeing all the incredible sights. They make me want to explore the world even more."

"Uh-oh, I think someone is catching the travel bug." Sam laughed. "It's contagious and never goes away. And can be very expensive."

Sophie giggled. "That's one disease I don't mind having."

We drove on in silence for a while until Sophie spotted a sign for an outdoor amphitheater. "What's that for?"

I checked the information we picked up at the visitor's center. "The park puts on a play called *Texas*, and it's a musical about the history of the state. Listen to this description: 'A lone horseman, carrying the flag of the great state of Texas, appears atop a 600-foot cliff, and, with a moving swell of the music, the horseman gallops across the rim. Suddenly, a cast of over sixty actors, singers, and dancers take the stage to kick off the show.' Wow, that sounds impressive."

"What time does it start?" Sam stopped the car as he waited for me to find the answer.

"Glad you asked. The gates open soon for a chuckwagon BBQ dinner, and the show starts about 8:15, once it gets dark. Do you guys want to go? If so, we can run back up to the visitor's center to see about tickets." I got a yes from both of them. "I hope they're not sold out. This show sounds so cool."

Thankfully, there were still tickets, and we settled in to watch.

Chills ran down my back, and goosebumps rose on my arms at the spectacle of this show. "What a perfect ending to our first day. I'm not sure that anything else on this trip can top that experience," I said while Sam drove back to the hotel.

"You might be right," Sam said as a soft snore arose from the backseat. "I think we wore her out."

"I'm exhausted too and so ready for bed and the A/C. We're making memories and I love them." I rubbed the sweat from my forehead. "What time do you think we should leave in the morning?"

"Since the drive is only five hours tomorrow, we don't need to leave too early. And between the heat and excitement of today, I think a little extra sleep might do us all some good. How about breakfast at about 9:00 a.m. and then try to leave around ten?"

"Perfect. We have nothing planned for tomorrow in Manitou Springs other than checking in to the rental. So that will work."

Sam woke Sophie and helped her get settled in her room at the hotel while I took a cool shower before hitting the sack myself. Sleep came easily as I snuggled up against Sam. "Thank you, Lord," I whispered.

CHAPTER FORTY-TWO

The sun sat high in the sky when we left Amarillo the next day. And with no stops planned, we made great time. Before long, I spied mountain peaks in the far distance. Sophie dozed in the back seat while Sam and I enjoyed some of our favorite Christian artist's CDs. I tried not to think about the work of the Gypsies and the conference, at least for the next few days. For now, I needed to care for my daughter.

"Are we there yet?" said Sophie.

"Almost. We're about an hour away," Sam said. "Since the sleepyhead is up, what is some of your planned fun?"

"Nothing's set in stone. I want to see how Sophie's leg does each day before heading out. Keeping that in mind, we could drive up to Pike's Peak one day. Another place I want to visit is Garden of the God's Park. They've got shuttle buses that circle the park, so less walking." I turned around in my seat to look at Sophie. "And if Sophie feels up to it, we can do some light hiking. Also, I think visiting Cave of the Winds Mountain Park might be something different to tour. It's a tour of a cave system below the mountain area. Another place to visit is the zoo in Colorado Springs, or there is a cool-looking North Pole amusement park and Santa village that's open year-round we could explore. And of course, rest and relaxation time daily for all of us."

"All sound fun, and I think I should be able to do most of the activities," Sophie said. "And don't worry, I'll let you know if my leg bothers me."

We made the final push to the rental. Sam hopped out of the car, opened the gate, and got the key out of the lockbox. A long, narrow dirt road wound upward. We bounced and climbed toward the rental. As I looked back down the path, trees filled my field of vision. The Aspen leaves shimmered in the breeze, and I exhaled. *This place looks like heaven.*

Before unpacking the car, we took a quick outside tour of the rental. Stunning views greeted us from many of the downstairs windows. A deck sat off the kitchen area with chairs and a fire pit for us to enjoy during the cooler evenings. This simple cabin in the woods above town thrilled me as much as some of the luxurious places we stayed throughout the years. But this place offered us something more—a blissful family holiday.

"Can we get stuff to make s'mores?" Sophie asked.

"I brought them with us already, and lots of other goodies to enjoy. I brought lots of breakfast food too. We can pick up lunch stuff or dinner stuff to eat in if we want, or we can eat out, depending on where we are and how we are feeling."

Sam did the bulk of the unloading while Sophie and I checked out the inside of the house and claimed our bedrooms—upstairs for Sam and me, downstairs for Sophie. I put things away upstairs until Sophie screamed, "Mom, Mom. Get down here quick."

I ran down the stairs two at a time. "What's wrong? Are you hurt?" I asked between gulps of air.

Sophie pointed out the back window. "It's a bear."

"What, where?" I shaded my eyes with my hand and stared into the trees. "Oh, my goodness, it is a bear." The beast lumbered across a field about one hundred feet behind the house. "Oh no, I better go warn Sam."

I yelled for him while I headed toward the front door, where I smacked right into him.

"What's wrong?" he asked.

"There's a bear out back." I pointed toward Sophie's room.

Sam ran downstairs to look. "That's so cool."

"Cool, as long as it doesn't eat us."

"Look, Mom. This place is well-prepared for this kind of situation." Sophie walked to the dresser against the wall opposite the window. "There's a can of bear spray on the island over here. We'll be fine."

"Oh, Lord," I prayed, "please keep us safe from the bears and other dangers that live up here in the mountains."

Sam and Sophie remained glued to the window and watched the bear move on.

After settling in for our five-night stay, we headed into town to a burger joint for dinner. On the way back to the house, Sophie asked if we could make s'mores.

"I'm not sure that's a good idea with the bear in the area," I said.

"Oh, come on, you big chicken. Where's your sense of adventure?" Sam grabbed my hand, as he turned to wink at me before the light turned green.

I glared at him and in a sharp tone said, "I don't want to get eaten by a bear. And I'll have you know, I've come a long way with my sense of adventure, thank you."

Sam laughed. "You've come a long way, baby. I'm just teasing. We'll keep the can of bear spray near us as we enjoy this beautiful night on the porch, okay?"

"Fine."

"I think you're very adventurous, Mom." Frowning, Sophie looked at Sam. "What did you mean by that comment?"

"Maybe you and Mom can talk more about this on your drive home from the conference," Sam said. "Your mom has grown a lot over the last few years. I think it's a great testament to the power of faith and prayer in her life, but she should tell it because it's her story."

"Okay, now I'm curious. But I can wait till our drive. Right now, I want to use my s'mores-making skills."

"Okay, okay. Let's go make s'mores." I kissed Sam on the cheek, then headed into the kitchen to get the bear spray and the stuff for s'mores.

The next morning, I found an incredible sense of peacefulness on the deck in the first light of day, sipping my coffee. The rustling sound of the wind in the leaves made me smile and shiver. A frost coated the ground in a glistening white all around me. A sigh slipped out, and I breathed deeply, pulling the cool air into my lungs.

The sun broke over the peaks behind the house and bathed the deck in amber light. I sighed again with a sense of deep fulfillment. I had come a long way from the person who'd lost the accounting job years ago.

God helped me to no longer doubt myself and my abilities, at least most of the time. I had lost my fear of unknown places and things. God granted me this tremendous gift of purpose in helping his children, and I found a satisfaction in the work. I made mistakes, but I did my best. That's all God needed. But now, I was struggling to balance all of God's work with being a good mom to Sophie. Just when I felt I had conquered one assignment, God changed everything.

I picked up my Bible and began reading the sixth chapter of Psalms. I continued reading through many of the Psalms and finished with Psalm eighteen. I closed my eyes in prayer—a lifetime of weight lifted off my shoulders at that moment, and contentment overflowed. *Amen, and thank you, Lord. But how will I explain my life to Sophie on our drive home from Denver and will she see me like the failure I feel I am?*

"Sitting here with all your friends?"

Sam. My love. My everything. "Ha, ha. You're so funny. No, just enjoying some peace and quiet." Sam bent down and kissed me. "Is Sophie up yet?"

"No, I didn't hear any movement from her. Mind if I join you with my coffee? This place is incredible."

"Just imagine the view we will get from the top of Pike's Peak. We should drive up there later today and maybe find some little café for lunch." I leaned over and rubbed Sam's arm. "How would you feel about grilling some steaks for dinner tonight?"

"Did someone say steaks?" Sophie chimed in. "I'm always up for steaks, and a drive up the mountains sounds great too."

"So, you're eavesdropping on us?" Sam laughed. "How bout I make some pancakes for breakfast before heading out?"

We both nodded, and my stomach rumbled in appreciation.

CHAPTER FORTY-THREE

Breathtaking scenery flowed past the windows while we wound our way up to the 14,115-foot summit of America's most famous mountain, Pike's Peak. The narrow road spanned nineteen miles with 156 harrowing turns and shoulders that dropped away to deep valleys below. And so did my stomach.

Sam pointed out a herd of bighorn sheep grazing on the narrow side of the road, but otherwise gripped the wheel tightly. When we approached the summit, patches of snow appeared scattered over the mountain.

The thin air at the top caused me to fight for each breath while we walked around. Dizziness and tunnel vision forced me to sit down for a moment when we entered the visitor's center. Sam got me a bottle of water, which helped. My head stopped spinning, so we continued to explore inside the visitor's center in case I needed to sit down somewhere.

A few hours later, the descent down the mountain became just as harrowing, as the burning, rubber smell of overheated brakes filled the air.

Sam cooked up a fantastic meal of steaks and corn on the cob, followed by a round of s'mores around the fire pit. I kept the can of bear spray right next to me the entire time. The fresh mountain air and altitude wore us out, so we all retired early.

I snuggled under the heavy down comforter, but the crisp coolness of the air blowing in through the open window chilled my nose. So I wrapped myself even tighter and moved closer to Sam to get some more warmth. I closed my eyes and inhaled the fresh scent of pine blowing in through the windows.

The following morning started in much the same way as the day before. After breakfast, a few rain clouds moved in, so we hunkered down at the cabin for some quiet time. We came prepared for just such a rainy event with books, because the cabin had no internet connection this high in the mountains. A comfortable silence filled the cabin. I wrapped myself in a blanket while I wrote and edited the information for the upcoming conferences. I hoped to finish today so I could read my new devotional book.

When the skies cleared in the early afternoon, we headed for the Gardens of the Gods Park. We caught an open-air jeep to tour the park. Again, we experienced dramatic views, along with three-hundred-foot towering sandstone rock formations that rose out of the ground against the backdrop of a snowcapped Pikes Peak. *Impressive*.

"How about some hiking?" Sophie asked.

I turned and looked at her. "Do you think you're really up to it?"

"Yes, Mom." Sophie rolled her eyes. "If it hurts, I'll tell you, and we can stop. Let's just do a short one to try it out."

Sam looked over the map from the tourist center and found one called the Siamese Twins trail. The trail map listed it as an easy one-mile loop, with only a slight rise, and we started up the hill. About halfway through, we came across "the window" rock formation.

The hole in the red sandstone provided a lovely family photo opportunity. Another family offered to snap a photo of the three of us while we sat inside the window with Pike's Peak looming in the backdrop. *I hope this photo comes out; it will be beautiful on my desk.*

Sophie's leg held up well for the hike but swelled later in the evening. I think I had made the right decision to keep the activities to a minimum each day.

We might try another hike before we headed to Denver, but I wanted to wait and see how she did with all the walking in the caves the next day. If she wanted to get a part-time job this summer, I wanted to make sure she did no further damage to the leg.

We headed to the Cave of the Winds just up the road from our rental for the next adventure. Apprehension set in when I stared down into the dark, black hole of the entrance of my first cave tour. Of course, my family made fun of me.

"Are you a chicken? Come on, you can do this, Mom," Sophie encouraged me, while I debated going on the tour.

I relented and bought a ticket for all three of us. "I hope I come out of this thing alive," I said when we started the descent into the cave system. "When did the last cave-in happen?" I asked the tour guide.

"The first tours started in 1880, and we've never had an accident," the guide said. "It's safe and cool even in the summer heat."

"Being hundreds of feet below ground feels unnatural," I muttered.

We walked through the maze and visited about twenty areas inside the cave. At one point, the guide turned out all the lights. The total blackness freaked me out. I yelled and grabbed Sam's arm. Now, they would make even more fun of me.

"Relax and look at all the incredible rock formations down here," Sam said. "Have you ever seen anything like this in your life?"

"Well, it's kinda cool down here. As long as the roof doesn't cave in on us."

Sophie giggled, and I glared at her. "You're funny, Mom. I'm enjoying learning about these stalactites and stalagmites. And think of all the great exercise we're getting with all these stairs."

I smiled but had to admit my leg muscles relaxed when we reached the outside again.

"Well, if you don't like caves, how do you feel about that ride over there?" Sophie asked.

I followed her gaze. "Look what that sign says, 'The Terror-dactyl ride sits on the edge of a 200-foot cliff in Williams Canyon. Those brave enough to ride it will get launched 200 feet into the canyon at nearly 100 miles per hour!' Do I look brave enough to try that thing? Nope, not interested in that either."

"I'll go with you, Sophie," Sam said, then turned to me. "I believe you're getting more adventurous these days, and I'm proud of you."

"Hey, I went into the cave, didn't I?"

We stood and watched a few people on the ride. I sighed. "They push you off the ledge, and you free fall. That looks fun to you two?"

Sam and Sophie nodded.

"The rope catches you before you hit the ground, and it becomes like a giant swing," Sam dismissed it with a wave of his hand.

"How about a zip line across the canyon instead of free-falling into it?" Sophie asked.

I watched a person ride the zip across the top of the canyon, and it looked a little more my speed. "I might if it didn't have such an enormous drop below the line."

"Mom's a chicken," Sam said, strutting around, acting like a chicken.

"I hate you two." I huffed. "Fine, if you're going to force me, I'd rather do the zip line thing."

"I'll admit that you are getting so much braver. So Sophie and I will ride the Terror-dactyl, and you'll ride the zip line." Sam ran toward the ride, screaming, "The first one to the bottom wins!"

"Is your life insurance paid up?"

Sam laughed.

My knees knocked, and my hands sweated when the attendant hooked me into the harness. I spotted Sophie and Sam getting strapped into their harnesses and said a quick prayer for their safety and mine. "Has anyone ever died on this thing?" I asked the man working the line.

"Not under my watch. It's perfectly safe. Just sit back and hold on to these handles above your head. At the other end, you'll feel a jolt as the brake grabs. My coworkers will help you get out of the harness and down from the pole at the end."

I nodded and looked over to the other ride in time to see Sam and Sophie fall away from the platform. Screams and yelps of delight echoed across the area between the mountains while they swung down through the valley. I laughed at their joy. *Boy, I wish their bravery would rub off on me.*

"Ma'am, are you ready?" the young man asked.

I nodded, and he pushed me a little to get me going. I gained speed and closed my eyes to block out my fears. But slowly, I opened them to watch the scenery fly by me. *This ride is kinda fun—what a rush.*

The end of the rope approached fast, and I gripped the harness as all the blood drained from my face, and I waited to hit the pole. But some hands grabbed me when I stopped and pulled me onto the platform.

Sam and Sophie waited nearby for me. Sam jumped up and down as I approached, and he yelled that he'd won the race while Sophie just rolled her eyes. We laughed at the amazing adventures.

"Want to try our ride, Mom?"

"No, I think that's enough fear conquering for one day. Maybe next time."

We headed to a little local diner before going back to the cabin. We laughed our way through lunch, as usual. *God has truly blessed me.* I looked around and savored the sounds of the beautiful laughter of my family. *And I'm glad for these adventures to take my mind off the upcoming conference.*

Before the time to go to Denver, the last family event was a trip to the zoo. It meant lots of walking, according to the map. Sophie's leg appeared to hold up to everything better than I expected.

We began the visit with a ride on the chairlift to the top of the park for a spectacular view of the surrounding area. Once back down, we wandered around for hours, seeing all the animals. I enjoyed the elephants, penguins, and the tiger the best. We found a little café in the park for lunch and enjoyed this gift of time together. In between bites, I looked at my little family and realized Sophie would head off to college in only two years. These times together would only be a memory. My eyes filled with tears.

"What's wrong, Mom?"

"I just thought about you going off to college in a few short years. So, our time together is getting shorter." A tear slid down my cheek.

"Don't worry. I'll come home on breaks and holidays and all summer long. It will be different, but that doesn't mean our life together will end. You're my family. You can't get rid of me that easily." Sophie leaned over and hugged my neck. "And someday, when I have a family of my own, you'll need to take your grandkids on adventures."

I smiled at that new thought. Grandkids. I had never thought of being a grandmother. I hugged Sophie back. "Just so you know, I want to be called Granny."

"Okay, let's not get ahead of ourselves, please." Now it was Sam's turn to roll his eyes. "So here we are, the vacation is not over yet, and you already have our daughter married off with kids. One event at a time, if you don't mind. Personally, I'm not ready for this to end."

We laughed again—one of the greatest blessings of being part of this family that God had put together.

We opted to skip out on the Santa's Village activities to enjoy another steak dinner cooked on the grill at the cabin. We lingered over our s'mores and talked about all the things we had witnessed together this week.

Nothing lasts forever, I told myself. Laughter brought my focus back to the moment. "I love you guys."

"I love you too, honey."

"And I love you too, Mom."

"Group hug," I said, and they moaned but complied.

On the last morning together, we enjoyed a leisurely breakfast before packing up and heading to Denver, about an hour away, for Sam's flight at 6:00 p.m.

CHAPTER FORTY-FOUR

We dropped Sam off at the Denver airport in the late afternoon on Sunday. After that, just we girls continued on for the next three days, then we would begin our drive home on Thursday morning.

But first, we headed to the hotel in downtown Denver to check-in because I wanted to polish up my speeches for the Gypsy conferences.

"Is it okay with you if we plan to eat dinner at the hotel tonight?" I stopped unpacking and looked at Sophie. "I want to go over my notes some more."

"Sure, I'm fine with that. I think my leg might need some rest too. If the hotel has a hot tub, I might go soak in it for a while."

"That sounds delightful. I might join you for that if I get finished in time."

"You seem a little nervous about this talk." Sophie scrunched up her face. "Follow the same script you shared before, and it'll all go well. Don't forget to address the problem of the stolen money head-on. Those who are open-minded will understand." Sophie stood tall and squared up her shoulders. "God made you for this project. I have faith in you."

"You just made me think of something to add to my speech. I'm reminded of the story of Esther in the Bible—

made for such a time as this. Maybe I'll add part of the story of Esther to my talk." I walked over and grabbed a notepad. "See, God put you in our lives for a purpose."

"I'm not sure I know the story of Esther or how it fits into this situation. Can you explain that to me?"

"In a nutshell, she was a young Jewish woman living in a city in the Persian area. She found favor with the king, became queen, and risked her life to save her people from disaster. A court official named Haman persuaded the king to allow a program that would kill all the Jews of the empire. Because of Esther, the plan failed. You should read the story in the Old Testament. The Book of Esther is only ten chapters long—a fast read."

I searched through my stuff to find my Bible. Then I fumbled through the pages looking for the right verse. *Does a sixteen-year-old really care about any of this stuff, or is Sophie just being nice to me?* I searched Sophie's eyes trying to decided before I plunged in.

"This is what Esther's uncle tells us in verse 4:14: 'For if you remain silent at this time, relief and deliverance for the Jews will arise from another place, but you and your father's family will perish. And who knows but that you have come to your royal position for such a time as this?' In my talk I will say to the crowd, 'For if you remain silent, someone else will get to do this work, and you and your family will miss out on the blessings God has planned for you. And who knows but that you have come to this meeting for such a time as this.' I want to believe this is my purpose but so often I doubt myself. Is it all just in my imagination that God could use me? Maybe, I'm too old or to set in my ways. What do you think?"

"I think it's great. And might I add, I think God made you for such a time as this too," Sophie said, the light dancing in her eyes. "He put you in the right spot to see all the lost children on your trips, start a program to help them, and rescue me when I lost everything."

"You know what? I think you are right. Thank you for confirming all of that for me. When I first lost my job, I thought my life had ended. I sank into deep despair because I lost hope in him. If you take nothing else away from our family, remember to never give up on God. No matter how terrible life gets." I hugged Sophie and stroked her hair.

"I bet Dad would be glad to miss this sappy moment." Sophie laughed.

"I think and hope you're right."

Monday started off with meeting the groups interested in the work of the Gypsies, the first of three meetings planned for each of the next three days. Monday's group comprised a women's group from a church in the Boulder area. The time together began with my talk, followed by Q&A time. Afterward, we took part in the social time. The sample food and dirty water displays from underdeveloped countries caused a few mouths to drop open.

Sophie and I spent the time mingling and answering more questions. Several complained about the missing money, but I did my best to reassure them. I glanced over and noticed several ladies at the sign-up table. They had cornered Sophie and bombarded her with more questions, but she handled herself so well. My heart swelled with pride for my daughter.

"Wow, a long day," I said when we were finally making our way up to the room. "It's amazing how talking can wear you out so much. How did you think it went?"

"The ladies provided us with lots of good feedback. And several of them signed up for more information. So ..." Sophie smiled. "A minor victory."

"Hopefully, the group will sign up to take on some projects. The more helpers, the more we can do."

"I think the story of Esther helped drive home the point. Since you're tired and we have two more of these to do, would you like me to speak in your place at the last meeting?"

"Really?" My little Sophie was taking a gigantic step. My heart overflowed. "Do you think you feel comfortable enough to do it? It would help me out. I'll be nearby and can help answer questions as needed."

We stepped into the elevator to head to the room. "Sure. I believe in what you're doing, and I want to be a part of it. So, yeah, I think I'm ready. And I've been praying about it too."

"Perfect. The final group is from a civic organization in Denver that's very active in this kind of work. I think it would be a good way to start." We got out of the elevator. "Do you want to practice some after dinner tonight?"

"Yes, please. And maybe you could start by offering a prayer."

I called Sam to check on him and Rex before dinner and told him about Sophie talking the last day.

"Wow, that's great. Sophie is following in your footsteps." I heard the pride in Sam's voice.

"I know, pretty awesome."

Sophie paced the near the back of the banquet hall while the ladies arrived for our Tuesday morning meeting. Other than the speaker, this day would mirror yesterday.

As the chairs filled, I walked over to check on her. "You doing okay?"

"I think so. I'm a little more nervous than I expected. But I think I have all the information ready to go."

"Great, we'll start in about five minutes. Do you want me to say a prayer over you before you start?"

"That would be wonderful."

I laid my hand on Sophie's shoulder and closed my eyes. "Dear Heavenly Father, we ask you to be with Sophie as she shares your work with children living in poverty with the group. Give her the words to say that'll move people to action. Confirm how you want her to live her life for you. I thank you for the gift of Sophie. In Jesus's name. Amen."

"Thanks, that will help a lot," Sophie said and climbed the steps to the podium.

I bite my lip to hide my growing smile.

Sophie appeared so relaxed and at ease while talking with the women. She could make a successful career with this kind of work. Her enthusiasm energized me. I sat down at the back of the room and watched instead of shouldering the load myself.

My heart swelled with pride as I watched this young woman speak like a professional. Her voice never quivered as she moved about the stage. Her warm smile and relaxed mannerism drew the crowd in as they sat on the edge of their seats to listen. *Thank you, Lord. I gave up hope on ever having a child and look what you did. Not only did you give me this child, but you gave me another helpmate who might continue in my footsteps. Thank you for my dual purposes, and thank you for changing my career path all those years ago.*

The applause brought me back to the conference.

"Okay, now will be a time for questions from the audience. My mom will come up to help provide any additional information as needed," Sophie said, and I moved forward to help my girl.

Finally, our time in Denver ended after three days of successful sessions. More than three hundred women had signed up for more information. When we returned home, I planned to ask Helen to sign them up for the newsletter and give them access to the website so they could browse the projects available.

After we loaded the luggage into the truck, Sophie asked. "Do you want me to do some of the driving?"

"Maybe later. I'm good for now, but thanks." I got in the driver's seat and pulled away from the hotel. "So, what did you think about everything?"

"I enjoyed it. Taking part in this work has me thinking about college and what I should major in."

"Makes sense. Next year will be your senior year, which means we should schedule some campus tours so you can narrow down the school too." I tried not to think about how I would feel once Sophie went off to college. "But no matter what you decide, we will support you. The money from your mom's life insurance policy should cover a sizable chunk of the cost, and we will cover the rest. So, no need to worry about anything."

"That's a relief. Some of my friends think they might have to work for a while to save up for school. Or go to a community college for the first year or two to save money."

"Do you want to go away to school, like, out of state?"

"I'm not sure. With everything that has happened in my life, I might like to be nearer to home than far away. I think I'd like to tour some close and some a little ways away, but not too far. I want to stay involved with the Gypsies, so it would be nice to come home most weekends."

"That makes me happy." My heart fluttered. "What about majors?"

"I've thought about this for a little while now. And I think I want to go with a degree that would help me do international work. I think with a Christian emphasis too. I want to follow in your footsteps by trying to change the world. Maybe international business, so I can work on the other side of the world for the Gypsies or something like that. I've researched schools like TCU or Dallas Baptist in our area. Maybe Southern Nazarene or Oklahoma Christian, both in Oklahoma, which would only be a three- or four-hour drive."

"Wow. I'm impressed. That all sounds wonderful. I think starting with four schools for tours would be manageable. We can set up some visits for the fall." I glanced over at Sophie. "I love the idea of international business for your major. Remember that once you start school, you can change it if something else catches your attention. The first two years of college are a good time to explore all the options and narrow them down as you find your interest."

Sophie nodded. "I think I won't change my mind about the degree part."

"I hope so. You also need to leave room for God to direct where he wants you to study. I thought I'd use my accounting degree forever. But God showed me he had other plans for my life. So be open to changes in college or later in your life. A good verse to remember is Proverbs 16:9: 'In their hearts, humans plan their course, but the LORD establishes their steps.' It took me the last few years to learn that I am happiest when I follow God's path instead of trying to go my own way."

"I've learned so much from you and Dad over the last several years. I won't say I'm glad that Mom is not here anymore, but I don't think I would be where I am without you two in my life."

"And I would not be where I am without you either, honey. You're part of the lesson of following God's path for life. Now, I can't remember our life without you."

The drive home allowed us to dig into and talk about the profound aspects of life. Sophie had grown into a beautiful Christian woman, and she would change the world for Christ. Again, my heart swelled with pride for this blessing.

At home, Sophie and I sat in the living room and spent the evening sharing everything with Sam.

"I'm sorry I missed out on the drive," he said. "But I'm glad you made it such a special time for bonding with you both. And I can't wait to visit the schools and help you into the next phase of life, kiddo."

CHAPTER FORTY-FIVE

Summer flew by. August brought the start of Sophie's senior year and all the pomp and ceremonies that go with it. And she now dated a boy from our church, Pete. He had started coming to our church a few months back. Both Sam and I liked him. They spent much of their free time together. I wondered if he might even play a part in the college Sophie chose too.

We planned the four visits to colleges during the fall break so Sophie would not miss school. Sophie also spent time with Pastor John and discussed her major. He also helped Sophie learn about the discernment process, and we all prayed for God's direction. Each of us spent hours online gathering the best information possible.

Having her stay in Texas would make my mom's heart lighter and full of happiness, but I truly wanted the best for Sophie. We first looked at Texas Christian University in Fort Worth. They offered significant financial assistance— up to half-off tuition—for those pursuing a religious major. Pete also planned to stay close to the area for his college career.

One Saturday, the three of us and Pete sat around the kitchen table and researched information about various colleges. "At TCU, you can pursue a Religious BA degree which seems very well rounded in many disciplines," I said. "As you move deeper into that program, you could narrow your focus if you wanted." I looked up from the computer.

"That sounds possible," Sophie said. "I'm looking at the Dallas Baptist website. They offer a BA in Christian Ministries that also seems to offer flexibility to tailor the course to any special area of interest down the road." She looked up from her computer screen. "I think I want to visit both schools."

Sam joined in the conversation as he looked at the two Oklahoma schools, Southern Nazarene and Oklahoma Christian. "Southern Nazarene has a degree in missions you might enjoy. At Oklahoma Christian, you can get a degree in the Bible and add on a second degree with an emphasis in an area like missions. The course load is hefty in the Bible area. Do you think that would interest you?"

"Maybe," Sophie said. "I would still like to check out all four of these schools. I think campus life and scholarships will also play a role in the one I pick."

With the visits planned, Sophie prepared the applications for the four schools. "I don't want to leave anything to chance, so I want to get these done," she said. "I just hope one of them accepts me."

"Now, you sound a little like the old me, honey," I said. "If none of these schools admit you, we'll find one that will. Trust God for the right option to rise to the top."

Sophie placed her head in her hands. "I know you're right, but it's all a bit scary. My future is in the hands of these schools. And their decision is based on how well I answer some questions. Scary. I'm not even eighteen yet."

"Trust God for the right answers."

"Ditto," said Sam.

During fall break in October, we toured each of the schools. Sophie liked some things at each campus, but not everything.

"Well, all pleasant visits, but they did nothing to help me narrow the list," she said, plopping into a living room chair one night after dinner. "I hoped something would stand out, like a neon sign saying 'Go here'."

"The acceptance letters go out in January," I said. "Let's see what they bring, and we can reevaluate."

All we could do at this point was wait. I prayed for the Lord's direction in Sophie's life as often as she popped into my head. The first letter arrived on a Monday, and by Friday, all four schools had accepted Sophie into their programs.

I walked into Sophie's room as she lay on the bed with her eyes closed. "Now what?" she asked.

"Look at this one, Sophie," Sam said. "TCU is offering you the best scholarship at a whopping 50 percent. I think that makes it a leader in my book."

"I really liked TCU, but I also want to stay in the dorms. But I would feel guilty for living on campus when home is less than thirty miles away."

Sam and I exchanged glances. "Look, Sophie," he said. "We want you to get the total college experience. Living on campus makes sense. And with this scholarship and the money from your mom's estate, it's very doable. So, please don't feel guilty about any of it. Pick the school that appeals to you most."

Sophie closed her eyes and said, "I really do like TCU and the programs. Plus, I can come home on weekends to help with the Gypsies' work. I really want to stay connected with it all, so the proximity to home is an added benefit."

"So TCU?" I asked.

"Yes!" She squealed, then jumped up and down before hugging both of us.

"To celebrate, how about dinner out? Then we can go buy some TCU shirts," Sam said, twirling Sophie around the room. "I guess my wardrobe will be home to a lot more purple."

With college and major settled, I fanned myself. A calm settled over the house.

Pete also planned to go to TCU in the fall, which made Sophie even happier. I tingled all over, watching Sophie blossom in her life and her faith. She was following her path in life, and despite all the difficulties she experienced, she understood she belonged to God as one of his children.

One evening, while Sophie went out on a date with Pete, Sam and I snuggled on the couch. I said, "I'm really going to miss that kid around the house. She brings such joy and energy into our home. What'll I do without her?" Tears welled up in my eyes as I snuggled closer to my husband.

Sam hugged me tight. "I'll miss her too, honey. But I feel so blessed we got to be part of her development. How different might life be for us if she hadn't come into our world? So I'm focusing on that instead."

Sam pulled away and gazed at me. "Besides, this is just the start of a new phase. Remember, Sophie told us a while ago that we would be the grandparents to her kids. So, we have that in our future. I guess this is what 'empty nest syndrome' feels like."

"True," I agreed. Our lives had definitely changed, but for the better. I was sure God would keep our family intact for many years. "I'm going to pray for something we can do together as a family one last time before Sophie goes off to college. Join me in prayer?"

"Sure. Are you thinking of vacation or Gypsy work?"

I smiled. "Whatever God has planned for us."

CHAPTER FORTY-SIX

Helen called early one morning in her usual chipper way, talking a hundred miles per hour while I sipped on my first cup of coffee. I tried to keep up with the conversation, but the early hour made it hard for my brain to function.

"Helen," I almost yelled to get her attention, "what are you saying?"

"A church in Thailand emailed the Gypsies' committee this morning," Helen said, more slowly this time. "This church needs help to put on a Bible camp for the poor children in the area."

"Okay, let's list it on the website to see if anyone will volunteer."

"We don't have time. Another group scheduled to go, but they just backed out. They reached out to us to see if we could help. The church is located in a suburb near Bangkok. The camp will last for a week, and they want to teach Bible verses, make crafts, play games, and provide some nutritious food for the little ones."

I put down my coffee cup, intent on the conversation now. "So, what are you thinking?"

"Well, I immediately thought of you, Sam, and Sophie. I thought this might be fun for you to do as a family. What do you think? Do you want to go?"

"Bangkok, Thailand?" My mind raced with questions. "Will anyone else be going?"

"The church needs the help next month, so I'm not sure if we can pull a group together that fast. Also, trying to raise funds and make arrangements with only a few weeks till departure seems impossible. I thought maybe you guys could pull it off with your background in travel," Helen said. "Besides, they said even a couple of people would make it a success. A perfect answer to your prayers about something you guys could do together before Sophie goes to college."

I pondered the idea for a moment. "It might be a possibility. Let me pray about it and talk things over with Sam. Would it be okay to get back to you tomorrow with our decision?"

"With Sophie heading off to college next year, this might be your last summer to make a trip like this as a family," Helen reminded me. "Just let me know soon, so I can let the church know."

I pictured Helen smiling on the other end of the phone.

"I'll look forward to hearing from you tomorrow."

After hanging up, I prayed about the need, asking God to confirm if he wanted us to do this trip. Helen had touched my heart with the comment about Sophie. This could be our last trip together before life changed for all of us. It was hard to wait for Sam and Sophie to come home to talk with them about the trip.

At dinner, I mentioned my conversation with Helen. "We would need to leave the last week of May and be gone at least a week. What do you guys think?"

"I'm in," Sam said almost immediately.

"Me too," Sophie added. "Question, do you think Pete could come with us? I've told him about the Gypsies, and he seems interested in the work."

"I'd be okay with it," I said. "But do you think Pete could raise or get that much money in such a short amount of time?"

"I'll check with him," Sophie said, already walking down the hall to call Pete.

Her eyes sparkled and gleamed when she returned a few minutes later. "He'd love to go, and he said that his grandparents always liked to help with such mission work, so he figured he could raise the money, no problem."

"Great." I shrugged. "Does Pete like working with kids? Does he have his passport?"

"Yup." Sophie nodded with wide eyes and a bright smile.

"Okay, I'll call and tell Helen tomorrow. Our small team of four people will have some fun with the kids in Thailand. Do you think Pete would be able to stay on to do some sightseeing?"

"Yes. I already asked, just in case."

The following day, I called the church office to talk with Helen.

"Hi, Kathleen, I prayed all night for you to say yes. I think God dropped this trip into your lap. Please tell me you are going."

"We all prayed about it and got the same feeling that we're supposed to go to Thailand. So, it's a yes," I said. Helen clapped her hands and yelled a loud amen. "Plus, we'll have an additional helper. Sophie's boyfriend, Pete, is going with us too."

"Great," Helen said, her enthusiasm coming through the phone while she spoke. "I'll email the group in Bangkok and copy you on the email as a way of introductions. And once you get your plans made, you can share all that information with both of us. We'll also add you guys and the trip to the Gypsies' website and the church's prayer list."

I smiled. "Do you know how many children will attend or any other details?"

"Not at this time. They told me they would provide that information soon." Helen paused before she continued. "They'll also confirm the exact dates of the program and if you need to bring any supplies with you to help them out. I'm so excited for you guys. I think you should start looking at travel arrangements while we wait to get the information back from the church."

"You're reading my mind, Helen. I'll work on options for flights and hotels since we know the approximate dates. Thanks for thinking of us for this project," I said before saying goodbye.

I leaned back in my chair and thanked God for this precious gift. This trip would be a great way to welcome Sophie and Pete officially into the Gypsies for God.

Back at my desk, I turned the page on my calendar and stared at it in disbelief. Seven years ago today, I had lost my job with the accounting firm. Back then, I thought it was one of the worst days of my life. Now I knew better.

God, you rescued me from a life of brokenness, fear, and failures. And look at me now. You gave me joy, peace, purpose, and motherhood. You blessed me beyond anything I could ever imagine. And even the fears of the unknown are slipping away as I put my trust in you. Thank you, Jesus. If I have you, then I have everything I need.

"Hey guys," I said as I walked into the living room a few minutes later. "Let's stay at the church in Bangkok instead of a hotel. That way, we can learn about the way they live."

Sam's and Sophie's mouth dropped open. Sam spoke first. "What about A/C, electricity, clean water, porcelain toilets, and all the other things you have worried about in the past?"

"I've got Jesus and you guys, so I have everything I need."

The End

ADDITIONAL RESOURCES

Maiti Nepal's list of the seven common warning signs to look for with human trafficking:

1. Traveler not dressed/prepared for travel—no luggage, wearing the wrong size or wrong type of attire for destination's weather.

2. Tattoo with a bar code or the word daddy, especially on a younger person.

3. Traveler doesn't know any details of their trip or travel plans.

4. Their story seems rehearsed or differs each time they tell it.

5. Traveler never moves around alone or freely—someone is always watching.

6. They appear afraid and won't discuss themselves or refuse to communicate at all.

7. Child dressed in a sexualized manner, appears malnourished, or has signs of abuse, like bruising.

OTHER RESOURCES

Author's charity organization—
https://orphan-relief-effort.org
Maiti Nepal—
https://maitinepal.org
Mother Teresa's Charity in India—
https://missionariesofcharity.org

Helping street children in Kenya—
https://chanceforchildhood.org/where-we-work/kenya
Compassion International—
https://www.compassion.com
Samaritan's Purse—
https://www.samaritanspurse.org/disaster/putting-a-stop-to-human-trafficking
Catholic Relief Services—
https://www.crs.org
Open Doors—
https://www.opendoorsusa.org

ABOUT THE AUTHOR

As an author and blogger, **Yvonne M. Morgan** writes stories to help deepen a relationship with God. On a personal level, she was born in Belfast, Northern Ireland. She is a wife, mom, and grandmother, but most importantly, Yvonne is a child of God who is passionate about prayer and missions. Her passion is to share stories of trusting the Lord and watching Christ in action. As a faithful prayer warrior, she trusted God when he called her to help orphans after losing her son.

Stay connected with the author through her social media accounts listed below:

Author's Page:

https://yvonne-morgan.com

Facebook:

https://www.facebook.com/YMMauthor

Twitter:

https://twitter.com/ymmauthor
INSTAGRAM:
https://www.instagram.com/yvonnemorganauthor
BLOG:
https://turningmountainsintomolehills.org

OTHER WORKS BY THE AUTHOR:

Turning Mountains into Molehills
Rest in God; A Prayer Journal
Finding Faith, Hope, and Love in a Broken World
A Sad Little Wildflower
ABCs of the Bible

Made in the USA
Middletown, DE
11 January 2024

47657425R00186